Shoot for the Moon

by Norma Howe

CROWN PUBLISHERS, INC.
New York

Published by Crown Publishers, Inc., a Random House company, 225 Park Avenue South,
New York, New York 10003.

CROWN is a trademark of Crown Publishers, Inc.

Manufactured in the United States of America

Library of Congress Cataloging-in-Publication Data

Howe, Norma.
Shoot for the Moon / Norma Howe.
p. cm.
Summary: The trip to Italy Gina wins in a yo-yo contest gives her
a new perspective on relationships, responsibility, and herself.
[1. Italy—Fiction. 2. Self-perception—Fiction.] I. Title.
PZ7.H8376It 1992 [Fic]—dc20 91-24585

ISBN 0-517-58150-7 (trade)
0-517-58151-5 (lib. bdg.)

10 9 8 7 6 5 4 3 2 1   First Edition

For all you amazing, mind-boggling paragons—
the Sicilian Safari Seven, the Unforgotten
Four, and the New Recruits, too—with love
and admiration from those longanimous and
punctilious folks at Unfriendly Tours, Inc.

("No, you can't! It is *not* included.")

1

I didn't believe in death until I was almost thirteen years old. By that I mean I didn't think death was possible. I know it sounds stupid, but that's what I thought. When I was in the fifth grade I started to read an old book of my sister's called *No Knights, No Dragons,* in which one of the main characters dies. My sister, Marie, saw me reading it and asked me if I liked it. I told her I didn't because one of the kids in it dies, and I liked more realistic books. Marie believed in death, I guess, because she gave me a funny look and said, "What are you talking about, lint-head?"

Marie has always talked to me like that, in hyphenated words. Lint-head. Potato-brain. Worm-juice. There are seven kids in our family, and she's the closest one in age to me. I'm sixteen, the youngest, and she's twenty-two. The others are all boys. (Men, actually.) But they're all scattered around now, and we don't get together very often.

There's an old family story that explains the reason that there were so many kids. The way it goes, my mother and her best friend from high school, Annie O'Rourke, were having a "baby race" all those years. Annie O'Rourke stopped at six, so that made me the winning baby. "Yes, but I'm a *Catholic,* Doris," Annie remarked in a joking manner once when the subject came up during a Saturday morning coffee klatsch at our house. "So what's *your* excuse?" The others all laughed, but I remember watching my mother stare at her coffee cup a moment before smoothing back her gray hair and saying simply, "Ignorance, probably. Ignorance—and carelessness." I didn't understand what she meant, being only about eight years old at the time, and I may have even laughed, thinking it was a joke. But then I saw my aunt give my mother a nudge and a disapproving frown, motioning over to me with a toss of her head. I think my mother had forgotten I was there.

In those early days we all lived with my grandparents (on my father's side) in their big two-story house near the Mission District in San Francisco. The old washer and dryer were going day and night, rattling the windows with their heavy unbalanced loads, and the whole house smelled like jogging shoes and shaving cream for all the years I was growing up. One by one, as soon as they finished high school, my brothers would pack up a few of their belongings and move out of the house. None of them went to college. I found an old postcard from my brother Tony in a drawer once when I was in the third grade. It was from Las Vegas and had a picture of a woman in a bathing suit surrounded by cactus. There was a scrawled message on the back that said: I'M DEALING BLACK-JACK AT THE DESERT INN. YOU SHOULD SEE ME IN MY SOOT. I was a pretty good reader by then, and I thought that was the funniest thing I ever saw. I pinned the card on my wall and laughed about it for weeks. A couple of years ago Marie left home, too, and now she shares an apartment with two other girls who work in her office. So by the time my parents and I moved to this hot, dumpy little town where we live now, I was the only kid left at home. That was okay with me. In fact, I was hoping that with all the others gone, maybe my parents would finally take note of my existence, but apparently in their eyes I had not yet outgrown the invisible bodysuit is-sued to me at my birth.

*　　*　　*

2

My grandfather retired about the time I was born, and somehow the responsibility of looking after me gradually fell into his lap. Although my mother never worked outside the home, after my brothers and Marie left it seemed like most of her spare time was taken up with telephone calls to her sisters, various daytime television shows, and, of course, gardening.

Grandpa and I always used to kid around a lot, and I would tease him by telling him he was my favorite grandfather, even though he was the only one I had. God, he taught me so many things, like how to bargain at flea markets, hang a spoon from my face, play the sweet potato, and yo like an expert. And yes, he taught me about death, too. It was Grandpa Gari who finally made me a believer.

Our usual meeting place was the swing in the shady corner of the front porch. There was one of those expandable wooden gates at the top of the stairs, and I remember when I was really little I used to climb onto it and almost rattle it off its hinges until my grandfather would come out and pluck me off like a big nubby hairball from the front of an old sweater. "Okay, okay, my little blond papushka," he'd say. "You don't have to shake the house down." My name is Gina, but he always called me his little papushka.

I can't think of my grandfather without thinking about yo-yos. He had whole cartons of them stacked in an old shed in our backyard, left over from his younger days when he was a traveling sales rep for Duncan. To my grandfather yo-yos were much more than mere toys. "Yoing is like music," he used to tell me, "or a handshake. It is a universal language, the same wherever you go." And he never went anywhere without a couple of them, one to play around with, demonstrating his flawless brain twister or Eiffel Tower to the little groups that always seemed to gather around him, and the other to give away to the last kid standing there with his mouth hanging open in awe. "Here you go, pal!" he'd say, handing over a shiny new yo-yo with a wink, at the same time pulling on the brim of that crazy Yo-Yo Man cap he always wore cocked over one ear.

He sure loved that old green and white cap. "A yo-yo in the cap is better medicine than tranquilizers in the bottle!" he used to say, tossing up his yo-yo in a high skyrocket and then catching it smartly in his hat. (It makes me smile now, remembering back to the time when I couldn't figure out what he meant by that.)

Of course I'll never forget the first time he put a shiny new yo-yo into my eager little fist, even though I was only four years old when it happened. "Here, hold your arm straight out, like this, Papushka," he said, placing my arm where he wanted it, looping the string over the middle finger of my right hand, and letting the yo-yo fall to the ground. Then he fished out his pocketknife and cut the string to fit. "Okay," he said. "Ready for lesson number one. Now watch me." With a gentle flick of the wrist, his own yo-yo sailed toward the floor and returned to his hand with a beautiful slapping sound. I tried it myself, catching it on my very first try, which prompted my grandfather to stare at me with a look of amazement and humor that I will never forget. In no time at all I graduated to a fancier yo-yo with a longer string and was throwing simple sleepers (or spinners, as they are sometimes called) that lasted nine or ten seconds, dangling the yo-yo over the edge of the porch. Grandpa always used to get such a kick out of that. By the time I was six I was hopping the fence and skinning the cat like an expert.

Back then I could never figure out why Grandpa would always make me stop practicing before I wanted to. But now I understand the psychology of what he was doing. By making me quit before I got too tired or bored, he was hoping there would be a better chance that I would grow to love yoing as much as he did.

4

It was a long time before he actually let me *keep* the yo-yo—more psychology, obviously—but eventually the great day came. To prevent Marie or my brothers from snitching it (not that they would have wanted to, all of them having grown bored with yo-yos long before), I slept with it hidden inside my pillowcase. And that's where I kept it for years, out of habit rather than fear of a midnight snatch by one of my siblings. Along the way I discovered something else: I loved yoing very much, but I loved my grandfather even more.

Sunday mornings were my favorite times. That's when we'd drop off my grandmother at mass, and the two of us would head on over to the Alameda Flea Market across the bay. Boy, what an old pill I thought my grandmother was! She was the only one left in the family who still went to church, so she felt it was her personal responsibility to "save" all of us, something she never let us forget. She often made snide remarks about my parents "living in sin," since they were never married in the Church—my mother not being Catholic and my father dropping out long before. I often wondered how my mother could just shrug and turn her head whenever my grandmother talked about her like that, but that's the way she handled it.

Another thing I couldn't stand about my grandmother was the way she criticized—even ridiculed—Grandpa's yoing. She called it a silly waste of time and even embarrassed him once in front of the grocery store (where he was entertaining some kids with his rattlesnake and Texas cowboy) by telling him he should have "outgrown his short pants by now." I was *so* mad at her for that! "Why don't you shut up, you old bag!" I muttered under my breath, just trying to show Grandpa that I was on his side. She didn't even hear me, but the whole thing backfired. My grandfather got really angry—not in front of everybody, of course. He wasn't like that. He just led me

5

by the arm away from the others and looked me straight in the eye. "I *never* want to hear you talk to your grandmother like that again!" he said. I think that's when I first began to realize that he actually loved her, but it would be years before I would understand how anyone could.

I don't know when my grandfather stopped going to church, but it must have been after he was married. Grandma never stopped nagging him about it. Her priest, old Father Rossi, was on her side, of course. It was kind of funny, though, since Father Rossi and my grandfather had grown up together on the same little street in Rome and even came over to this country on the same boat with their families when they were kids. They had never agreed on anything, and they argued for nearly seventy years about everything from the Holy Trinity to the World Series. Both the old priest and my grandmother never stopped telling Grandpa that he would surely go to hell if he didn't buckle down, confess his millions of sins, and attend mass regularly on Sundays like a good Catholic should. But my grandfather would have none of it.

So every Sunday we'd dutifully drive over to the church and drop off my grandmother. I couldn't wait for her to cover her head with her ugly black lace scarf and then knot it under her chin with her fat little fingers. After she finally got out of the car, I would scoot up over the front seat and plop down in her place (sitting way over on the edge by the door for a while because I didn't want to sit on the part that was still warm from her body) and wait for my grandfather to ask the familiar question: "Well, how about the flea market today, Papushka? Feel like making some deals?"

He liked to buy really unusual and funny stuff, most of which he stored in the little shed. Once in a while he would mail something crazy to one of his friends from the old days— always anonymously—or else, if they lived in town, he would double-park the car while I ran up and left mysterious packages at their doorsteps. He particularly liked original (but terrible) art objects, like oil paintings of bathroom sinks or ballet dancers wearing pink tutus. He loved to bargain for unfinished paint-by-number pictures—especially huge ones of the Last Supper—and felt he was doing people a big favor by buying them for fifty cents and then taking them home and disposing of them, since, he said, they could never bring themselves to do it after all the work they had put into them. One time he found a really hideous homemade table lamp constructed out of seashells and marbles. I distinctly remember the table lamp, because that was also the day we found the big flimsy carton of Groucho glasses—you know, those big noses with the fake eyeglasses attached. The same guy was selling the lamp and the noses.

"Take seven bucks for both?" my grandfather asked.

"The lamp *and* the noses? Nope. Sorry, pal. Can't do that. Ten's the lowest I can go."

"Eight fifty, then," Grandpa said, digging deep into his pocket. "That's all I've got."

"Aw, all right." The man shrugged.

Then my grandfather handed him a ten-dollar bill. The guy gave him his change without batting an eye. On the way home we each put on a pair of Groucho glasses and stopped for french fries and a large chocolate shake, which we split, as always, exactly halves.

I was almost thirteen when my grandfather died. For the first time in my life death actually became a reality. How could he be gone, I kept thinking, just gone forever, never to return? I still didn't understand death, but at least I believed in it.

It was my grandmother's fault—Grandpa's death, I mean. Everybody knows that, but I'm the only one with guts enough to say it. The two of them were crossing the street in front of our house (this was when we still lived in San Francisco) and Grandma Gari very carelessly dropped a small paper sack of avocados that she was carrying home from the store. My grandfather let go of her arm—they were jaywalking at the time—and started after the avocados, which were rolling all over the street by then. (I saw it all from our front room window, so this is exactly the way it happened.) Grandma Gari hurried up on her short banty-hen legs and made it safely to the curb, but my grandfather was hit by a guy in a Napoli's Pizza delivery truck that came around the corner "like a bat out of hell"—as he told us afterward in a throaty whisper from his hospital bed. I screamed and screamed, and my mother came running to the window and called an ambulance right away. Grandpa wasn't killed instantly, but he was all messed up inside. He lingered on in the hospital for several weeks, but there was nothing the doctors could do for him except hook him up to an IV and keep the pain to a minimum. When his kidneys finally gave out, he was gone. Although he was an old man—seventy-six years old when he died—he was just about the neatest human being I ever knew.

My grandmother really put a damper on the elaborate gag he planned for his funeral with that typically sourpuss attitude she had about everything. My grandfather had planned the really funny (but totally *bizarre*) episode while he was dying in the hospital. I mean, there he was, with "one foot in the grave and the other on a banana peel" (his joke), and yet he was still able to come up with an idea designed to shock and amaze his old nemesis Father Rossi one final time. Grandpa knew for certain that whether he liked it or not, he was doomed to be buried with all the regular Catholic fanfare, presided over by an ultimately victorious Father Rossi. He knew that my grandmother and Father Rossi would definitely see to that, and there was absolutely nothing he could do about it—until he came up with his plan. Three days before he died, he picked me (his trusty, longtime pal) to help in carrying it out.

"In the backyard," he started telling me softly when I was alone at his bedside, "in the backyard, out in the shed—"

I leaned my head closer to his. "Yes—out in the shed. Go on, I'm listening."

"Those old Groucho noses—remember, a long time ago, from the flea market?"

I nodded. "Yes. I remember."

He put his hand up to his throat and swallowed several times. "I want you to pass them out at my funeral—"

"Oh, Grandpa!" I interrupted. "Don't talk about your *funeral!*"

He pressed my hand and said, "Shh, shh! Listen to me, now. Pass them around—the Groucho noses—without Father Rossi seeing you, and tell the people to slip them on while his head is bowed in the final prayer.

"You can tell them it's my last request," he added weakly, a pained smile twitching around his wrinkled mouth. "They'll understand."

I'm proud to say I didn't cry. Not then, anyway. Instead I told him I thought it was a *fabulous* plan and that he could count on me.

After that he talked to me about death—and heaven. That's when I started to cry. We both did. He knew he didn't have much longer to live because all his organs were failing and he was in so much pain. I was holding on to his hand and crying and trying to tell him that maybe we would meet again—like in heaven or someplace. "That's possible, isn't it?" I pleaded, as if his agreeing would make it so.

"Well, I don't know, Papushka," he whispered. "I hope so, but I don't think so." He swallowed a couple of times. "Listen, I'll tell you what. I'll try to come back and tell you what it's like if I make it to heaven."

My heart seemed to swell up in my chest. "You *will*? How will I know? Will you appear to me, or speak to me, or what?" All of a sudden I was having trouble with my breathing. I took several deep breaths, but that only made me feel weak and dizzy.

My grandfather closed his eyes and was silent for a long time. It scared me after a moment because I was afraid that he had died right there and then, but soon he squeezed my hand and I knew it was okay. "No," he said finally, "on second thought, I won't do that. In fact, I promise I *won't* appear to you as a ghost or speak to you in the night. Even if I can, I won't. If they make me the offer, I will refuse. So don't you be looking and listening for me and imagining that I'm there." Now his own eyes were watering.

Suddenly there was the rustling sound of people entering the room. I looked up to see my mother and Grandma Gari. My grandmother was holding her rosary, and my mother was carrying a single pink rose from her garden. I went and stood

by the window and tried to concentrate really hard on the moving patterns that the shadows of the trees made on the tops of the cars in the parking lot below.

The last time my grandfather spoke to me was after school on the following day. I thought he was sleeping when I first walked into the room, so I decided I would go to the cafeteria and come back a little later. But as I was walking out the door I heard him call to me. For once he didn't call me Papushka. He said very softly, almost in a whisper, "Don't leave, Gina. Come here. I want to tell you my dream." He was lying on his back with his eyes closed, and when I came near, his hand groped for mine. "I dreamed I was a boy again," he said in a hesitant monotone. "I was a little boy again in Rome. I was running past the large fountain and heard a strange sound. But familiar. A sound I knew." He paused and opened his eyes, then laughed a short, tight breathless laugh. "The sea god was holding a yo-yo, Papushka, and he was very, very good."

I forced a smile for his sake and gently squeezed his hand. He winked at me then—I'm sure it was a wink—and with just a trace of his own sly smile, whispered softly, "Heading for my longest sleeper yet, and no rewinding allowed." His eyelids slowly closed and soon he was asleep.

The next morning the nurses told us that he had gone into a coma during the night. Three days later he was dead.

Oh, those noses! They worked like a charm! At the funeral, after Father Rossi finished the final prayer, I thought I saw a self-satisfied little smile starting to form around his mouth just before he looked up ↵ face the sea of mourners—fifty Groucho Marxes and my grandmother. (Even my parents agreed to wear the silly things, which really surprised me.) How I wish that Grandpa could have been there to see the expression on Father Rossi's face! It must have been exactly as he had anticipated.

Naturally my grandmother was disgusted over what happened at the funeral and blamed me for the whole thing. But I didn't care. As far as I was concerned, she had about as much sense of humor as an aspirin tablet. The important thing is that I did what Grandpa Gari wanted, fulfilled his last wish, actually, and I was honored to be the one he picked to carry out his plan. And anyway, the friends and relatives who really knew and loved him—well, they thought it was a wonderful stunt. "Just like the old so-and-so," they said afterward. "What a guy! What a guy!" And even Father Rossi turned out to be a good sport about it. When I saw him coming toward me as we were leaving the cemetery, I thought for sure I was really in for it, but all he did was put his hand on my shoulder and whisper, "Gina, my dear, your grandmother has had a heavy cross to bear for many, many years. Heavier than you will ever know. We must be extra kind to her in her time of sadness."

Well, I didn't know what he meant by that "heavy cross to bear" comment, and at the time I mistakenly took it as a direct insult to my grandfather. I could feel the anger boiling up in me. I couldn't think of anything nasty to say, so I just stared at him for a few seconds, then turned on my heel and rudely walked away. I still feel bad about that (even though it wasn't completely my fault), and I'll never get a chance to apologize, since Father Rossi himself died early the following year.

One thing that really got to me was that Grandma *still* ate avocados in spite of all that had happened. God, I can still see her, the day after the funeral, even, sitting at our yellow Formica table in the kitchen and smacking her lips over a mushy, disgusting avocado. A few months later she surprised us all by announcing she had purchased an airline ticket for a visit back to Italy and was leaving on the second of July. But she suffered a mild heart attack the very next day and was forced to cancel the trip. The best thing about it (in my opinion—and I must be a terrible person for thinking this

way) is that right away the doctor put avocados on her limited-foods list. I'm really ashamed at how much secret pleasure I experienced over that.

As for my yo-yo, well, just looking at it during the long, quiet afternoons following the funeral made me so sad that I finally wrapped it carefully in tissue paper and saved it in a little box, where it remained for many months—along with my Groucho glasses and Grandpa's Yo-Yo Man cap, which I rescued just in time from the Goodwill bag where my mother had tossed it along with the rest of his clothes.

Of course, I had no way of knowing then how my special talent for yoing would be responsible for changing my life so drastically in the not-too-distant future.

After Grandpa Gari's death I really went into a prolonged tailspin, emotionally speaking. I dreaded going to school; and I dreaded coming home because I couldn't bear not seeing him waiting on the porch for me with that crazy cap cocked over his ear and his yo-yo spinning all around the place. I couldn't forget how he used to light up his cigar and tell me to "fork over" my school papers for his inspection and comments, or how we would stay out there until dinner, talking and telling jokes and doing yo-yo tricks by the dozen.

My grandmother and I rarely exchanged more than occasional grunts, and my mother and father never inquired about my day at school or asked to see my papers. Nobody noticed the little blob spending more and more time in front of the television set. Finally I found a way to deal with my parents' disinterest. Naturally I got the idea from a TV show. This guy was lying in traction with two broken legs after a skiing accident, obviously in enormous pain. His wife had just taken the children and left him, and he had been fired from his job. His friend was trying to cheer him up. "Hey, just try not to think about it!" was his friend's advice. So that's what I did. I just tried not to think about it.

3

Three years later the firm my dad works for—the Frank and Frank Sausage Company—suddenly closed down its San Francisco plant and we had to move to this hot, sleepy little town in the San Joaquin Valley, about ninety miles away. The best thing about it was (hurrah!) my grandmother was not going to be living with us anymore. She decided to sell the old house in the Mission and move into a retirement home full of old widows just like her. My mother got on the phone and was lucky to find a place that filled both of my grandmother's requirements: the apartment had to be near her church, and it had to have a sunny outdoor patio area where she could place her life-size statue of Saint Francis of Assisi and grow sunflower plants in huge redwood tubs. Those sunflowers! It seemed like she had this almost *neurotic* need to grow them every single year, harvested from the *original* seeds she brought over on the boat from Italy. In some mysterious way there was a connection in her mind between those seeds and Saint Francis, who was both the special saint of her childhood and the patron saint of San Francisco, her adopted home. Every October 4 (Saint Francis's Day), after going to early mass in his honor, she would corner Marie and me and any of my brothers who were around and relate the story of his life *again*. And after that, she'd launch right into the sunflower story, telling us how she brought the original little bag of seeds all the way from Assisi, secretly tucked away in the pocket of her navy-blue jumper. Oh, but we were rude little buggers, and we'd all roll our eyes and say, "We *know*, Grandma, we *know*! You tell us the same thing every year!" Somehow, though, I always had the feeling that she wasn't telling us *everything* about those seeds.

The funny thing about our moving is that for months before I found out that we were going to leave San Francisco, I had been praying for that very thing—a chance to get a completely new start at a brand-new school. I think now, after all that's happened, I can finally admit to myself the real reason I wanted to move. My problem is that when I'm away from home I'm a real talking fool, and the kids at school were just plain sick of listening to me. What I needed, I thought, was simply a bunch of fresh ears.

After our move I was assigned to San Joaquin High School, a two-story building with peeling gray paint, surrounded by dead hedges and foot-high weeds. What was worrying me most—as I climbed up the cracked cement steps and walked into the school building—was lunchtime. Who would I eat with? I felt sick just picturing myself sitting alone in some strange, noisy cafeteria with nobody to talk to. Shyness has never been a problem with me, but all the same, you just can't barge right in on people and expect them to start listening to you right off the bat.

One of the classes they put me in was called cultural geography. (They said I needed credits in the social science department, and that was the only class that had room for me.) Toward the end of the period on the first day I was there the teacher, a nice guy named Mr. Costello, gave us a short quiz, and afterward he asked us to pass our papers to the person in front of us for correcting. I passed mine to this girl named Tammy Hudson. Lunch was right after cultural geography, and when the bell rang and Mr. Costello waved us off, Tammy stood up and smiled at me.

"Hey, Gina," she said, "do you want to come over to McDonald's for lunch with us?"

"Gee, sure," I answered, trying not to let on how relieved I was, which was just short of falling right down and kissing her shoes.

All the way over to McDonald's, Tammy kept talking about a Molly somebody. She just got a letter from Molly; Molly said that in San Diego you didn't have to wait six months to see first-run movies; Molly's dad finally bought her a CD player, but not the one she really wanted. Well, it turns out Molly had been Tammy's best friend, and she had just recently moved away.

At McDonald's, Tammy introduced me to some of her friends ("This is Becky and Jenny, and that's Georgia over there with the really short haircut—"), but mostly the two of us just talked together. I could tell right away where Tammy was coming from: she had just lost her best friend and was struggling to find a replacement. My first impression of her was that she was pretty scatterbrained and severely boy-crazy. I could deal with that, though, because I felt in my bones that somewhere under all that dizzy exterior were the makings of a very good listener.

I had no sooner bitten into my hamburger than Tammy suddenly collapsed into a little fit of shivers and muted squeals of delight. "Ohh, ohh," she said, ducking and hiding her pointing finger behind her hamburger. *"There he is!"*

I moved my head around, trying to see who she meant. "Where?" I asked. "Who?"

"P.J. Gannon!" she whispered. "Over there. Just sitting down over there by the windows!"

"Hey, yeah!" I answered, partly playing along with her. "I see what you mean! I noticed him right away in Mr. Costello's class! What a doll!"

Actually the guy she was pointing at *was* a real darling. His complexion was gorgeous, and his hair, parted on the left side, fell across his forehead all brown and shiny, just missing his eyes, which—even from across the restaurant—looked as blue as the violets in my mother's garden.

"Is P.J. his real name, or what?" I asked. "Reminds me of pajamas. And who is that beautiful girl he's sitting with?"

"Oh," Tammy said, recovering from her fit just as quickly as she had fallen into it. "That's Justine Kim. They're married."

"*Married?*" I exclaimed. "Really?"

Tammy laughed. "No! Hey, I didn't mean really *married*. That's just what we say, like, when people are going together. You know."

"God, her hair is so black and so long!" I said. "Look at it. It reaches clear down to her butt, for God's sake."

"She lives across the street from me," Tammy said. "She's a model. She does modeling for a big department store in Stockton. P.J.'s nuts about her."

"Yeah." I watched him open her milk carton for her and stick in the straw. "I can see that."

"But I don't think it's going to last too much longer," Tammy whispered.

I was intrigued. "Really? How come?"

"The white Camaro," she said mysteriously, rolling her eyes.

"The white Camaro? What white Camaro?"

"Some guy in a white Camaro. He's been coming to visit her. I see him through my window."

"No kidding! Wow! Then P.J. will be up for grabs, huh, Tammy?" I kidded.

Tammy giggled at the thought, and I must say it sent a little shiver down my own spine, too.

Two seconds later Tammy was having another little squealing fit.

"Now what?" I asked, still playing along.

"That guy over there!" she whispered, covering her mouth. "The one taking a bite out of Jenny Olson's hamburger. His name is Mark Jarvis. Isn't he just *fabulous*?"

Before lunch was over I had Tammy figured out. She was crazy about boys, but only if they were unobtainable, because actually she was scared to death of them.

It took two months—all the way to that stifling-hot week before finals—but Tammy's prediction eventually came true: P.J. and Justine Kim really did split up. And a nasty "divorce" it was too, with a lot of shouting and name-calling and even a slap on the face, according to some of the talk going around school.

It was hard enough to think about finals coming up without having the weather in the 90's for eight straight days. In fact, on the Friday before finals week, the thermometer in Mr. Costello's room read 85 degrees, even though the so-called air conditioner was blowing full blast. That was the day he was reviewing some of the questions he was planning to ask on our test, and I was just sitting there, bored out of my gourd. I knew that even if I flunked the final I would still squeak through the course with a D, so I wasn't *that* worried about it. And after all, my main goal then was just to hurry up and get out of school any way I could, since it seemed like such a gigantic waste of time. I was hoping that after I graduated I could get a job someplace—like The Video Store, for instance, where they let you check out all the tapes you want at no cost for your own viewing.

I was aware of a sudden silence in the room. I looked up. Mr. Costello was staring right at me. Oh, God. My mind had been drifting again. As usual, I just couldn't seem to pay attention in that class. And besides, I think that I had a really bad case of spring fever. I just stared out the window a lot, my mind a complete hopeless blank.

"Are you with us, Ms. Gari?" Mr. Costello asked, raising one eyebrow in that funny way he has, half-joking but half-serious, too.

"I'm sorry," I said, giving my usual excuse with my best apologetic smile. "I guess I didn't hear the question."

Mr. Costello sighed and shook his head. "Oh, come on, Gina. It's an easy one. You *did* hear me say that the final is going to be only on our European unit, didn't you? The one we started shortly after you joined us?"

"Yes, I heard that," I answered, trying not to sound sassy. I really liked Mr. Costello. Now he was perched on the edge of an unoccupied desk by the windows. He put his hands on his slim thighs, hunched up his shoulders, and leaned forward. "All right, Gina. One more time, then. On what occasions does a typical Italian Catholic require the services of a priest?"

I couldn't believe he had asked me that question. I felt a sharp stab of pain right square in the center of my chest, followed suddenly by a big lump in my throat. What he had asked me was the exact same straight man's line to a joke Grandpa Gari used to tell when I was just a kid. I swallowed the lump while my heart started to pound and I felt my face flush. I knew I was going to get a laugh.

"Yeah, well," I started, "a typical Italian Catholic sees a priest when he's baptized and when he makes his Holy Communion, when he's married, and uh"—I tried to sound as matter-of-fact as possible—"and, oh, yeah . . . when he's hanged."

Just as I expected, everybody laughed, especially the five or six Italians in the room. Old Costello was pretty cool about it. After the class quieted down, he said that next Thursday (the last day of school before summer vacation) would be a good time to have a class discussion on the causes and effects of ethnic humor. "I'm curious," he said. "Where did you hear that joke? I'll bet it was from another Italian."

I nodded and blinked my eyes real fast a couple of times. "My grandfather used to tell it."

"And is he Italian? Is his name Gari too?"

"No, not originally. He changed it from Gari*baldi*," I said, rolling my eyes up and patting the top of my head. That got a few laughs, but I just kept on talking over them. "See, he and my grandmother came over on a boat from Italy in the twenties or thirties sometime. Not on the same boat, though. They got together later. Their parents matched them up. You know, the way they used to do in those days. He's—uh, he's dead now, but she's still alive."

Once I got over that hurdle, the rest was duck soup. I took a deep breath and plunged in. "But anyway, he changed their name just before the war. World War II, that is. He thought his real name sounded too Italian, what with that Mussolini guy running around loose and everything. In fact, after he came to this country and learned a little English, he didn't even *speak* Italian anymore. My grandmother told me that whenever she'd start to speak in Italian, he'd say to her, 'You're in America now. So talk American!' As a result of that, my father, well, he doesn't know any more Italian than, uh"—I racked my brain—"than Mickey Mouse! But then, you know," I added quickly, trying to keep up the momentum, "about changing his name—well, he told me once that he was sorry he did it. He really wanted to change it back to Garibaldi again, but he just never got around to it." I paused, but when I saw I still had the floor, I just jumped right in again and started talking about my grandmother. "My grandmother never did like him cracking jokes about Italians," I rattled on. "She still lives in San Francisco. See, she has this thing about San Francisco because she came from a little town in Italy called Assisi, and you know, that's where that saint is from— that patron saint of San Francisco—Saint Francis of Assisi, the animal lover—"

All of a sudden there came a loud, gruff voice from somewhere toward the back of the room. "Hey, magnum-mouth, give us a break, and *cork* it!"

I was a little surprised by that outburst, but then again I'm always prepared for put-downs. They hurt, but I pretend they don't. I timed my pause like a pro, then I answered indignantly, as if showing off my big vocabulary, "Hey, I *represent* that!"

It's a little play on words, of course, and the kids had probably heard it millions of times before, but it got me a few hoots anyway. At least it was an answer, and helped me save a little bit of face—probably my chin, that little mole on my cheek, and my left eyebrow. (Ha-ha.) And that certain guy named P.J. Gannon looked like he appreciated it. As I glanced over at him, his eyes met mine in a long, steady gaze, and he gave me the barest hint of a wink, all the while those blue eyes of his holding mine like a magnet.

I picked up that "I represent that" crack from TV. That's where I get lots of my stuff, from sitcoms and late-night talk shows. So the people who think I'm the funniest generally aren't the television watchers. For example, when Mr. Costello came back to school after spring break with a beard, I pointed to it and repeated what I had heard the night before on some show or other, which was, "Hey, there's *more* of you!" Jim Peters (one of our school's few A students) thought that was very clever of me, so I knew right away *he* hadn't stayed up all night watching television.

Tammy turned around in her seat and tapped me on the arm. She put her finger to her lips in a shushing gesture. "We just want to hear what he's going to ask on the final, Gina," she explained in a loud whisper.

Well, now, that surprised me, her saying that, since up till then Tammy was an even worse student than I was. (We made a pretty good pair, even though we didn't have that much in common and I still didn't have anyone on God's green earth that I could *really* confide in.) All the kids knew that Tammy wasn't exactly Miss Studious, and that's probably why they laughed again when I stared at her with a really exaggerated incredulous look on my face and said, "We *do*?" By the way she blushed and looked down I know she resented it. But I snuck another look at P.J., and at least *he* thought it was funny. He even gave me a *real* wink this time.

"Well, Garibaldi's a noble name, all the same," Mr. Costello said, going back to his notes. "A very noble name." I didn't know what he meant, and at the time I really didn't care.

I guess I started daydreaming again, because the next thing I knew, the bell rang and everybody closed their books and started leaving the room. I looked down at my notebook. It was blank. I hadn't even written down one question that Mr. Costello might ask on the test.

Honestly, if I were Tammy, I would have had nothing to do with me after the way I embarrassed her, but she waited for me anyway. We didn't bother going to our lockers but just headed straight over to McDonald's for lunch.

She started off the conversation by criticizing my eyes. "You could really use some eye shadow," she said. "And liner, too. Your eyes look all naked."

"Well, maybe I like naked eyes," I answered.

"They look small, too. They look like small, squinty little beans. Little white bean-eyes."

I knew what was happening, of course. Tammy *was* upset with me after all, and was getting even in her own pathetic way. "Well, thanks, Tammy," I said, deciding to play it cool and not let this turn into a big fight. "Thanks a lot. It was *very* nice and thoughtful of you to say I have little white bean-eyes. *Squinty* white bean-eyes."

We didn't say anything for a while. Then she broke the silence. "I noticed P.J. was winking at you in class."

I perked up. "Yeah? You noticed that, huh?"

"It doesn't mean anything, you know."

"Oh, really?" I tried to sound just mildly sarcastic.

"He winks at everybody."

"*Really?*" By now I was starting to get annoyed, but I tried not to let it show.

"Didn't you see him winking at Becky, too? Jeez, you must be blind." Then she added her clincher. "If you ask me, I think he's only pretending to come on to you because of your hair."

"My hair? What's my *hair* got to do with it, for God's sake?" I was really mad now.

"Because you're a blonde, dummy! He's just trying to make Justine jealous. She did the breaking up, you know, and he's just trying to make her think he doesn't care. That's why he's just pretending to like you. God, it's so *obvious*, Gina! He's just *using* you!"

As it turned out, she was right, but I was just too stupid or naive or something to realize it then. I guess she got me more upset than I thought, too, because about half a block before we got to McDonald's, I was suddenly overtaken by such a feeling of utter loneliness, I thought I might burst into tears and collapse in a big wet heap on the sidewalk. But I didn't. Instead I made it to McDonald's and had a cheeseburger, fries, and a Coke. And afterward, just for kicks, I hung a couple of spoons, one on my nose and one on my chin. My grandfather taught me the hanging-spoon trick at my brother Benny's wedding dinner. (God, my grandmother was mortified, but everyone else almost died laughing.) Those plastic spoons at McDonald's are a cinch. Just barely exhale on them, and they'll stick every time. The kids thought it was hilarious.

*   *   *

Dinner that night was the same old thing—my parents and me just sitting there, biting and chewing, chewing and biting. I started to think about what Raymond Keefer had called out in class—"Hey, magnum-mouth, give us a break, and *cork* it!" (At least I *think* it was Raymond Keefer.) I knew a magnum must be something large, but I didn't know what exactly. I looked over at my dad. Somebody had forgotten to turn on the TV, but he was just kind of staring at it anyway, in a vacant, absent-minded way.

"Hey, Dad," I said finally. "What's a magnum, anyway?"

"Whatcha mean, a magnum?" He looked over at me, both of his hairy forearms resting on the edge of the table. "What kind of a magnum?"

"Well, that's what I'm asking you. Is it just a word that means big, or is it some kind of a real *thing*?"

"You talking about guns or bottles?" He finished off a huge piece of French bread, and it made his cheeks bulge out.

I shrugged. "I don't know."

He shrugged too and speared another piece of fried chicken. I watched him without saying anything, then glanced at my mother, who was just sitting there quietly going about the business of eating. How long have I felt that these people, somehow, are not my real parents, I wondered. Have I always felt this way? Why don't we ever talk? Why don't we ever laugh? Who are these people, anyway?

When my dad still didn't say anything, I said, "Okay, then. Guns."

My father looked over at me as if he had never seen me before. "What are you talking about?" he asked, and the mixture of annoyance and rudeness in his voice seemed to crush my lungs and stomach and heart all together in a lump about the size of the yellow sponge on the sink board when all the water is squeezed out of it.

I took a deep breath and said, "Magnums. You know. You

24

asked me if I was talking about guns or bottles. So I'm talking about guns."

"Well," he said with a wave of his hand, "it's a big gun. A big revolver. Like on TV. You know."

"Oh. So what about bottles?"

"A big bottle, too. Like what they put booze in. Champagne, mostly."

Like champagne, I thought. Sure, that explains it. *Cork it, magnum-mouth.* Darn it! How come Raymond Keefer is not even that smart and yet he knows things I don't know? Like, the time we were talking about the difference between similes and metaphors in English class, one of his examples of a simile was "as noisy as Guy Fawkes Day," and I didn't even have a clue as to what he meant. Ms. Vickers asked the class to comment on whether that was a good example, and I had to make myself invisible so she wouldn't call on me. (That's one thing I'd gotten very good at!) But really, there are so many things I don't know. Even at McDonald's, when one of the kids starts to tell a joke, I begin to get that scared little nervous feeling I hate, like maybe they'll refer to something I don't know anything about, and I'll laugh in the wrong place, over nothing. That's happened lots of times, and it's embarrassing and hard to cover up, although I try. How am I ever going to catch up, anyway? Am I going to be an ignoramus forever?

My dad suddenly scraped his chair back and reached for the remote control. Click, click, click in rapid succession.

Oh, shoot, I thought finally, wondering what channel he would settle on. Who cares, anyway? Who cares?

My dad hogged up the tube all night watching some dumb basketball game, so I went to bed early, even though it was Friday. But I didn't get to sleep until after midnight, and then I kept waking up all the time. Finally at about six in the morning I just decided to get up and go for a run before it got too hot.

For a long time I had been wanting to go and find something I read about in an old newspaper that was lining my closet shelf the day we moved in. It was a little story about something the local people called the Thing. The photo next to the article was of a funny-looking building that looked like a cross between an abandoned grain elevator and an early rocket-launching pad. The article said the Thing was located past the old airport on the east side of town.

I knew that the quickest way of getting to the airport was to jog past Flipper's Family Creamery (where I had just recently applied for a summer job), the Laundromat, and Gannon's Hardware (a dinky little store owned by P.J.'s father). The frontage road that led to the airport started at the dirt parking lot behind the Leaning Tower of Pizza Parlor.

It was too early for the stores to be open, and the streets were deserted. I could tell by the feel of the air that it was going to be a real scorcher in a couple of hours. As I jogged past Flipper's, I wondered if they had decided to hire me or not. I had turned in my application as soon as I saw the HELP WANTED sign in their window. They said they would call me, but so far I hadn't heard from them.

Before I knew it, I was way out in the middle of nowhere. The scenery was flat farmland with a few big trees here and there, and once in a while there was a farmhouse needing paint, with odd machinery parts and boards and junk scattered around. I saw a couple of big dogs lying on porches or under trees, but luckily none of them came after me.

Finally I saw it—*the Thing*—looking like some kind of mirage in the desert. It was at least four stories high, all rusted and dilapidated, surrounded by a chain-link fence. I just stood back and stared up at it with my mouth hanging open. The Thing, I thought. What a perfect name!

There didn't seem to be a soul around for miles. The only sounds I could hear were those of a couple of small airplanes circling above and the usual buzz and hum of field insects. I must have stayed there about ten minutes just gazing up at it in a kind of trance. The more I looked, the more beautiful it became, especially if I squinted my eyes, which gave it a really romantic, blurry effect. The stairways were fascinating. The first group was very narrow, and the steps were high. Broken guardrails leaned every which way. Then there was a little catwalk thing leading to the second set of stairs. The third level was trickier. It was a lot narrower and more like a slanted ladder than a staircase. I decided the whole thing must have been painted blue at one time, but now the rust had taken over. For a second I got a crazy urge to climb up to the top, but then I figured I'd better not. Instead I contented myself with just looking at it.

I don't know how to explain it, but there was something about that old building that brought out in me some kind of deep, vague feeling that I couldn't put into words. I felt it rising up from the middle of my chest somewhere, like a big bubble of emptiness longing to be filled. I couldn't figure it out, because I had never felt that way before. All I knew for sure was that something big was missing from my life.

Finally I turned around and started to walk back home. For some reason I just didn't feel like running anymore.

The first thing I noticed when I got within sight of our house was Marie's car parked in our driveway. That meant my sister had brought Grandma Gari over for a visit. Well, there goes the whole day, I thought. Right down the drain.

"Hey, Gina!" Marie yelled as soon as I came in. "How come *you* get to walk right in the front door as big as life, and all *us* kids had to go around to the *back* door? Explain *that* to me, please!"

I sighed to myself. *Oh, brother!*

"So how come, Mom?" she persisted in her slightly whining tone. "How come Gina doesn't have to go around to the back door like we all did?"

They were sitting around the kitchen table drinking coffee—Mom, Marie, and Grandma Gari, whose fat little body was all decked out in black, as usual. That's what a lot of "Old Country" widows do, I've noticed. They just can't wait to get into their black clothes. And they wear black for the rest of their lives. Once when we still lived in San Francisco, I had to go with Mom to pick up my grandmother after a rosary one Saturday afternoon. As I watched her walk out of the church with her clutch of widow friends, it occurred to me that they all wore identical black dresses with absolutely no shape to them at all, and their wide, heavily stockinged legs sticking out from the far edges of their skirts hardly bent when they moved. "Little walking wine barrels!" I exclaimed. "That's what they look like!" My mother didn't answer, but maybe she didn't hear me.

I used finals week as an excuse to get out of the house that afternoon. I muttered something about having to go to the library to study, but instead I went to the movies.

Since Grandma Gari was visiting, we naturally had spaghetti for dinner. I was just waiting for her to comment on the sauce. Every time she eats my mother's spaghetti, she says there's something wrong with the sauce. I looked across the table at Marie, hoping she might be waiting to see what was wrong this time, too, and maybe we could share a little secret joke. When Grandma Gari made her inevitable pronouncement, maybe I could give Marie a little kick under the table. I kept staring at my sister, waiting for her to look at me. Finally our eyes did meet, but she just looked at me for half a second and turned away as if I were just another piece of furniture. Suddenly I thought I must be going crazy, because

I felt like any minute I might scrape back my chair, rush from the table, and jump right through the dining room window into my mother's favorite rhododendron bush. I could see it all like a slow-motion movie—the splintering glass flying everywhere, me sailing through the air in a magnificent leap, and everyone at the table exclaiming, "What was that? Was that Gina going through the window?" But it didn't happen, since I have a good trick for keeping myself under control whenever I get crazy ideas like jumping out of windows. I just pretend my shoes are glued to the floor.

The announcement came after her first few bites. My grandmother moved her tongue around in her mouth and then kind of licked her lips with an expression even more disagreeable than her usual one. "Too sweet!" she said triumphantly. She reached over and touched the arm of the world's most perfect man. "Don't you think it's too sweet, Salvatore?"

"Nah," my dad said, looking up from his plate. "The sauce is okay."

Obviously disappointed with his response, my grandmother looked at me next, the unspoken question still on her lips.

"Don't look at me, Grandma," I said, rearing back a little in my chair. "I think it's great. And anyway, I like it sweet." And I do, too. I thought it was delicious. If there's one thing about being a housewife my mother doesn't mind, it's cooking. And her spaghetti sauce is even better than my grandmother's famous recipe, in my opinion. She uses all kinds of homegrown herbs and spices, plus lots of sausage (Frank and Frank, of course). She makes it about once a month in a big kettle and then freezes it in peanut butter jars, permanently ruining all the lids by both color and smell (red and garlic). The only problem I have with my mother's spaghetti sauce is that I'm sort of trying to be a vegetarian, and her sauce is so good it's practically impossible for me to resist. We had a speaker at school last year who was a vegetarian, and after hearing him I decided I'd become one too. The speaker convinced me that killing and eating animals is cruel and unnecessary. I still haven't forgotten the video he showed us. God, it was so gruesome! The video proved that there are plenty of other ways of getting the protein our bodies need without resorting to butchering animals, and if we spent all the time and money we use on growing grain for cattle on growing grain for *people*, we could help feed the starving millions in the world. Well, my father won't even listen to "vegetarian garbage," as he calls it, and I guess that's understandable, since he's worked for Frank and Frank Sausage for more than twenty years. To hear him talk, eating meat is as natural as breathing. So half the time I don't know what to do. I think I'm truly a vegetarian at heart, then I usually cave in and just go ahead and eat meat anyway.

After dinner, while everyone was sitting around watching television, I got the bright idea that if only we had a big bowl of popcorn, we would magically turn into a typical happy family. Unfortunately, nobody else wanted any.

4

I could tell Sunday was going to be another scorcher even
before I got out of bed, which was about ten o'clock. I wandered like a zombie around the house in my pajamas, half-
heartedly looking for my slippers, thumbing through
magazines, throwing out old *TV Guides*, and otherwise pro-
crastinating. Something told me I should at least start *planning* to study for that cultural geography final, not to mention
my other classes, but I just couldn't seem to get up any steam.
For one thing, I didn't even have all the worksheets I needed.
At first I had tried to keep them all straight, but then I started
leaving them at school and throwing some out by mistake and
all that. What a nightmare.

I could tell where my parents were by the sounds I heard.
My mother was out watering her flowers. Whenever the hose
outside is running, you can hear it echoing through the inside
water pipes like some kind of organ from hell. My mother is
nuts about flowers, especially violets, which she calls her ba-
bies. (That gets to be mighty old after a while. Once I even
dreamed about them—little purple violets with real baby
faces in them.) I could hear my dad out in the garage working
on his car, his usual weekend occupation. (Whung! Kerplunk!
Whang!) I don't know how that poor car manages to survive its
weekly sessions with old Mr. Fix-it. Anyway, that's what was
happening, until I got my little brainstorm, which was to go to

the phone and call up Tammy and see if I could talk her into going over to Waterworld for a while and then maybe to Flipper's so I could check on my job application.

At first she said she couldn't because she had to study. "My mom and stepfather, well, they're really ganging up on me. They're even talking about college! Duane said he'd help pay for it if I got my grades up."

Just for a moment I felt a little shiver of jealousy. "Really? That's great, but—"

"And I think I *can*, too," she said. "Get my grades up, I mean."

Naturally I didn't want to go to Waterworld alone. "Hey, I've got it!" I said. "Let's go to Waterworld *now*, and then later, *tonight*, we can study together! That'd be better, anyway. See, we could ask each other questions and stuff."

"Well . . ." she said, hesitating, and I knew I had her in my clutches.

We had a pretty good time. A bunch of kids from Stockton were there, and we sort of made friends with them. Well, actually, all we did was splash around and push each other down the slide a couple of times. Mostly I did the splashing around and pushing, since Tammy seemed content to stay in the background and just watch, at least when the boys were around.

Afterward, according to my plan, I suggested to her that we go to Flipper's. "We can have some ice cream, and then I want to remind them about my job application. They were supposed to call me, but they haven't yet."

While we were walking from the bus stop to the ice cream store, Tammy started talking about her father. "You know, Gina, I'm really scared about going to New York this summer," she said softly, looking down at the sidewalk.

If there was one thing I didn't feel like doing, it was getting into a big boring discussion with her again about her father and his new wife and all that, so I started humming under my breath and doing a little sidewalk dance step as we walked along.

But that didn't stop her. "He's married again now—oh, but I guess I told you that already, didn't I? But anyway, I don't know if I'm going to get along with—"

"Oh, sure you will," I interrupted, and quickly changed the subject. I can't even remember what I started talking about. I only know that Tammy turned and stared at me, and that hurt, pitiful look in her eyes still haunts me whenever I think about it.

Tammy obviously gave up on me, because she heaved a big sigh and started walking about sixty miles an hour without waiting for me or even looking back.

It was really noisy and crowded at Flipper's when we got there a little after four. The PLEASE SEAT YOURSELF sign was up, so we found a table near the little glassed-in room where they make the ice cream. Flipper's is a really neat ice cream parlor that specializes in huge servings. Their banana split, which they call the Gargantuan, is as big as a football. They have to put a plate under the banana split dish to catch all the syrup that slops over the sides. Some people (a minority, the skinny, finicky types) are disgusted by those mounds and mounds of ice cream melting all over the place and after trying it once they never go back again. But most people think it's great.

After about five minutes someone came over and waited on us. Tammy ordered a caramel sundae, but I only had enough money left for a small Coke.

We sat there waiting without saying anything, with Tammy beginning to drum her fingertips on the tabletop in a very annoying manner.

"Do you have to do that?" I asked. "It's very annoying, you know."

"Oh, *sorry*," she said very sarcastically. Then she let out

33

another big sigh and muttered, "What am I doing here, anyway? I should be home studying. I don't know how I let you talk me into things like this. Next time I'm just going to—"

"Well, well! If it isn't Gina and Tammy! How did you girls find out I was working here? Word sure gets around fast, doesn't it?"

"P.J.!" Tammy and I exclaimed together, attracting the attention of the people sitting at the neighboring tables, and then I laughed outright while Tammy giggled and hid her face in her hands.

P.J. is a master at performing his little conceited act. He's very cute at it, and he can get away with it. But then P.J. can get away with a lot of things, as I was about to learn.

"Hey, I didn't know you were working here!" I said before Tammy could even gather her wits about her. "When did you start? Gee, I have my application in too! How do you like it, anyway? Do you get to eat all the ice cream you want?"

P.J. shrugged. "It's okay. They hired me for the ice cream machine, but now Vera thinks I'd do better waiting on tables. And that's fine with me, since the ice cream machine doesn't dispense very big tips."

"Uh, who's Vera?" Tammy asked.

"Vera? She's the assistant manager. Anyway, she said they've almost finished hiring their whole new summer crew, and that—"

"They've almost *finished*?" I interrupted.

"Yeah. That's what she said. Like, my shift ended at four today, but I'm supposed to come back at seven tonight and be in on the training session for new builders. Vera said they like the waitpersons to know how to build in case someone's sick or something." He pointed to the people behind the counter who were busily dishing up the ice cream and syrups into various concoctions. "Looks like fun, doesn't it?"

I suddenly stood up and said, "Hey, I'd better go talk to Vera!" I looked at P.J. "Is she still here, do you know?"

P.J. said he thought she was in the little office in back, and that's where I found her, sitting at a cluttered desk and talking on the phone. She motioned for me to come in and sit down.

There was a big poster on the wall in back of her. I can mention that poster now. I mean, I can talk about it *now*, but when I was actually *there*, when I first saw it, I just looked right through it without letting it really register deep down in my brain. It was such a surprise, and it hurt so much that I looked at it just long enough to see what it was, and then I lowered my head and looked down at my hands until Vera was off the phone.

"Yes? Hello there! What can I do for you?" she asked, adding, "say, are you all right?"

I nodded. I was about back to normal. I can be really good at that. I have little tricks I use to not think about things I don't want to think about. That time I promised myself I wouldn't think about that poster and all the memories it dredged up until bedtime; I would save it for bedtime. And that's what I did.

"Oh, yes. I'm fine," I answered, still nodding. "I guess I was daydreaming or something." I told her my name and reminded her about my application.

"Gina Gari, hmm," she said, and started shuffling through a pile of papers. "As a matter of fact, I've been trying to call you all afternoon, believe it or not." She pulled out a paper from the stack. "Here it is!" She took a pencil from behind her ear and made little scribbles on the paper. "We do have an opening," she said, smiling at me. "But you do understand you'll start as a builder, not as a waitperson?"

"Oh, that's okay!" I quickly assured her. "That's no problem."

"I know it's terribly short notice, Gina," she continued, "but could you possibly come back at seven this evening? We're having a special training session for the new people."

"Oh, sure!" I said. "I can make it! That's no problem, really!"

In the back of my mind I was thinking that I could ask P.J. if he would give me a ride. I was pretty sure my mother wouldn't object to that. After all, it would save her the trouble of driving me. I thanked Vera and rushed back to where Tammy and P.J. were sitting.

"I got it! I got it!" I said, jumping up and down. "I'm supposed to come back at seven tonight—same as you, P.J.— and get trained!" I put my hand on his arm. "Do you think you could give me a ride? And what are we supposed to wear, anyway? Vera didn't mention anything about that. Where am I supposed to get a uniform? Well, for you *guys*, P.J., it's no big deal. You just wear jeans and those blue aprons. But look, see? The girls have those pinafores, and—"

"Gina!" Tammy said, her face flushed and angry. "Don't you *ever* shut up?"

I stopped talking and looked at her, surprised at her outburst. "What? What's wrong?"

"Oh, I knew it!" she said with a disgusted look on her face. "So what about studying together, huh? What you *promised*— that we'd study together tonight! You forgot all about that, didn't you?"

It's true. I had completely forgotten all about that. I got defensive right away. "Well, hold it, Tammy. I can't help it! I mean, this is a job! A real *job*. I don't tell them, you know. They tell me!"

"Well, just the same—"

"What do you mean, *just the same*? You talk as if I *planned* it this way!"

Tammy shook her head and turned away, saying, "God, Gina, you're really something, you know that?" She glanced at P.J., who was just sitting there watching us. "I can't believe this! First she promises me that we're going to study together tonight, and then she just waltzes over here like some princess or other and conveniently forgets all about it! But I don't know why I'm so surprised. After all, Gina *never* keeps her promises."

"How can you say that?" I answered. "When did I not keep a promise? Before now, I mean. Just tell me when?"

"Simple! I suppose you don't remember last Tuesday, when I was sick? You said you'd stop by Thrifty and get that lipstick for me that was on sale? No, you don't remember that, probably. Well, what about that night I had to go to my cousin's house, and you said you'd tape my program for me, and you forgot all about it? Don't remember that, either?" I think I saw a few tears in her eyes then. She wasn't actually crying, but she was very upset. Finally she just turned away and said, "Oh, what's the difference! I'll just study by myself. I'll probably get more done that way anyway." She took out a tissue and blew her nose.

I didn't know what to say. I was about to take another sip of my Coke, but just as I reached for the straw, P.J. playfully grabbed the glass and moved it out of my reach. "Hey, quit that!" I laughed. "Give that back!" I stretched out my arm, nudging his shoulder with mine. Instead of giving the glass back to me, he lifted it to his lips and took a couple of swallows. "P.J.! Stop that!" I laughed again. "Get your own drink if you want one, but keep your cottonpickin' hands off—"

Tammy suddenly stood up. "I'm going home," she said. "See ya." And she walked straight to the door and opened it so hard it practically swung off its hinges.

"Poor Tammy," I said. "I guess she's mad."

"What makes you think that?" P.J. said, and then he laughed.

P.J. came to pick me up in his father's old delivery truck a little before seven. He seemed glad to see me, but all we

37

talked about was how lucky we both were to get hired and how nice Vera was.

The training session lasted almost two hours. The most fun part was putting on the toppings. The idea was to have all of our "creations," as Vera called them, looking "absolutely decadent." Then, as a final check, we had to weigh them. For example, a Gargantuan had thirty-two ounces of ice cream.

"Wow!" this new builder named Lester said. "How many calories are in that thing, anyway?"

Vera said she didn't know about the sauces, but the ice cream itself contained about two hundred twenty-five calories per half cup. "So how many is that in a Gargantuan?" she asked us. "Can anyone figure it out?"

Whenever I heard a question like that, I automatically tuned out and let someone else come up with the answer. Someone always did.

"About two thousand?" someone guessed.

"I think it's more like eighteen hundred," another person chimed in. "Not counting the sauces. There's eight ounces in a cup, so that's four cups of ice cream at four hundred fifty calories a cup. Four times four hundred fifty is eighteen hundred."

Just like I said, I knew somebody would come up with the answer. No sense in me taxing my brain for nothing, I thought.

Vera smiled. "Yes, that's correct. However"—she held up a warning finger—"remember, if a customer asks about calories, you just smile and joke with them. Say, 'Luckily Flipper's ice cream is nonfattening!' "

By the time the training session was over I felt like I was covered with sticky sauce up to my armpits. We all sat around a big table while Vera explained about our uniforms, which for the girls are checkered blue pinafores and white blouses. She issued us two blouses and two pinafores each and told us that it was our responsibility to wear a clean outfit to work every day.

Then everyone got an individual evaluation for the night. I fared very well. Vera's only suggestion was that I gather my hair up somehow, like with a rubber band or something, since it would look and feel a lot neater that way. "Oh, this stupid hair," I agreed, reaching up with both hands and pulling it away from my face. "Maybe I'll just go and get it cut."

P.J. was sitting next to me, and when I said that, he leaned forward and whispered in my ear, "Don't you dare! I love your hair! Cut that hair and we're through!" And he made a slashing gesture with his forefinger right across the front of his throat. (Of course he was joking, but was he really? I felt a deliciously warm glow all over my body.)

The last thing Vera did was pass out two items to everyone: first, a thin blue binder called "The Flipper's Information Manual" (which she said we should all read thoroughly as soon as possible), and then our work schedules for the next two weeks. My first day would be June 8, the following Saturday.

P.J. drove me home after the session, and I think I came within an inch of getting kissed. I think if I had lingered there beside him on the front seat of the truck for just a second or two more, it probably would have happened.

After I got ready for bed I went and dug out what notes and worksheets I had in my cultural geography notebook. Unfortunately, I was just too tired to concentrate. I started thinking about how close I had come to being kissed by P.J. Gannon. Could it be that maybe—I mean, it seemed like he had been paying an awful lot of attention to me since he and Justine broke up. Could it be that he had gotten over her *that* fast?

An outline map of Europe slipped out of my notebook and floated to the floor. I was supposed to have located the major cities and filled in their names, but it just didn't seem to make any sense to me. Who could remember anything like that? Besides, those countries seemed so far away from California, they might as well not even exist at all. That's the way I felt about it. Circles on a blank outline map—that's all they were. And Mr. Costello probably wasn't going to ask us to do that on the final anyway. I picked up the map and stuffed it back into my notebook. Then I shut off my light and got into bed.

And then the time had come to think about the poster in Vera's office. I got the tissue out of my pajama pocket because I knew I was going to need it. Even though I had barely glanced at it, I could practically see it in living detail. In the foreground was a close-up, larger-than-life photograph of a huge yellow yo-yo with the words "Fly-by-Nite" spelled out in a circle on the face of it. Around the edges of the poster were pictures of kids in Flipper's uniforms doing various yo-yo tricks, or at least pretending to. Big white letters at the top of the poster spelled out the words:

YO-YO CONTEST FOR FLIPPER'S EMPLOYEES! WIN A TRIP TO ITALY! ENTER TODAY!

Oh, Grandpa! I thought, tears finally flooding my eyes. Grandpa, I miss you so much!

5

The next morning I tried to ignore that sickening, unprepared feeling that had become so familiar to me on test days. I got up too late to wash my hair, so I just brushed it back and tied it with a red bandanna. I was shocked when I looked into the mirror. Boy, my eyes were red and swollen from all that crying the night before, but at least I got it all out of my system.

I sighed and held up my hand mirror to check how my hair looked from the back. Hmm, I thought. Not bad. That's when it dawned on me that since P.J. had come into the picture, making such a big deal out of my blond hair, I didn't feel so cheated for not inheriting that luxuriously thick dark hair that hangs from the heads of all my brothers and Marie.

Except for Grandma Gari, I'm the only blonde in our family. What a downer it was when she informed me I must have gotten my hair from her! Her ancestors, she explained, came from northern Italy, where there are lots of light-haired people. And then she added the clincher: she herself had hair *just like mine* in her younger days. "So curly and fluffy," she said, reaching out to touch it while I tried not to cringe.

Well, I certainly didn't want to believe *that*, but I was finally forced to on the day we were helping her move out of the old house. My job was to pack up the things in her dresser, and there in the bottom drawer, wrapped in tissue paper, were two ancient photographs framed in dark gray cardboard folders. One was my grandparents' wedding picture, and the other was a photograph of my grandmother alone, sitting beside a large potted plant. The name of a photographer in San Francisco was printed in fancy type in the bottom corner of the wedding picture, but the one of her alone was stamped ASSISI, ITALIA, on the back.

I sat down on the bed and studied the wedding photo first. It fascinated me, but strangely enough it made me more curious than sad. The young man in the photograph was not the grandfather I knew.

"Oh, Grandma!" I called out. "Look! I found your wedding picture!"

I couldn't believe how young they looked. The man was so proud and serious, and the woman peeking out from behind her wedding veil reminded me of a frightened fawn. My grandmother came into the room and, panting slightly, lowered herself into the chair next to the bed.

"Look," I said. "It's you and Grandpa! It's your wedding picture! Where did you meet him, anyway? You didn't know him back in Italy, did you?" I really didn't expect an answer. I had often wondered about the beginnings of their romance, but neither one of them ever seemed to want to talk about it.

My mother and Marie had come into the room by then. "What's going on?" Marie asked. "We've got a lot to do yet, and here you two are—just sitting around." Then she saw the photographs. "What are those? Are those of you, Grandma?"

I looked at my grandmother again. She was a million miles away. "No," she said, shaking her head slowly. "I didn't meet him in Italy. We met here in San Francisco."

She paused, and I held my breath. Could it be she was ready to talk about it now? "So you met in San Francisco?" I repeated gently, hoping that would spur her on.

"His father knew my father," she said, brushing her hand

over the photograph like she was trying to brush away the years. "And one day he came with his father to my house. Soon he was coming to see me every Sunday afternoon. We would sit in the parlor and talk, with my mother crocheting nearby. A few months passed. He said he loved me. He had a steady job and a little money in the bank—so the two families arranged for us to marry." She looked away for a moment. "I was only seventeen, and Anthony was twenty-one." She looked over at me almost defensively, I thought, and added, "There was nothing I could do about it. My father was determined, and I was just a girl."

"*Really?*" I exclaimed. "They really *did* that in those days? Sort of *arranged* marriages like that! Wow! That's hard to believe!" I paused. It was unusual for my grandmother to be so talkative about the old days instead of complaining about everything in the here and now. I had more questions. Actually, what I wanted to ask about was love. But she had gotten up from her chair by then—after positioning her feet just so—and was slowly walking out of the room, dabbing at her nose with her lace-trimmed handkerchief.

Then I looked closely at the other photograph, the one from Italy, and that's when the stick hit the gong. There was no longer any doubt about it; except that her hair was a lot shorter than mine, in that old picture Grandma Gari looked exactly like me.

I was sure glad I had done my crying the night before, or I would have been a real basket case at McDonald's that day when I saw all the guys at P.J.'s table taking turns with a bright yellow yo-yo. I did my best to ignore them, but after lunch, when Tammy and I went outside, some of the boys were standing in the parking lot watching Raymond Keefer fooling around with the yo-yo. He did a fairly passable gravity pull, and then tossed it back to P.J., who seemed to amaze everybody just by doing a couple of round the worlds. I suddenly wanted to get that little disk in my hand so bad I could taste it. I walked up to them with Tammy following a few steps behind.

"Hey, P.J., let me see that a second, okay?" I asked.

"Didn't you get one? Vera has a boxful."

"No, I didn't get one. Come on, let me see it."

P.J. held out the yo-yo in front of me, teasing. "See? It's a Fly-by-Nite. It lights up. It glows in the dark." Then he added in a singsong, mocking way, "You didn't read your information manual, did you? You were supposed to read it, you know. If you did, you would have found out how to get your very *own* yo-yo."

P.J. was right. I hadn't read my manual yet. I shrugged and reached for the yo-yo again. "Come on! Let's see it! How does it light up?"

He backed up a few steps and threw a sleeper. "Little power packs. They plug into little power packs. So you didn't read about the contest, either," he teased. "And the trip to Italy! The trip to Italy that I'm going to win!"

By then my hand was aching to hold that little yellow charmer. "Give me that!" I said, making one final grab for the yo-yo.

But P.J. was too fast for me. He twirled himself around in a complete circle, avoiding my attempted snatch.

"Darn it, P.J.," I said. "I'm not kidding! I want to show you something! Give it to me!"

"Vut do you vant to show me, my little darlink, my little pussycat?" he said, pursing his lips and coming toward me as if he were about to kiss me. Tammy squealed in a fit of vicarious delight, but I didn't think he was funny at all. "Come on," I said to her. "Let's go."

*   *   *

44

Three hours later, as Tammy and I were walking home from school, who pulls up beside us in his father's beat-up delivery truck and offers us a ride home? That's right. Old P.J. Gannon himself.

"Hey, Gina!" he called out. "Come on! Hop in and I'll give you a ride home." He glanced at Tammy. "You too. Come on."

Tammy was standing closest to the door, but she hesitated a trifle too long. So I just brushed past her and opened it and slid over on the seat next to P.J. while she scooted in after me. Was she weird. She accidentally slammed the door shut so hard I thought she had broken the window. Both hands flew to cover her mouth, and her shoulders hunched over in embarrassment.

"Shut the door, why don't you?" P.J. said dryly, giving me a conspiratorial nudge with his leg as he pulled away from the curb.

P.J. passed right by my house without stopping. Instead, he took Tammy home first.

"Do you have to go right home, Gina?" he asked as I waved good-bye to Tammy and settled back in my seat.

I shook my head. "No. I guess not. Not *right* home, anyway."

"Good. There's something I want to show you."

At first I thought he meant the yo-yo. But I just asked, "What?"

"Oh, just something. You'll see."

"Mysterious, huh? Hmm."

He stole a quick glance at me, then looked straight ahead again. There was something odd and different about him, I thought. He seemed keyed up, kind of flushed and nervous. My heart started beating faster, and I felt a sudden wave of shyness.

We drove the few blocks to the center of town without

speaking. He pulled into the Leaning Tower of Pizza parking lot, missing the driveway by a couple of inches, and the wheels on my side hopped up on the curb with a lurch.

"Damn!" he said with a little nervous laugh. "Who put that curb there, anyway?"

I had a weird premonition as soon as he turned onto the frontage road in back of the parking lot. I held my breath and didn't speak, fearing that my words might somehow jinx the wonderful, strange ways of fate.

"It's called the Thing," P.J. said a few minutes later as the little truck pulled up right in front of it and he shut off the engine. "It's—it's like, well," he stammered, "it's like a local landmark."

"I know!" I said excitedly. "I was here on Saturday. I think it's so—"

"You were here?" he said loudly, interrupting me. "You were *here* already? Who with?"

I was surprised by his tone. "Well, nobody," I answered defensively. "I wasn't here with anybody. I came by myself. On Saturday morning. I, well . . ." I shrugged. "I just came over by myself."

He acted like he almost didn't believe me. "How did you hear about it? Did the kids tell you, or what?"

"No. I read about it in the paper."

"In the paper! It's in the *paper*?"

"Well, yeah. An old newspaper, a really old one, that I found in my closet the day we moved in."

P.J. laughed then. "Well, come on. Let's go up. Did you climb up on it when you were here before?"

"Oh, no." I shook my head. "No, no. I didn't go up. I—"

"Do you want to go up there now?"

"Well, sure. I guess so. I mean, can we? There's that fence and everything. I don't think I can get over it."

"There's a way," he said. "I'll show you."

46

He led me around to the back and in through an unlocked gate, and we slowly started climbing up the first cluster of stairs, with me leading the way. The next level of stairs was harder, and by the time we reached the last level, I was actually getting a little scared, to tell the truth. The breeze was suddenly stronger, almost a wind. We had finally run out of stairs, and now we were faced with an actual ladder. It was made of wood and partly rotted away. I wasn't sure it was all that safe to climb.

"Are these little thingies going to hold?" I asked, touching one of the rungs with my foot.

"Sure. But let me go first now," P.J. said, slowly inching past me on the narrow ladder. I wasn't sure if the twinge of excitement I felt was because of the height and danger or because of P.J.'s body brushing up so close to mine. But it was a wonderful feeling all the same.

In a few more seconds he had reached the top, where there was a small windowlike opening. P.J. was motioning to me. "Come on," he urged. "It's okay." Then he disappeared head-first through the opening. A moment later he leaned out, his arms resting on the weatherbeaten sill.

"Watch that rung there. It's a little loose," he cautioned. "Here!" He stretched out his right hand. "Take my hand." He reached for me and gently pulled me through the opening, his other hand gripping me firmly around the waist.

"We made it!" I said, my voice vibrating loudly in the small room. I dropped to a whisper. "We made it."

"Yeah."

"And look! It's like a hayloft! How neat!"

The tiny room was filled with bales of hay about knee high, with dry loose hay piled on top. P.J. sat down and sighed, "Whew! Some climb, huh?"

I sat down beside him. "Yeah, really," I answered, trying to control the sudden tremor in my voice.

"Just look at that view," he said softly, bringing his face

alongside mine and raising his arm to point out the little window. "You can even see the river over there."

I could feel his breath on my face. He smelled like peppermint, my favorite flavor. He was silent a moment. We both were. And then he spoke again. "It doesn't even look like our town, does it? It's almost like being in another country."

I'm not sure how it happened, but somehow P.J. was facing me now, and his arm again encircled my waist, and we were sharing a lingering kiss, and then another. The smell of the warm hay mingled with his sweet breath, and for a few seconds I actually felt like I was about to faint. I guess P.J. sensed it, because he just held me close a moment. I thought I was in heaven for sure. The next thing I knew, he was reaching into the front pocket of his white polo shirt. The material was thin, and I can still remember how I could see the outline of his fingers, reaching down there in the pocket and taking something out. It was a ring, a gold ring, set with an amber-colored stone. As soon as I saw it I knew I had seen it someplace before.

"It's my birthstone," he said softly. "My parents gave it to me on my twelfth birthday. It's too small for me now, but I'd really like you to wear it. Would you, Gina? Would you wear it?"

I looked down at the ring in his hand, and suddenly in a flash I remembered where I had seen it before. It was on Justine Kim's finger, of course.

"That's—that's the ring Justine used to wear, isn't it?"

P.J. drew back slightly, and I felt him take a quick breath. "That's over! That's over and done with!" he said—a little bit too defiantly, I thought.

"Oh," I said meekly.

Still holding the ring, he took my hand and singled out my fourth finger. "Can we just see if it fits?" he asked. "I really do want you to wear it, you know."

I looked into his eyes for a long, long moment. Of course, I knew what wearing his ring would mean and all that it implied. I also knew what I was going to say. It just felt so *right*, somehow. "Yes." I nodded. "Yes, I'll wear it."

After he slipped the ring on my finger, he stood and slowly pulled me up beside him. "I really have to go now," he whispered. "My dad's expecting me at the store."

I swallowed hard and forced myself to answer. "Yes. I should be going, too."

I really don't remember going down those flights of steps at all. It seemed like I just floated magically back to the ground. When we got to the truck, I turned around and gazed up again at the Thing. "It's so beautiful," I heard myself say. "I don't want to leave. I want to stay here forever and ever."

P.J. took my hands in his and bent down for one last kiss. "We'll be back, Gina," he said. "I promise you, we'll be back."

I was overflowing with happiness, and I was sure that at last I had found what I had been searching for. And what an omen! What a wonderful omen it was, I thought, that I should find such happiness at the very same spot where just a few days before I had reached the depths of loneliness and despair.

Three days later, on the last day of school, P.J. asked me for his ring back. It was humiliating and hurtful, and it certainly shattered into smithereens my hastily formed belief in omens.

"Gina, there's been a terrible mistake, and I'm in big trouble," was the way he broke the news to me the first thing in the morning on the front steps of school. Tammy was with me at the time, and the fact that he didn't even make an effort to catch me alone just added to my disgust. I was a partner in one of the shortest "romances" in history, and the experience of being dumped so unceremoniously left me with the feeling that guys in general were untrustworthy slimes and fickle as the day is long. What happened, of course, is simple. Justine Kim wanted him back, and got him.

That night, just before bedtime, I reached up on the top shelf of my closet and got down the little tin box that held my special treasures. I had been tempted to open it on the day we moved, but I just didn't have the heart.

I had a little trouble with the lid but finally got it off. And there they were, the Groucho nose, just as I left it, my grandfather's old cap, and finally, wrapped in tissue, my old yo-yo. I made a slipknot and stuck my finger through the circle of string. Then I threw a tentative sleeper. Then I threw a couple more. I walked the dog and rocked the baby just to warm up. Next I did a perfect Confederate flag. I didn't have room to try any astro loops or three-leaf clovers, but I knew right away that yoing was like riding a bicycle. It was a skill that once mastered, you never forgot.

With my yo-yo still cupped in my hand, I reached under my bed and dug out that information manual and quickly flipped through it. In just a second I found what I was looking for. It was a full page, and here's what it said:

Fly-by-Nite Toys (a division of TATER TOYS) and
Flipper's Family Ice Cream Parlor announce an exciting
YO-YO CONTEST
WIN AN ALL-EXPENSE-PAID TRIP TO ROME!
TEN WONDERFUL DAYS IN SUNNY ITALY
JULY 1 THRU JULY 10

- Open to all employees of Flipper's Family Creamery!
- Contest to be held at Flipper's on *Sunday,
  June 9, at 1 P.M. sharp!*
- Lots of free Fly-by-Nites and Sailing Circles
  to be given away!

Without even knowing the details of the contest, I was sure there was no chance in the world that my parents would allow me to go to Rome. But all the same, I knew my grandfather would have wanted me to enter. Even though he had said he would not speak to me from the dead, I thought I heard him anyway.

Okay, Grandpa, I answered. I hear you. I'll enter, and I'll win it—for you!

6

My first day at Flipper's was the day before the contest. The phone rang about nine thirty in the morning, while I was still getting ready. It was Tammy. "I'm leaving for New York tomorrow," she said. "Are you busy? Maybe we could do something today, you know, since I won't see you again until August."

I couldn't believe she had forgotten that I was supposed to start work that day. I was pretty short with her. "No, I can't, Tammy! Don't you remember? I start my job at Flipper's today. In fact, I have to be there at eleven, and I was about to take a shower."

"Oh." She made a little sigh. "I forgot."

I looked at the clock on the kitchen wall. It was almost a quarter to ten. I had to get going. "Listen, I have to go, Tammy," I said. "It's getting late. I have to take a shower yet and get dressed, and then I have to walk over there."

"Yeah. Okay. Well, I guess I'll see you in August, then."

"Okay. Have a good time," I said more or less offhandedly, since I was wondering if I had a clean slip to wear under my pinafore.

"Maybe I'll write to you," she added hesitantly, as if she didn't want to hang up.

"Okay," I answered simply. "So long, Tammy." And I hung up the phone.

Luckily I did have a clean slip, and a little before ten thirty I was all ready, and went out to the backyard to tell my mother good-bye. She was on her hands and knees, weeding between her rosebushes.

"How do you like my uniform?" I asked, since she hadn't seen it yet. "It's a pinafore. Isn't it cute?"

She made a slight effort to turn her head, but her blouse caught on a thorn near the back of her shoulder, and she just said "Ouch, damn!" and never did look directly at me.

I watched as she jabbed her little green garden shovel into the ground with her right hand and pulled out the weeds—roots and all—with her left one. Then she would toss a handful of weeds into a yellow bucket without missing a one.

"So I guess I'll be going now," I said, bending to retie my shoelace, even though it didn't really need retying.

"All right," she said, and threw another handful into her bucket.

My first day at work was hard but fun. I couldn't believe how fast the time whizzed by, and I couldn't believe how tired I was when I got home. I practically fell into bed, and then before I knew it, it was Sunday morning and back to work again.

There was more commotion than I expected in front of Flipper's when I arrived, and I realized that the yo-yo contest was a much bigger deal than I had thought. A good-looking guy wearing a red, white, and black TATER TOYS ARE TOPS T-shirt and a matching red, white, and black Tater Toys visor cap had just finished setting up a portable table and a little raised platform on the sidewalk in front of the creamery under the big elm tree. Two large easels with huge posters showing the whole Fly-by-Nite line of toys were already standing, but now he was putting a big display board on the table with sample Fly-by-Nite spinning tops and yo-yos and things called

Sailing Circles, which were actually saucer-shaped disks like Frisbees. Everything really looked spectacular. The yo-yos and Sailing Circles had all been charged up on their little power packs, I guess, because even in daylight you could tell they were lit up. The name Fly-by-Nite was spelled out on the yo-yos and Sailing Circles in a rainbow of colors.

"Hi there!" the guy said with a typical public-relations-type person's enthusiasm. "I see you're an employee! You're entering the contest, I hope?" He pointed to a clipboard with a list of names on it. "We've got eight people signed up so far."

I added my name to the list. "Well, you can count me in," I said just as P.J. walked out of the employees' entrance carrying a stapler and a large roll of tape. "Will this be okay, Donnie?" P.J. asked. Then, noticing me, he added, "Oh, hi, Gina."

"Fine, that's fine!" the guy he called Donnie answered, taking the tape and throwing his arm around P.J.'s shoulder. "This guy's a winner!" He beamed, looking at me. "Great yo-yo talent! He *really* impressed me! Wouldn't surprise me at all if we found ourselves together in Rome in about three weeks' time," he said, grinning and clapping his hand on P.J.'s back with a loud thumping sound.

My heart sank all the way down to my socks. That clinched it. Any glimmer of hope I might have had that *maybe* my parents would allow me to go on the trip vanished into thin air. (*"What? Did you say Rome? You want to go to Rome with a man named Donnie? Have you lost your mind?"*)

Some people were beginning to gather around Donnie's table, mostly customers from the Laundromat next door, along with the usual assortment of boys with skateboards and kids on bikes. One of the kids suddenly pointed toward the street and called out, "Hey, look! There's Channel Seven's mobile truck!"

Donnie perked up his ears at that and quickly made a circle of his thumb and index finger, stuck it in his mouth, and let out a shrill whistle. Then he took off his cap and waved it in the air, shouting, "Over here! Channel Seven! Over here!"

The TV van went to the corner, made a sharp U-turn, came back, and parked at the curb right in front of us. Both doors of the van flew open and two guys jumped out. And then this really cute short woman with reddish-brown hair slid off the high seat on the passenger side and landed lightly on her feet. She was wearing white jeans and a red, white, and black TATER TOYS ARE TOPS T-shirt and cap just like Donnie's.

Donnie seemed surprised and took a couple of steps toward her. "Maddy! I was wondering what happened to you! You're late, you know. What were you doing, anyway?"

She gave him a quizzical look, as if she didn't understand what he was talking about. Then she put her hands on her hips, took a deep breath, and answered, "Oh, nothing. I wasn't doing much. Just arranging for TV coverage, that's all. What were *you* doing, Donnie-poo?" Then she shrugged and grinned at me and started walking toward the front door.

"Oh, that door's locked," I said. "They'll open it at eleven, when the creamery opens. You have to go around to the side."

She squinted her green eyes in the bright sunlight and nodded. "Oh. Okay. Thanks."

I looked at my watch. "I should be going in too," I said. We headed for the side door together.

"My name is Maddy," she said with a smile. "I'm working on this contest with Donnie." She pointed to her T-shirt in a cute, funny way, making her finger go around in a little circle before landing right in the center of her chest. "For Tater Toys. That's us."

I smiled back at her. "I'm Gina," I said. "It's nice to meet you."

"It's very nice to meet you, too, Gina," she said. "Gosh, I just love Flipper's pinafores," she added, reaching out to touch mine. "They look so cute and old-fashioned. Have you been working here long?"

"This is only my second day."

"Really!" she exclaimed as if I had announced that I had just won the lottery. Then she said something that sounded like "Cripes!" Only she pronounced it in two syllables. "Ka-ripes! You must be excited! And still a bit nervous, too, I'll bet! But not as bad as your first day, huh?"

"Yes," I agreed, nodding. "That's right. That's exactly right."

She gave my arm an encouraging little squeeze, then held the door open for me. Vera waved as we walked past her office. I was waving back when I noticed a couple of bright yellow yo-yos on her desk. "Oh, excuse me a second, Maddy," I said, stopping and touching her arm. "I think I'm supposed to get one of those yo-yos."

"Oh, didn't you get one yet?" Vera asked, getting up from her desk and handing me one. "Are you going to enter the contest, Gina?" she asked politely. (How could she know she was talking to a champion!)

"Yes," I answered demurely. "I think it would be fun."

I loved the way that Fly-by-Nite felt in my hand, and I was really eager to give it a whirl. But before I could make the slipknot and loop it over my finger, Vera looked at her watch and said briskly, "Two minutes to eleven! Time to open up!"

Boy, were we busy! I didn't have a moment's rest for more than an hour. At twelve thirty Vera came up to me and said, "It's getting close to contest time. Why don't you take your break now—get washed up and so forth. I can handle things fine back here. Once the contest starts I don't imagine we'll be too busy."

I went to the restroom and washed the syrup off my arms.

It's surprising how that stuff gets all over you. Then I walked through the creamery again and outside into the sunshine. The crowd was growing larger by the minute. I guess people noticed the television van and the guys with the camera and were wondering what was happening.

I stepped aside out of the crowd to test my fancy new yo-yo. Wow! I couldn't believe the duration of my first sleeper. I threw another one and counted the seconds. I was amazed. That little yellow marvel slept for *fifteen* seconds. That was two seconds longer than the best I ever did with my trusty Duncan.

Several people were walking by on the far edge of the sidewalk, but I ignored them as I continued experimenting with that little gem. First I did a fine brain twister and an excellent flying saucer, and then I felt myself begin to tingle all over as I realized that maybe with this wonderful new yo-yo I could do what was for me the hardest trick of all, the one trick that for some unknown reason I had never completely mastered. I looked down at the sidewalk and concentrated as hard as I could, rehearsing the trick in my mind. It's called shoot for the moon, and it's a real zinger. You have to shoot the yo-yo almost straight up in the air to the right of your body, and as it starts to fall you snap it back up to a point behind you, and as it starts to fall again you snap it back up to the left of your body, then finish by catching it in your hand. I mean, that ain't no simple task! In fact, it's so hard I chickened out at the last second and did a skyrocket instead. That's the trick my grandfather always liked to do. You throw a very fast sleeper and then remove the loop of string from your finger. Just before the yo-yo hits your hand again on the return trip, you let go of the string. The yo-yo shoots straight up in the air like a skyrocket and you catch it on the way down. My grandfather always caught it in his cap, but I just caught it in my hand. I was thinking of him all this time, of course, with a quiet kind of happiness, but with a lump in my throat, too.

I turned around, intending to head back toward Flipper's, but instead I suddenly found myself standing face to face with Maddy, who appeared to be absolutely transfixed.

"*Ka-ripes*," she breathed. "Am I seeing what I'm seeing, or what?"

I laughed. "That depends on what you're seeing, I guess!"

"What I'm seeing is the answer to my prayers! How many lunar loops can you do?" she asked suddenly.

"My all-time record was two hundred thirty-seven," I answered, somewhat startled by her question. Why would I be the answer to her prayers? I wondered.

"Two hundred thirty-seven!" She hit herself on the forehead, pretending to knock herself out. She "came to" quickly, though. "Have you signed up yet?" she asked, all excited. "Is your name on Donnie's clipboard?"

"Yes. I just signed."

"Do you realize what's happening?" she said, practically jumping up and down.

"Well." I smiled. "Not exactly."

"I've just checked out the other contestants," she said. "They're all over there with Donnie, practicing, and from what I can tell, there's only one guy who can even do the basic five—"

"That must be P.J.," I interrupted. "He thinks he's going to win."

She grabbed my hands. "But we know better, don't we?"

"Yeah, I guess we do." I smiled again. But I still couldn't figure out why she was so excited. It wasn't like we were friends, or anything. After all, we'd just met. Then I started asking her about the contest.

It all began, Maddy explained, when her boss at Tater Toys mentioned at a sales meeting that he had two round-trip airline tickets to Europe that he couldn't use. That's when Donnie—she motioned over to him with a toss of her head—came up with the idea for the contest, since he knew Tater Toys was about to test the Italian market. The connection with Flipper's happened because Vera is Donnie's aunt.

"I'm ashamed to admit it, Gina," Maddy said, "but all of us at the meeting that day just naturally thought it would be a *boy* who would win a yo-yo contest, and so that meant Donnie would be the one to accompany the winner to Italy. But it was also decided, as a kind of joke"—she laughed gaily—"that if a girl *should* win, *I* would be the chaperon! So what do you think of that?" She gave me a quick impulsive hug. "An all-expense-paid trip to Italy for both of us! Can you believe it? Two hours ago I was admiring a stranger's uniform, and now we're going to Europe together! *Ka-ripes!* You know, that's what I love about life! It's so unpredictable!"

Well, that explained why she was so excited. I had to laugh at her, the way she was jumping up and down. But to me Europe was just a name and Italy just a country. And I didn't have the heart to tell her about my parents. They were probably the real reason that I couldn't let myself go all-out crazy like her. I realized that getting my parents' permission would definitely be a major problem. But at least with a female chaperon I might have just a glimmer of a chance. I decided I would concentrate on winning the contest first and worry about my parents later.

"Now tell me," Maddy said as we started walking back to Flipper's, "*where* did you learn to yo like that?"

"Oh, I learned a long, long time ago. I was only four years old when I first started. My grandfather taught me when we lived in San Francisco. He was a Duncan pro in his younger days. God, when I think of the hours we spent on that big old front porch, practicing one trick after another! My grandfather told me once that I was one in a thousand! He said that yoing required perfect timing and hand-eye coordination, and that it was a rare gift, probably inherited from him." I paused. "He was always joking around like that."

Maddy just rumpled up my hair, and a minute later she was saying, "Two hundred thirty-seven lunar loops! Unbelievable! It's amazing enough that you'd even know the simplest of tricks. Yo-yos have been out of style for years. Leonard Tater is taking a chance, but I think he's on to something. Even with computer games and all, I think yo-yos still have enough old-fashioned appeal to make a real comeback. And then there's this business about the Italian market. Leonard wants to give Rome a shot—so there you go."

"Well," I said, "I think it's a great idea." I paused a moment and added, "Yo-yos are like music or a handshake. You know, kind of a universal language . . ." I could almost see Grandpa's smile of approval.

"Say!" Maddy exclaimed. "A universal language! I like that!" She glanced at her watch. "But hey, it's almost one o'clock! Come on, champ, let's go show 'em how it's done in the big time!"

I only wish my grandfather could have been there at Flipper's that afternoon. God, he would have been so proud of me! And not just for the way I handled the yo-yo, either. I also remembered a lot of the stuff he told me about yo-yos and their history, and I'm glad I was able to pass that on, too. Grandpa would have liked that.

Donnie started off the contest by lining up all of us contestants and telling us each to do the five basic yo-yo tricks. The five basic tricks are the gravity pull, the sleeper, walk the dog, forward pass, and around the world.

The gravity pull is just throwing the yo-yo down overhand with your palm up, then turning your hand over and catching the yo-yo on the way back. The sleeper is when you throw the yo-yo and let it spin around at the bottom of the string. The trick there is to be sure you pull it up before it dies. Walking the dog is just what it sounds like. While the yo-yo is sleeping, you touch it to the ground and let it roll along by the force of its spin. A forward pass is when you throw the yo-yo out horizontally and let it come right back to your hand. An around the world starts out like a forward pass, only you let the yo-yo sleep, and while it's doing that you make it go around in a big circle before you pull it back in.

Well, believe it or not, P.J. and I were the only ones left after those five basic tricks. The other kids were laughing and giggling and getting their strings all tangled up with one another. That builder named Lester was really funny. When he was supposed to walk the dog, he just dragged the yo-yo on the sidewalk behind him and said, "Heel, Rover! Heel!"

The first trick Donnie called for after the five basics was rock the baby. To rock the baby, you throw a good sleeper and make a kind of pyramid, or triangle, out of the string and let the sleeping yo-yo rock back and forth within the pyramid. Well, poor P.J. messed up on his first try.

Then it was my turn to rock the baby. I gave it the required four rocks and an extra one for good measure, and when I finished, some people in the crowd actually whistled and applauded.

By that time it must have been obvious to Donnie that if he expected P.J. to win a trip to Italy for him, he was in serious trouble. (And from the way he kept staring at me with that incredulous look on his face, you'd think I was a two-headed monster from Mars.)

After that, it was just no contest. I mean, P.J.'s warp drive was a disaster, and his double-or-nothing stank, to put it mildly. I did both of those with no trouble at all, and then just to show off while the crowd was still applauding, I calmly shot the teacher and split the atom. God, it was fun yoing again!

I was disappointed that I didn't get a chance to demonstrate my lunar loops, though. They're used as the traditional tiebreaker. Actually they're just forward passes, one right after another without stopping. Instead of catching the yo-yo when it returns, you let it pass your hand on the inside and flip it out again. You do that over and over. The problem is that every time you do it the string gets a little tighter and the trick gets a little bit more difficult. And you break a lot of strings that way, too.

But I was so far ahead we didn't need a tiebreaker. Donnie just announced that we'd go right into the *second* part of the competition, which, he explained, was "a little quiz on yo-yo lore and history." Poor Donnie. He knew by then, of course, that I had already won the contest and (he thought) his free trip to Italy had vanished into thin air, but as a professional, he had to continue to the bitter end.

"Since the winner of this contest will represent Tater Toys on foreign soil, we feel that some knowledge of yo-yo history is essential to enable the winner to, uh, communicate effectively with those with whom he comes in contact."

"Yay!" Maddy exclaimed loudly from the sidelines, raising her arms in a victory salute.

Donnie gave her a very dirty look but kept on talking. "So for that reason, several days ago we asked our contestants to review an information sheet containing some pertinent facts about yo-yos and their history."

Well, that was news to me! And then I realized that since I was a "late entry," I obviously missed getting the information sheet. I decided to announce that fact as soon as I had the chance, since I didn't think that was fair at all.

"Now, then," Donnie was saying as he unfolded a scrap of paper, "I have five simple yo-yo questions for our remaining two contestants.

"I will alternate between you," he continued, speaking directly to P.J. and me now. "You will get one point if you answer your own question correctly and two points if you answer a question that your opponent has missed. Is that clear?"

I nodded and looked at P.J., who quickly averted his eyes. That's when it dawned on me that I had really beaten him. I have to say I didn't feel sorry for him at all (or Donnie either, for that matter), especially since even if they didn't realize it, they would still get to go on the trip—as soon as my parents nixed my going. But for the time being, let old P.J. suffer. Let them both suffer.

"First question for Gina," Donnie said. "What does the word 'yo-yo' mean, and in what language?"

"Well, I didn't get an information sheet, but I know that yo-yo means 'come-come' or 'to return' in Tagalog, the official language of the Philippines," I answered.

"That's—that's correct," he said with a somewhat surprised expression.

Did he think I didn't know the answer to such a simple question, or what?

"This one's for you, P.J. In the British Museum there hangs a painting of what monarch playing with a yo-yo?"

"King George IV?" P.J. asked sheepishly.

"Correct!" Donnie exclaimed enthusiastically. "That is correct!"

"Now, Gina," Donnie said. "Maybe you can make a guess on this one. In what other country besides England did the yo-yo become popular with the aristocracy?"

"In France," I replied. (That was an easy one. My grandfather had told me all about how the members of the French aristocracy were very fond of their expensive ivory yo-yos, and when the French Revolution forced the nobles to flee Paris, they took their toys with them. That's how the yo-yo came to be known as *l'emigrette* in French—from the word *emigre*, or "emigrant.")

Donnie cleared his throat. "France," he repeated. "Good."

Then he asked P.J. what the French word for yo-yo was. Well, too bad for poor P.J.! If he had learned it, he forgot it. My grandfather had only mentioned it to me once, but I remembered it. But then I usually remembered the things he told me.

"Well?" Donnie asked. "What's your answer, P.J.?"

"I—I don't know," P.J. said, blushing. "I forgot."

"They called it *l'emigrette*," I said calmly. "So that's two extra points for me, isn't it?"

"Right," Donnie said, looking like he just wanted to get this thing over with as fast as possible. He consulted his notes again, then asked me in a dull monotone, "I suppose you know the name of the man who first introduced the yo-yo into the United States?"

"As a matter of fact, I do. He was a Filipino by the name of Pedro Flores." Then I added offhandedly, "My grandfather knew him personally."

"Your grandfather," Donnie repeated in the same disinterested monotone. "I see. Well, I think it's obvious to everyone here that we do indeed have a winner. Congratulations, Gina, and have a wonderful time in Italy." Then he stepped down off the platform with that fake smile pasted on his face until he was just out of camera range, when it vanished like a bubble. And then he went over and kicked the tree. Most of the people in the audience were still facing me, so they missed seeing that. Actually, it was funny as heck.

Suddenly everyone gathered around me and took turns shaking my hand and congratulating me. I don't know what happened to P.J. He just disappeared into the crowd.

Then Maddy and I were interviewed on TV and had our picture taken for the newspaper. I was kind of flabbergasted by the whole thing, but Maddy, well, judging from the look of her, Maddy had simply died and gone to heaven.

7

Maddy and I were still standing arm in arm, the way we were for the newspaper photo, and Donnie was leaning on the portable display table a few feet away, mad as a wet hen, as my grandfather would have said.

"So where do I pick up the airplane tickets, Donnie?" Maddy asked, walking over to him with a wary smile.

Donnie didn't answer her for a moment. Then he began throwing yo-yos and Sailing Circles back into the brown plastic demo kits.

"Well?" she repeated. "The plane tickets?"

Donnie threw the last of the Sailing Circles into the kit and flipped down the lid. "They're at the travel agency, dumbo."

"Which *one*, Donnie?" Maddy turned and looked at me, rolling her eyes and mouthing the now familiar "Ka-ripes!"

With a loud sigh Donnie reached for his wallet and took out a business card, which he more or less tossed at her.

"Thank you," she said very politely, adding, "do you need some help packing up?"

"Just finished, thanks," he said coolly, snapping shut the second case. Then he scooped up the easels and posters and everything and headed for his car.

"Whew-ee!" Maddy grinned and spoke in a funny, lisping baby voice. "He *mad*, ain't he? No more fwee twip to Wome for 'ittle Donnie-poo."

That's when it finally sunk in. I mean, I really *did* win a free trip to Rome, and I wasn't even sure my parents would let me go!

I guess I was looking very somber about then, because Maddy suddenly poked her face up close to mine and said, "Hey, what is it? What's wrong, Gina?"

"Well, I was just thinking—about my parents, actually."

"Your parents?"

"They're really old-fashioned, Maddy, in a lot of ways. I mean, if you want to hear the worst, I don't even know if they'll *let* me go to Italy with you!"

Maddy knit her brows, and her green eyes looked deeply into mine. "My God, you're serious, aren't you?"

I nodded. "I'm serious. Like, they never let my sister go to the beach with her friends during spring breaks while she was in high school. She still complains about it. She says she was the only one whose parents wouldn't let her go."

Maddy raised an eyebrow. "Well, what about you? Do they let *you* go to the beach on spring breaks?"

I hesitated. "It's never come up, really. See, I've only gone to this high school for a little while, and before that—well, it never came up."

Maddy scratched her head. "It sounds like we may have a real problem, then. Listen, what time do you get off work today?"

"At five."

"Well, what if I come home with you? I could sort of, you know, talk to them. Your parents, I mean."

I thought about that a second. "Gee, I don't know. I suppose it *could* help. Maybe."

Maddy shoved her hands into the back pockets of her white jeans. "I think I understand how they feel, though," she said, nodding. "I know if I ever have a daughter, I'm going to be pretty careful about where I let her go and what I let her do.

I mean, hey, I know I'll love her enough that I'll try to protect her as much as I can." She shrugged and turned away with a blush. "God, listen to me."

But I had my own problem. I was starting to feel that familiar little gnawing hurt somewhere around my heart. "In this case," I said, choosing my words as carefully as I could, "I don't know how much of it has to do with love, exactly, and how much with—well, just taking the easy way out. It's like my mother is not so concerned with *me* getting into trouble—it's more like *she* just doesn't want the trouble of dealing with it. So she just says no all the time. We never discuss the pros and cons of anything. She just says flat-out *no*."

Maddy was really listening to my little speech, watching me intently and nodding her head. "Well," she said, "we'll see what we can do. This trip would be a wonderful opportunity for you, and I'm pretty confident we can talk them into letting you go."

I looked at her in her Tater Toys T-shirt and cap and tight white jeans. "I hope so," I said, "except that—" I shook my head. "I don't know. You really don't look like a chaperon or anything. Hey, how old are you, anyway? You almost look younger than me."

"Come on! I'm twenty-eight!" She looked down, giving herself the once-over. Then she nodded. "I see what you mean, though. Not too responsible-looking at the moment, am I?"

I smiled. "You said it, Maddy."

Just then Vera poked her head out the front door of the creamery. "Gina!" she called. "As soon as you're through out there, we could use you back in here."

"Oh, sure!" I said. "I'll be right there."

Maddy and I went back inside, and Vera came over. "Over there," she said. "You can help the people in the back station. They're swamped."

I looked over to where she pointed me. One of the builders had just put the finishing touches on a chocolate Super Soda by precariously hanging a scoop of vanilla ice cream the size of a softball over the edge of the glass.

Maddy touched my arm. "Listen, I've got an idea. If I'm not back by five, wait for me."

"Okay," I answered as a waitperson almost ran into me, carrying in her hands a dish containing a definitely decadent-looking, calorie-free Gargantuan piled high with thirty-two ounces of ice cream, oozing tons of strawberry, pineapple, and chocolate syrup and topped with a mountain of whipped cream, chopped nuts, and two cherries.

Maddy returned a few minutes after five, but at first I didn't recognize her because she was dressed in completely different clothes. She stopped to talk to Vera while I stared at her with amusement and wonder. She was wearing dark-rimmed glasses, no makeup, and a dowdy plaid cotton skirt with a simple white blouse. And then I looked at her shoes. I couldn't believe what I saw. Oh, no! It can't be, I thought. Not *those* ugly things! For the shoes she was wearing were brown chunky crepe-soled loafers with fake golden buckles just pasted on, identical to a pair I once had—a pair of shoes that were loaded through and through with bitter memories.

"Well, how do I look?" Maddy asked me in a prim, subdued voice. "More responsible, maybe? Chaperonish, even?"

Those shoes really knocked me for a loop, and I couldn't answer her for a moment. But then somehow I pulled myself together and said as brightly as I could, "You remind me of Miss Ragland, my old sixth-grade teacher! And you sound like her, too. Where'd you get all that stuff, anyway?"

Maddy laughed. "At that little thrift store around the corner. And I got it all for less than five dollars. How 'bout that?"

"Amazing," I said, forcing a smile. "The glasses, too?"

"No." She shook her head. "The glasses are mine. I just removed my contacts. Pretty good, huh?"

"Maddy, you look perfect. My mom will—well, I think my mom will love the way you look," I said, my voice cracking just a bit.

Maddy gave me a long stare. "Are you okay, Gina? Is something wrong?"

"No," I answered. "It's—it's nothing."

We started to plan our strategy in her car as we drove to my house. I told her that we should concentrate on Mom. Dad would take his cue from her. And I would be careful not to act too excited, since I've discovered through the years that when I'm really excited about going someplace, it's more difficult to get my mother's permission.

"But that's going to be really hard to do," I said, "acting like I'm not excited, I mean, since I'm getting more excited about this trip every second!"

Maddy looked at me and smiled. "Same here, Gina."

"You look great!" I told her. "I think those clothes will make a big difference." And especially those *shoes*, I thought.

"Well, I sure hope so," Maddy said. "After all this, it would be a terrible disappointment if they didn't let you go."

I nodded and bit my lip. "Yes. I know." Then I laughed hollowly and added, "Gee, if by some miracle they *do* let me go, I can just see Marie's face when she finds out. She won't believe it! Old Marie will probably stand there whining, 'How come *she* gets to go to Rome, and I couldn't even go to the beach!' "

"Let's not get overconfident now," Maddy advised, pulling up in front of my house.

I jumped out of the car and ran up the front steps two at a time. But Maddy, in keeping with the part she was playing, climbed the steps in a very subdued and ladylike manner.

I tried the front door, but it was locked. "That's strange," I said. Then I rang the doorbell a few times in rapid succession. I turned and looked at Maddy. "That's really strange. They're always home on Sunday afternoons."

"Do you have a key?"

I got out my key and unlocked the door, and Maddy followed me inside. The house was hot and stuffy. The air conditioner hadn't been on all day. There on the spindle by the phone was a scrawled note.

11:30 A.M.

Gina:

Marie just called. Grandma Gari has been taken to the hospital. They think it's a minor heart attack. Your father and I are driving over. You can try to reach us at Marie's when you get home.

I read the note quickly. "Oh, *no!*" I said.

"What is it? What's wrong?" Maddy exclaimed.

"My grandmother. In San Francisco. She's had a heart attack. My parents are over there."

I began to read the note to her, and when I finished, she took it from my hand and read it again herself.

"Oh, God! You'd better call!"

But I was already looking for Marie's number in our little blue book. I don't call her very often, and when I do, I usually get the wrong number and end up talking to some guy at a place called Corky's Used Cars. I wanted to be sure I got the right number this time.

Marie answered after the first ring. "Hello?"

"It's me," I said. "How's Grandma?"

"Gina! We saw you on TV!"

"You *did?* When? It wasn't supposed to be on until the news." I covered the mouthpiece with my hand and practically shrieked at Maddy, "Marie said we were on TV already! She said they saw us on TV!"

Maddy looked puzzled. "But your grandmother. How's your grandmother?"

70

"Oh, yeah." I took my hand away from the mouthpiece. "But Grandma, Marie. How's Grandma?"

"Oh, she's fine. They're not even sure it was a heart attack. You know how she exaggerates all the time. She just had some slight pains and was feeling dizzy. She called me up and told me she wasn't feeling well, so this time, instead of going over there and all that, I just called an ambulance. The doctor did say he wanted to keep her in the hospital for a couple of days, though, for tests and stuff, just to be doubly sure."

"Oh." I glanced at Maddy. "It's sort of like a false alarm. Marie says she's okay."

"But listen, you little brat," Marie was saying. "You're going to Italy! What a lucky stiff! And all because of your silly yo-yo tricks, too! You should have seen Mom and Dad! We were all just sitting around in the waiting room while Grandma was having her EKG and stuff, and the TV was on, and all of a sudden there's a shot of Flipper's and you with your stupid yo-yo and some woman with her arm around you talking about going to Rome! Mom and Dad were so impressed! God, the power of television. It's really disgusting. Anyway, they said they didn't even know about that contest. How come you didn't tell them?"

"Well, it's a long story. See, uh, I didn't even know about it myself until—"

"Listen, Gina, I really don't have time for all that now, okay? Mom and Dad went back to the hospital to see about getting Grandma a private room, and when they get back we're supposed to go out for dinner. I want to wash my hair and do some stuff around here before then."

So what's new? I thought. Nobody in my family ever wants to listen to what I have to say. "Okay, I'll tell you about it later," I said, even though I knew the subject would never come up again. "But now the big question is will they let me go? You know how they are."

"What are you talking about, lamebrain? Sure they'll let

you go! And I'll tell you what did it. Appearing on TV, that's what! A bunch of other people were in the waiting room, and when they heard Mom and Dad saying, 'Look! That's our daughter on TV!' well, they all came over and started congratulating us, and the nurses and orderlies and everybody started coming in, and God, it was wild! So don't be silly. They're going to let you go. You've got a proper chaperon, and everything. It's a lead-pipe cinch, for God's sake."

"Yo, Maddy!" I called out. "Marie says they're going to let me go! Yip-*py!*" I started dancing around with the phone in my hand.

"Gina! Toad-face! Where'd you go?" Marie was trying to get my attention. "Hey! Listen! There's something else, something very weird. When we finally got to see Grandma and told her what had happened—about how you were going to Italy and all—she almost had another attack! I'm telling you, it was *scary.* She started praying and kissing that necklace she always wears and muttering stuff like 'Oh, thank you, Saint Francis! Thank you!' over and over. She even started to get out of bed, and when Dad asked her what on earth she was trying to do, she said she had to get down on her knees and give thanks. Can you believe it?"

"Sure," I said. "I can believe it. The praying part, at least. That's nothing new."

"Yes," Marie said impatiently. "That's nothing new. But the thing is, why should she be so excited about your going to Italy? That's what I'd like to know!"

"Search me. I don't know."

"And there's more. She said she wanted us to tell you to be sure to see her in person before you leave. She says she absolutely *has* to see you. But she wouldn't say what for."

"Oh, yeah? And she wouldn't say what for?"

"That's right. Well, listen. I've got to get moving here. God, my scatterbrained little sister's going to Europe before

72

I do! You know something? When I was your age, Mom and Dad wouldn't even let me go to the *beach*, for God's sake!"

After I hung up the phone, I smiled at Maddy. "She said when she was my age, they wouldn't even let her go to the beach, for God's sake."

Maddy grinned back at me. "She did, huh?"

We went into the kitchen and I poured us some lemonade, and then we sprawled out on the couch in the front room. Maddy took a few sips of her drink and then suddenly looked at her watch. "Hey! It's just six! Turn on the TV. Let's see if we're on the news!"

I reached over, snapped on the television, and turned to Channel Seven, saying, "Gosh, we were already on once today. Do you think we'll be on again?"

Maddy picked up the *TV Guide* and ran her finger down the listings for Sunday afternoon. *"Out and About with Terry Trout,"* she read. "Sunday at three thirty. That must have been it. That's probably the program your family saw at the hospital. Darn!"

"What's wrong? We're still going to be on the news, aren't we?"

"Well, that's just it. I'm not sure. Especially since they've already aired it. See, the problem is, nobody watches those Sunday afternoon time-fillers. Especially with baseball on Channel Twelve." She opened her purse and pulled out a little red spiral notebook, all the while keeping her eyes on the television. We sat there and watched the entire six o'clock news—right down to the sports and weather. A few more commercials, and it was over.

"I'm going to call the station in Stockton," she said, checking the number in her little red book and then reaching for the phone. "I'll put it on my credit card."

"Hello?" she said after a moment. "This is Maddy Meyers with Tater Toys. May I speak to Vincent, please? Oh, he's

73

not? Well, I was wondering if you were going to run the Flipper's yo-yo contest on the late news tonight. The guys told me this afternoon they'd try to fit it in this evening, but apparently—" She paused and made a face at me. "Oh," she said very sweetly. "It was already on this afternoon? I see. Well, darn, I guess I missed it. Anyway, if you can possibly fit it in the *late* news—" She paused again. "Oh, I see. Yes. Well, thanks very much, anyway. Bye now." She hung up the phone very gently, and then she exploded, "Those cretins!"

I had to laugh. "You were so nice to them, and then you say that."

She looked at me with a sheepish grin. "That was only my public-relations niceness," she explained. "No sense burning bridges, right? The thing is, I might have talked Vince into it, but this babe couldn't care less."

"You mean they're not going to show it later either?"

"No, it doesn't look like it."

"Oh, nuts!" I said. "I wanted to see myself on television."

Maddy smiled. "Yes, I know." She shrugged. "Well, that's how it goes." Suddenly she jumped up. "Ka-ripes!" she said. "Passports! You and I need to get our passports!"

"We do? Right now?"

"Well, not this minute, silly, but soon. We're supposed to leave on July first, remember? And today's the ninth of June! Listen, you're going to need your birth certificate. Do you know where it is?"

The phone rang suddenly, making both of us jump. I picked up the receiver. "Hello?"

The voice on the other end was so faint I could barely hear it.

"Hello? Hello?" I said. "I can barely hear you." And then I realized who it was. "Grandma?" I said. "Is that you, Grandma?"

"I'm calling from the hospital," she said. I heard another voice in the background—probably a nurse—saying, "Speak

74

right into the phone, Mrs. Gari. Here, let's sit you up a little higher."

"Yes, yes. All right," my grandmother said. Then, to me again, "This is your grandma." Pause. "I can't hear you."

"Yes, I know!" I practically shouted into the phone. "How are you, anyway? Are you feeling better?"

"I have my own room now," she said. "A private room. Your father fixed me up in a private room."

"Well, that's very nice," I said (knowing that my mother had probably done the fixing up but that my father got the credit, as usual).

"What's that?"

"That sounds nice!" I repeated even louder.

"You are going to the Old Country," she said. "They explained to me about the contest. I don't understand all of it, but is it true you are going to the Old Country?"

"Yes! That's right. On July first. Isn't it wonderful? I'm going to Italy for ten whole days. And I'm going with—"

"*You come and see me!*" she interrupted.

"Well, I—"

"The saint has answered my prayers! Now you must come and see me as soon as you can! Do you hear that?"

"Yes," I said, shrugging at Maddy. "I'll try."

"No trying! *Coming!*"

"All right," I said finally. "I'll come to see you."

A few minutes later, after I hung up the phone, I told Maddy what my grandmother had said. "I don't understand it. She's so insistent!"

Of course, Maddy couldn't make any more sense out of it than I could. She looked at her watch again. "Listen," she said, "I've been thinking—what are the chances of your coming back with me tonight?"

"Back with you where? Do you mean to San Francisco?"

"Yes. To my place. We've got some heavy planning to do, kiddo. So this is what I have in mind. You can come back with me tonight, see. I'll take tomorrow off, and we can pick up the plane tickets at the travel agency and get our passports and all that. We can plan what we're going to take, maybe do a little shopping, and you can visit your grandmother. You can get that out of the way."

"How?" I asked, wide-eyed. "I don't even know which hospital she's at."

Maddy dropped her chin to her chest and stared at me from under her reddish-brown eyebrows. "You don't know which hospital she's at?" she asked in a breathless whisper. "Gracious me! Now we're in a fine pickle, aren't we? *She doesn't know what hospital her grandmother's at!*" she repeated like an actress in a soap opera. "*Oh, dear! Oh, dear!*"

"Okay." I laughed. "I get the point. So I can *find out* what hospital she's at."

"Wonderful," Maddy said dryly. "You find out where she is, and I'll drive you there tomorrow for your command performance. After we do all our other business, I'll drop you off at the Greyhound depot. You'll be back here tomorrow before dark. How does that sound?"

"That sounds great, Maddy. I'll call Marie again and see if it's okay with my mother."

"Perfect," she said.

A little while later I got my mother on the phone and she actually agreed to Maddy's plan, but not until she had spoken to Maddy herself and gotten her address and phone numbers (both home and office) and repeated everything about fifty times to make sure she had it straight. When she starts acting like that it usually annoys the heck out of me, but this time— with Maddy nodding and winking at me and being so patient—it hardly bothered me at all.

8

It was dark by the time we finally got on the road heading toward Maddy's condo in San Francisco. She took the freeway that goes right through the middle of the windmill farms in the Altamont Hills. They were so beautiful—row after row of twirling windmills all silvery in the moonlight.

"Oh, look at that!" I said. "Isn't it neat the way they shine? I've never been on this road at night before."

"Really? Yes, they are pretty, aren't they?"

"Boy, you know, Maddy, my heart's beating a mile a minute! I'm getting really excited about this trip."

"Same here, Gina," she said. "We're going to have a great time."

I sighed, folded my arms, and settled back in my seat, still watching the windmills, until I suddenly remembered that I was supposed to report for work at Flipper's at eleven o'clock the next morning.

"Uh–oh," I said. "I'm supposed to work tomorrow. I forgot all about it."

Maddy quickly turned and looked at me. "Oh, no!" she said. "How could you forget that?"

I shrugged and looked out the window again. "I don't know. All the excitement, I guess. I just forgot." After a moment I added, "Well, I guess they can get along without me all right."

But Maddy had already changed lanes and was pulling off the freeway on a long, curving off-ramp. "What did you say?" she asked as if she didn't hear me right.

"I said they can probably get along without me okay."

She was really shocked. "Hey, Gina!" she said. "That's *not* the way to go! We're going to stop here and try to find a phone. And if you don't get permission to miss work tomorrow, we're turning right around and I'm taking you straight back home."

I looked at her in amazement. I couldn't believe she'd actually do that. "Does it really matter *that* much?" I asked, genuinely puzzled that she was ready to chuck all our plans just because I was scheduled to work the next day. "I mean, what if I were sick or something? They'd get along without me then, wouldn't they? We have plans! We have things to do! What about our passports? What about my grandmother?"

Maddy pulled up in front of a pay phone in the far corner of a Mobil station and shut off the engine. "Those are good questions," she said. "However, we're just going to sit tight in this car until you can figure out where your basic loyalties should be."

"What do you mean by my basic loyalties?"

"Which word are you having trouble with?" she asked with slight sarcasm. "Basic or loyalties?"

I slumped down in the seat. Suddenly Maddy was not being much fun anymore. "Both," I said, choosing to match her sarcasm with stubbornness.

"Okay, then, if you insist. 'Basic' means fundamental, or primary. You know, like *first*. That's not too difficult, is it? And the word 'loyalty' refers to things like trustworthiness and dependability. Your employers are depending on you, Gina. It's like you have a contract with them. You go to work, and they pay you. What would you think if they reneged on *their* part of the contract?"

"What do you mean?" I asked. I couldn't believe I was sitting there arguing with Maddy. I wanted her to start up the car again. I wanted to go to her condo. I wanted to start planning our trip.

"I mean," she explained patiently, "what if you worked your shift, for instance, and then they said you weren't going to get paid?"

"After I worked, you mean?"

"Exactly."

"Well, that's different. If I work, they should pay me."

"But don't you see, Gina? It's a two-way street. You trust them to pay you if you work, and they trust you to report for work as scheduled."

I didn't answer.

"It's like an equation," she continued. "A balance. Don't you understand?"

"Well," I said grudgingly, "since you put it that way, I guess I do. It's like when I took the job, they agreed to pay me, and I agreed to work. I can see that, I guess. Only it seems like their agreeing to pay me is a lot more important than my agreeing to work."

"Aha!" she said. "That's because it's not your creamery. Just put yourself in their shoes. That's all you have to do."

Neither one of us spoke for several minutes. Finally Maddy said, "So out you go! Do you have change for the phone?"

I sighed. Maddy wasn't kidding. I was going to have to phone. "Yeah. I have change, but I don't know the number."

"That's easily remedied," she said, reaching onto the back seat for her memo book. "I should have Vera's home number in here someplace. Yes. Here it is." She jotted down the number on a scrap of paper and handed it to me with a big smile. "Good luck," she said.

Vera was great. I told her about how I was halfway to San Francisco and that I had to get my passport and everything, and how I just forgot about having to work. I used the fact that I was so excited as an excuse—which was, after all, the truth. "I'll find someone to fill in for you," Vera said. "Thanks for calling, and let me know when you get back."

Maddy leaned over and opened my door when she saw me hang up the phone. "It's okay," I told her as I climbed back in the car and buckled up my seat belt. "She said she'd take care of it."

"Well, that's fine." Maddy paused a moment before starting up the engine. "Gina, I didn't mean to lecture you like that, and I hope you don't resent—"

"Hey, you weren't lecturing. You were just explaining. And I don't resent it. I—well, I appreciate it," I added, sincerely meaning every word.

Maddy reached over and patted my hand. Then she started the car and made a wide U-turn in the empty parking lot. For some reason I felt like I had finally started to grow up.

After we returned to the freeway, Maddy turned on the radio to some soft music and I settled way back in my seat. I started thinking about the contest again. "Maddy," I asked, "what did Donnie mean this afternoon when he was talking about the winner representing Tater Toys on foreign soil, and being able to communicate with the people over there, and all that? Am I supposed to sell yo-yos when we get there, or what?"

"Oh, no," she answered, shaking her head. "Nothing like that. It's just that this is conceived as a business trip, at least partially, and it's my chance to make some real points with Leonard. So I'll probably want to set up a little demonstration in one of the larger toy stores in Rome—with *you* there doing your thing, of course—and perhaps see if they can help with a little free newspaper coverage. If the stores advertise at all, they're bound to know someone at the paper. That's just the way those things work. I can almost see the headline now, with an accompanying photo: *American Teen-ager Wows Them with Yo-yo Magic!*"

"Wows them!" I laughed. "I wonder if there's a verb for 'wow' in Italian."

"Well, anyway, you get the idea. I'm certain the two of us can stir up something once we're there."

"You sure sound confident! Where did you learn about stuff like that—publicity, and all? Do they have a major in that at college? You did go to college, didn't you?"

"Certainly I went to college," she answered. "I was a psychology major with a minor in business administration. I had really planned on going into counseling work—like in family relations, for instance, but somehow I ended up in sales and public relations instead. The job at Tater Toys just sort of fell into my lap." She paused and then asked, "So what about you, Gina? Have you decided on a major yet?"

"Oh, no. I'm not even planning to go to college. I just want to get a job and buy a car so I don't have to beg my mother to drive me places anymore."

"Oh?" Maddy said, obviously surprised. "What will you do then, after you graduate from high school? What kind of job will you get?"

"I wish I knew. Anyway, I don't have to worry about it for two years yet."

She glanced over at me. "Oh, *really*?" she said quite sarcastically. "*That* long?"

I shrugged and closed my eyes. We didn't talk for a while. I was just listening to the music on the radio and thinking about the great adventure that lay ahead. I only knew of two kids at my school who had already been to Europe. Marian Tyacke went to visit some relatives in Denmark or somewhere over Christmas vacation, and David Lundgren (the richest kid in school) spent a month touring France by bicycle with his parents. They visited the grave of his grandfather, who was killed during the Second World War. Now I was sorry I didn't pay more attention to what Marian and David had said about their trips. I guess that at the time I never dreamed that I would ever travel out of the country, so I just tuned out. I mean, how could I have known that I was destined to win a trip to Italy in a yo-yo contest, of all things?

Maddy suddenly reached over and shut off the radio. "That music's putting me to sleep." She rolled down her window, let in a blast of fresh air, and rolled it up again. "So tell me about your mother, Gina," she said. "What is she like?"

"What?" I asked, even though I had heard her perfectly well.

"Your mother. When I talked to her on the phone, I thought she sounded a lot like my own mother."

"Well, I doubt that," I said. "My mother is definitely one of a kind."

To my surprise, Maddy laughed a sharp little laugh. "Don't be too sure about that," she said. "So what's she like?"

"I wouldn't know where to start," I answered, stalling for time. The fact is, I wasn't sure I could talk about my mother to Maddy. How do you tell someone that your mother doesn't really care about you? Oh, she doesn't whip you and lock you in your room and make you go hungry or anything like that; she just doesn't *care*. How do you go about telling that to someone like Maddy, whom you desperately want to have a good opinion of you? It's embarrassing, and it hurts.

Maddy seemed to sense my hesitation. "Well, some other time, maybe," she said. "How about when we're leisurely strolling along the *Via Veneto* in Rome?" She laughed. "Eating raspberry *gelati* and fending off legions of young Roman swains!"

I knew she was just being funny, but a little wave of apprehension washed over me. What if there *was* a little bit of truth in what she said? I thought, squirming around in my

seat. Legions of young Roman swains? My God, what was
going to happen on this trip, anyway? Could Maddy be thinking of me as a contemporary—a kind of partner in romantic
conquests, maybe?

She turned to me and smiled. "Hey, relax. I'm only joking,
you know."

It was uncanny the way she seemed to know what I was
thinking. I laughed a partly forced little laugh, but I felt relieved all the same.

I just loved Maddy's condo. It's on two levels, with a darling
front room on the bottom floor and the bedroom and kitchen
on the top. You can even get a tiny glimpse of San Francisco
Bay from her bathroom window.

"I don't know about you," she said, collapsing on a chair in
the kitchen, "but it's been a long day. I'm pooped."

"Yes," I agreed. "Me too."

"Why don't I take the first shower then, and while you're
taking yours, I'll put a pizza in the microwave."

"Okay," I said.

Later, after we had finished our pizza and were talking
about what kind of clothes we should take, Maddy's mother
called. Maddy had called her earlier to tell her the big news,
but apparently her mom wanted to talk to her some more.
They were on the phone for quite a long time, with Maddy
doing most of the listening, it seemed to me. After she hung
up, she just sat there at the table resting her chin in her hands
with a faraway look in her eyes—as if she could see right
through the walls and out across the bay all the way to the
bridge. "The thing about my mother that drives me absolutely bonkers," she said suddenly, getting up and heading for
the bathroom, "is that she would gladly suffer any pain or go
through any deprivation—all for me. In fact, I think what she
would *really* like is to make the ultimate sacrifice and live my

whole damn life for me." Maddy closed the bathroom door, leaving me sitting there with my mouth hanging open about a foot.

I had to search around for a while before I found her remote control, and then I lay down on the bed and turned on the television. When Maddy came out of the bathroom, she started poking around the bedroom in her bare feet, straightening things and hanging up loose clothes. Suddenly she stumbled.

"Damn!" she said, flopping onto the bed and cradling her foot in her hand. After a few seconds she leaned over and picked up the offending object. It was one of those stupid brown clodhoppers that upset me so much when I first saw her wearing it at Flipper's that afternoon.

"You know, these old things are surprisingly comfortable," she said, waving the shoe in the air. She impulsively grabbed hold of one of my ankles and raised my foot off the bed. "Well, I'll be darned! Look there! Our feet are almost the same size! Ka-ripes! I knew I had big feet, but you're six inches taller than me, for God's sake. Hey," she said, reaching for the other shoe, "do you want to try these on? They're *really* comfortable."

I was just wishing she'd throw those stupid shoes back under the bed and forget about them. "No, Maddy," I said as plainly and forcefully as I could. "I *don't* want to try them on."

I guess she thought I was just egging her on or something, because she started to get playful. She made a grab for my foot, but I was too fast for her. I quickly flopped onto my stomach and buried my face in the pillow. Suddenly the words my mother said to me at the shoe store that day came back to taunt me, as they had done countless times before: *You've been nothing but a royal pain in the ass since the day you were born.* As much as I tried not to, I still started to cry.

Maddy must have thought I was just horsing around. The

bed moved, and I felt her leaning over me. In a few seconds she had a hold on my right foot and was shoving that ugly brown shoe over my instep. I rose up as if I'd been shot. Maddy, laughing, took one look at my face, and suddenly her whole body stiffened and the shoe dropped to the floor. "What's wrong, Gina?" she breathed. "You're crying!"

Still keeping her eyes on me, she went to her dresser and got me a tissue. "Tell me what's wrong," she pleaded. "What have I done?"

Well, after I calmed down a bit, I told her the whole pathetic story about the shoes with the golden buckles. I told her how my mother and I were shopping for my new school shoes—I was just going into the sixth grade—and she wanted me to try on a pair of those ugly things just because they were on sale. Well, I did try on a pair, but I couldn't stand them. I knew my mother wouldn't care about that. She would want me to get them anyway. So I lied and said they were too tight. Her solution to that was simply to have the salesman get a larger pair. The only thing I could do then was to just bite the bullet and tell her outright that I hated those shoes, that none of the kids at school were wearing that kind anymore, and that I wasn't going to wear them either. "What do you mean?" my mother said. "He just went in the back and found a larger size. And they're on sale. Put them on." I argued about it some more. I told her no wonder they were on sale, they were ugly and stupid, and nobody would buy them.

"Yes," Maddy said softly. "What happened then?"

I didn't know if I could say the rest. I just sat there swallowing.

"Gina," Maddy said finally, putting her hand on my back. "You don't have to tell me any more if you don't want to."

But the strange thing was, I *did* want to tell her. It was just so hard getting the words out. "She—my mother—she threw the shoes down on the floor and said, 'To hell with your new

shoes!' " I wiped my eyes with the tissue Maddy had given
me. "And then," I continued, "my mother called me a royal
pain in the ass. Isn't that awful? She said I'd been nothing but
a royal pain in the ass since the day I was born."

"Oh, Gina, she didn't mean—"

"Oh, yes, she did. Anyway, I finally told her I'd *take* the
shoes. I thought maybe she'd say she was sorry or something
if I agreed to get the shoes. But she didn't."

"Well, listen. I'm *sure* she didn't mean—"

"But wait," I said. "There's more. See, a couple of days
later I happened to be at the mall by myself—in a different
shoe store, since I would rather die than go back into a Kin-
ney's again—and I was beginning to feel a little better. I had
told myself over and over that my mother and I were certainly
not the only mother and daughter who ever had a fight in a
shoe store. But then here I was in another store, and there's
this other mother and daughter looking at shoes together. The
daughter was about my age, maybe a little younger. There
was nothing special about her. She certainly wasn't very
pretty or anything like that. Anyway, what happened was"—
and here I started having trouble keeping my voice steady—
"this mother took up a pair of the exact same shoes I had
wanted and said to her daughter, '*I notice a lot of girls your
age are wearing shoes like these.*' Then the daughter took
them from her mother's hand and started to look at them."

"I think I get it," Maddy interrupted with a huge sigh.
"Like, what a contrast, huh? Your mother and this other kid's
mother—"

"Yes, that's part of it," I agreed, "but here's the part that
just kills me. The mother smiled at the daughter and said
something like, '*I think these would be fine, honey, but if you
don't like them we can try some other store.*' You know,
Maddy, actually it was the 'honey' that really got to me." I
took a deep breath. "My mother has never ever called me

honey in my whole entire life," I managed to say at last, since it was the whole point of my story.

After a moment, Maddy got up from the bed and padded into the kitchen. "I'm going to make some nice hot chocolate," she called out. "Do you want some?"

So we drank hot chocolate at the kitchen table, and soon we were comparing our all-time-favorite-movies list. Hours later we were still sitting there, but by then the conversation had become much more personal, and Maddy was idly toying with her hair and telling me fascinating stories about the "three serious men" she had had in her life up till then, and how—each time—she had thought for sure that Mr. Right had arrived. And then I told her about P.J. and my three-*day* romance, and I couldn't believe I actually laughed about it, but after hearing her sad sagas, I realized mine was really just minor-league stuff. Finally, after agreeing that men were as fickle as fleas, we decided we'd better get some sleep.

Back in bed I fluffed up my pillow and pulled up the sheet around my shoulders.

"All settled?" Maddy asked.

"Yes, thanks. Good night."

"I left the bathroom light on and the door ajar, so you won't have to stumble around in the dark."

"Okay," I said. "Good night again."

Maddy reached over and shut off the lamp. "Good night to you, honey," she said.

9

What a strange sensation that was—sitting on an airplane for
hours and hours and still not believing I was really there. On
our first flight that morning—from San Francisco to New
York—Maddy had explained all the little details of the plane
to me, like where to find the blankets and pillows and how to
work the light switch and adjust the air vent over our heads.
Then, after a few hours' wait in New York, we had to get on
a different airplane.

"Now this is a *nice* airplane," Maddy remarked as soon as
we had gotten settled in our seats. "A wide-bodied Boeing
747."

"As opposed to what?" I asked, smiling. (God, I was so
happy. So excited and carefree and *happy*.) "And anyway," I
added brightly, "I thought we were on TWA."

Maddy looked at me for a moment, as if making up her
mind about something, and then she just shrugged (in a
friendly, slightly put-upon way) and started to give me a lesson on airplane identification. She pulled her small red spiral
notebook out of her shirt pocket and removed the pencil from
in between the coils. "First of all," she said, "TWA is an
airline *company*; they *fly* the airplanes. Boeing *manufactures*
them. TWA buys airplanes from companies like Boeing. Get
it?"

I grinned and nodded. "Yep! Got it!"

She gave me a sideways glance with a funny, skeptical look on her face.

"I got it! I got it!" I laughed.

"Good. Now this is what a 747 looks like." She started to sketch a rough outline of an airplane. "There's probably a diagram in there," she said, indicating the seat pocket in front of her, "but I can draw it for you just as easily. Notice the front end here? See how it looks swollen, sort of? There are two levels up here." She quickly penciled in an upper row of little windows. Then she flipped over a page and made another drawing. "Now, a DC-10, for example, looks something like this. The tail is kind of funny, like so." She traced over the tail part of her sketch, refining it a bit. "See the difference?"

"Um, I guess," I said, letting my eyes drift away from the sketch and not making any attempt to keep the growing boredom I felt from creeping into my voice.

Maddy picked up on that right away. "I seem to sense a bit of disinterest here," she remarked, raising an eyebrow.

I shrugged. "Well, it is sort of boring, you know. Like, who cares about airplanes?"

"Oh, I see." She paused and then asked, "Can I tell you something, Gina-girl? Without your getting all mad and taking offense?"

"Oh, no!" I joked, covering my mouth. "Bad breath!"

She flipped her notebook shut and put it back in her pocket, ignoring my bad breath comment completely. "How can I put this?" She sat there thinking for a moment. "Well, okay." She cleared her throat. "I've noticed during the times we've been together that you seem to have, uh, well, let's see—" She hesitated again. "Let me put it this way. You seem to have an aversion to any sort of mental exertion. Do you know what I mean?"

"Not exactly," I answered, feeling slightly insulted.

"Okay, then, to put it bluntly," she said, laughing and

placing a hand on each side of my head and giving me a light massage with her knuckles, "I keep wanting to say, *Wake up in there, lazy brain! Wake up!*"

I just looked at her.

I think she was a little embarrassed. She removed her hands from my head and said earnestly, "It's just that life can be so much more fun when you make an effort to take an interest, you know? There's so much going *on* in the world." She raised her hands palms upward, as if searching for the right words, then smiled and added, "Like shoes and ships and sealing wax—"

She was drowned out in midsentence by the sound of the engines firing up, and in a few minutes we were lifting off the ground in a breathtaking climb. And that was the end of our "lazy brain" conversation, at least for the moment.

After a while they brought us some dinner, and then I watched the movie while Maddy drifted off to sleep. I just loved sitting there on that airplane with Maddy asleep at my side, listening to the deep droning of the engines and watching as the reading lights were extinguished one by one, until we were all riding in an eerie half-light, traveling through the sky somewhere high above the earth. Every so often I would see the shadowy outline of fellow passengers carefully making their way up or down the aisle, walking stiff-legged, hands touching the tops of the seats for balance. In the front of the plane, in the first-class section, I heard the muffled whimpering of a baby.

Even though I was worn out, I was still much too excited to sleep. I leaned my head back and closed my eyes and began to relive that event-filled Monday in San Francisco when Maddy and I went to the travel agency and the passport office before she dropped me off at the hospital, where my grandmother made her weird and mysterious request.

*   *   *

How surprised Maddy had seemed at the travel agency when she saw the destination on the plane tickets! "Are you sure this is correct?" she asked the agent. "It says Zurich here. I understood the tickets were to be for Italy."

"Well, let me check on that," the agent said, picking up the phone. She cleared up the matter in just a few seconds after talking with Mr. Tater's secretary.

"Well," she explained, "Zurich is correct. He got these on a special deal the airline offered last February." She started typing some information into her computer. "Let me get your seat assignments now, and you'll be all set."

"Hey, Maddy," I whispered, "where *is* Zurich, anyway? Does this mean we have to change all our plans about Italy?"

Maddy turned and stared at me in disbelief. "Zurich's in Switzerland, Gina. Where do you *think* it is?"

"Well, then, how do we get to Italy?"

She raised her eyes to the ceiling for a moment and swirled her head around in a circle before starting on that same routine she did before, when I said I didn't know which hospital my grandmother was at. She hit herself on the forehead with the palm of her hand, opened her eyes really wide, and said, "*I don't know!* Jeez, do you think it's possible? Maybe we'll be stuck in Zurich the whole time! Does anybody *ever* get out of Zurich? Oh, *dear!*"

The travel agent obviously didn't know what to make of Maddy's little performance. She was sitting at her desk with her hands pressed tightly together, looking anxiously first at me, then at Maddy, then at me again. "What is the question, ladies?" she asked. "Is there a problem about Zurich?"

I started laughing. "No," I said. "There's no problem about Zurich. But there is a problem with my friend here. She's insane."

Maddy winked at me and gave me a little punch, but I was just realizing what I had said. *My friend,* I had said. *My friend.* It suddenly occurred to me that even though Maddy was more than ten years older than I, and I had known her only two days, she was already more like a sister to me than Marie, and more like a friend than Tammy.

From the travel agency we went directly to the passport office, where we learned that I couldn't possibly get my passport that day. I was a juvenile and needed the signature of a parent or guardian.

"Boy, did I goof!" Maddy exclaimed. "I should have known that."

Not to worry, the clerk said. I could apply at my local post office the next day, as long as I brought along my parent or guardian. But I should be sure to take care of it the very next day, she said, since time was growing short.

"So you made the trip here for nothing," Maddy said, very upset with herself. "Damn! Missing work and everything."

"No, I didn't make it for nothing," I answered. "I still have to see my grandmother, remember? I still have to find out what she has to tell me that she feels is *so* important."

"Let's have a quick bite to eat," Maddy suggested, "and then I'll drop you off at the hospital. I'll do a few errands and pick you up later."

Grandma Gari was taking a nap when I entered her room. I didn't know if I should wake her. There was a chair by the window, so I quietly moved it close to the head of her bed and sat down. I was shocked at how old and frail she looked.

A soft chime sounded from a loudspeaker above the door, followed by a woman's voice, quiet and soothing. "Dr. Peabody. Dr. Peabody, please—"

My grandmother stirred but didn't wake up. I kept looking at her face. Would I ever get that old? Would ugly little black hairs like the ones peppering the skin above her upper lip sprout out on my face, too? God, I hoped not. And then there was her winning personality. When I got old, would I also get so unhappy and disagreeable about everything?

It was as if she had heard my thoughts. Her eyes suddenly shot open, and she slowly turned her head toward me. "Gina!" she accused. "How long have you been here?"

"Oh, not long, Grandma," I answered quickly, hoping I wouldn't have to kiss her. Sometimes she insisted on a dutiful kiss, but that was usually when one of her old cronies was around to observe.

This time I was saved. "Now tell me again," she demanded without any preliminaries. "You are going to Italy—when?"

"Well, we're leaving on the first of July, and we'll be there for ten days."

"Yes," she whispered to herself, closing her eyes and turning her head toward the ceiling. "Blessed holy saint," she muttered, resting her clasped hands on her stomach, "you've answered my prayer!" After a few moments she opened her eyes again. "There's a button here someplace to raise my head," she said, all business now, her stubby hand groping along the side of the bed. "I want to look at you while we talk."

"Okay." I pushed one of the buttons, and the foot of the bed slowly started to rise.

"What are you *doing*? You've got the wrong button!"

"Whoops," I said. "Sorry." I lowered it back and pushed the other button.

"All right, stop!" she ordered. "Now you've got it too high!"

Eventually we got the bed adjusted the way she wanted it, and after I had fluffed up her pillow and straightened out her sheets, she *finally* got around to telling me what I had to do. And that's exactly how she phrased it; I *had* to do it, because according to her, Saint Francis of Assisi himself was directly responsible for my winning the yo-yo contest! And the reason he did it was so I could "fulfill a mission" for my grandmother. Those were her exact words—*fulfill a mission*.

"What do you mean by a mission, Grandma?" I asked, trying my best to be civil, since it sounded like such a stupid word for her to say. "What kind of a mission?"

Before she answered, she asked for a glass of water. I poured her a glass from the pitcher on her nightstand and helped her hold it while she drank.

She took only a few sips before resting her head back on the pillow. "I have told you many times about the *Eremo delle Carceri*," she said, "have I not?"

"Well, I guess so," I answered vaguely.

"It is the hermitage high above the town of Assisi," she said impatiently, "where the saint himself would go to meditate and pray with the birds. I have told you about that many, many times."

"Oh, sure. The hermitage. I remember now. I just didn't recognize the word in Italian, that's all."

But wouldn't you know it—she had to tell me the whole Saint Francis saga *again*, starting with his birth in about 1181 in her own hometown of Assisi. She went on about how his father was a well-to-do cloth merchant who traveled to France a lot, and that's why he called his son Francesco, which means "the Frenchman." Well, old Francesco led a wild life until he was about twenty-five, going to parties and getting drunk every night and squandering his father's money on his good-for-nothing friends. But then he became gravely ill and almost died. After he got his health back, he really changed. That's when he stopped seeing his former friends and started giving all his money to the poor. He traded all his fine clothes for rags and began begging for alms himself. Finally, my grandmother continued (her cheeks getting all rosy, since for her this was the exciting part), he heard "a voice" speak to him from a crucifix. It said, "Francis, go repair My house." (That was Jesus talking, and by "My house," he meant the church.) So what else could Saint Francis do? He obeyed the voice and started to rebuild a little broken-down chapel in Assisi, all with his father's money. The last straw was when he sold some of his father's most expensive bolts of cloth and spent the money to help restore the church. His father took him to court to get his money back, but Francis said, "I'll not only give him his money back, but I'll do more!" And after saying that he went inside the house, only to reappear in the town square a few minutes later, stark naked. (My grandmother always blushed when she came to that part.) Well, soon Francesco came to be known as *il Poverello*—Little Poor Man. He gathered other men around him and finally got approval from the pope in Rome to start his own religious order, which he called the order of the Friars Minor—now famous all over the world and known as the Franciscans. I had to admit it was a pretty interesting story. And every time my grandmother told it she would emphasize a different part—sort of elaborating, trying to keep me (or whoever else was lucky enough to be present) from nodding off.

But this time she forgot to mention the basilica built in honor of Saint Francis in Assisi. It seems that the pope at the time of Saint Francis's death authorized the building of a really expensive and showy church in his memory. That is where the body of the saint "reposes," as my grandmother said, and it made her heart ache whenever she thought of it. In fact, she said when she was a young teenager in Assisi, she wouldn't even go near the place if she could help it. Saint Francis would have hated that fancy and expensive basilica, she said. It's just not in keeping with his simple life of poverty. And so *il Poverello*, who loved to go alone up into the hills above the town and feed and preach to the birds, was not allowed to be remembered in the way he truly wanted to be—in poor and simple surroundings.

And it was on that very mountain where Saint Francis used to go to the *Eremo delle Carceri*, where my "mission" was to take place.

My grandmother leaned forward and clasped my hands, her unblinking eyes staring into mine. "You are to climb up the hill to the hermitage on the *fifth day of July*," she said. "Do you hear me, Gina? The date is very important. *It must be on the fifth day of July and no other!*"

The intensity of her gaze sent goose pimples up my arms. "Well," I started, "uh, I don't know if I can do that. See, we're going to Rome, mostly. I mean, what if—"

"*You will be there! Saint Francis of Assisi has arranged for you to be there!*"

A passing nurse poked her head in the opened door. "Is everything all right in here?" she called out cheerfully.

"Oh, yes!" I answered. "Everything's okay. We're just, uh, talking." But I was thinking, God, this is crazy! How am I going to do that? I don't even know where we'll *be* on the fifth of July! I mean, Grandma's always been very religious. My whole family knows that. But *this* is beginning to border on pure craziness.

But since she wouldn't relent, I thought it would be best to humor her—at least for the time being. Pretty soon she began talking about those wonderful sunflower seeds of hers, the ones she had kept growing and reseeding ever since she had come to this country. But this time she told me more about them, adding something that she had never mentioned before. She said she was just sixteen and ready to leave for America when she had found them growing wild near the cemetery gates and took them first to the Convent of Saint Damian, where the crucifix had "spoken" to Saint Francis. When she got to that part, she paused, and her eyes searched mine again. "I have told you the wonderful story of the crucifix at Saint Damian?"

"Yes, Grandma!" I said, trying to keep my patience, since I really wanted to hear about the seeds. "You just *told* me that part. Don't you remember? You just told me the whole story—"

The strange thing is, I don't know if she even heard me. She was a million miles away. "The Convent of Saint Damian," she whispered. "Where we—" she broke off suddenly, covering her mouth with her hand.

"Yes, Grandma, go ahead. The Convent of Saint Damian, where you—" I paused. "Where you what?"

She coughed slightly and asked for more water. Then she began again. "That's where I first took the seeds to be blessed at the crucifix at Saint Damian. And then"—she paused again and pressed her fingers against her lips for a moment—"and then I made the steep climb up the mountain to feed the birds of Saint Francis and to pray that one day I would return to my home." I was shocked to see her eyes suddenly fill with tears. "To my home and to . . . to my friends in Assisi."

I was embarrassed to see her crying, but I didn't know what to do about it. And then she started acting very peculiar. It was like she was trying to speak, but something kept her from saying the words. Several times her lips would start to move and little hesitant sounds would come out, but it was nothing I could understand. Finally she just shook her head and murmured, "No, I cannot tell you—"

"What is it, Grandma?" I asked, bending down close to her. "What are you trying to say?" I was so curious I could hardly stand it. "You can tell me, honest—"

She raised her hands to her watery eyes and covered them with her short, pudgy fingers. "You will know what to do," she said finally as she slid her fingers up to her forehead and began drumming away. "The saint will tell you what to do."

Well, that was *it*, as far as I was concerned. I was really starting to lose patience with her.

"Grandma," I started to say, "I don't know what the saint has to do with—"

But before I could finish my sentence, she suddenly began reaching her shaky arms awkwardly up to her neck, fiddling around with something.

"What are you doing now, Grandma?" I asked, thankful to see that at least her eyes had stopped watering. And then I saw she was trying to do something with her necklace. I had noticed that tarnished silver necklace before, but I had never asked her about it. As a matter of fact, the first time I noticed her wearing it was the day after Grandpa's funeral, when she was sitting at our kitchen table eating those mushy avocados. I think she wore it all the time after that, sometimes on the outside of her dresses and sometimes on the inside.

"What's the matter?" I asked. "Is your necklace coming undone or something?"

"I am taking it off," she said. "Help me take it off."

"Well, okay, if you want me to." It had one of those old-fashioned little ring-type clasps that you have to slide with your thumbnail. It took several tries before I got it to work, but finally off it came.

"There!" I said, catching the necklace in my hand. "It's undone now." I turned it over in my hand and saw that the pendant part was actually a locket. It was about as big as a fifty-cent piece, but thicker. Some sort of figure was engraved on the front, but it was hard to make out because it was so tarnished. I bent down to take a closer look, and then I realized who it was. It was Saint Francis, of course. I mean, who else could it be—a figure in a monk's robe, with a bird perched in one hand and several others pecking around at his feet? I turned it on edge and saw that there was a tiny keyhole there.

"Did Grandpa give this to you?" I asked. I figured he gave it to her many, many years ago, probably before he stopped going to church.

"Put it on," she said, ignoring my question. "Put the necklace on."

"What?" I couldn't believe my ears.

"I said, put it on. I want you to wear it now."

"Your necklace? But why?" I didn't want to be caught dead wearing that thing, but naturally I didn't tell her that.

"You have to be wearing it when you climb the hill to feed

the birds," she said simply, like I was a stupid oaf not to realize that fact.

She's really off her rocker now, I thought. But there was even more. She had asked one of her old lady friends to bring some of her sunflower seeds to her in the hospital. She told me to look in the drawer of her nightstand, and sure enough, there they were, a handful of sunflower seeds safely stored away in a Ziploc plastic sandwich bag.

"You are taking a camera on this trip?" she asked me then with a sly glance.

"Yes," I answered, knowing what was coming. She was going to want proof.

"I will expect photographs," she said with narrowed eyes. (Did I know my grandmother, or what?) "I want to see photographs when you return," she continued, pausing between each phrase, "photographs of the birds of Saint Francis eating these seeds on the hill high above Assisi, taken on the *fifth day of July* by you, Gina, my granddaughter, wearing the necklace I have just entrusted to your care."

Holy smoke, I thought. The lady's nuts for sure. But in spite of what I thought, she still made me promise that I would follow through. And another thing she made me promise: this was strictly between her and me and did not concern the rest of the family in any way.

Well, of course I promised. What else could I do? When your grandmother is lying there in the hospital, no matter what she asks you to do or how you feel about her, how can you refuse?

"Sure, Grandma," I said finally. "Sure. I'll do it. Just like you said. Don't worry," I assured her. "I'll do it. I'll do it."

And, you know, I think she actually believed me.

10

I had no idea what time it was, but the blackness of night had somehow turned to a grayish light. Here and there window shades were being raised with little snapping noises. I looked up to see the flight attendant pushing his serving cart down the aisle, passing out paper cups of orange juice as he went.

Maddy was awake now, too, sitting up and untangling herself from the blanket.

"Oh, I'm so stiff," she said, turning her head from side to side in an exaggerated stretching movement. "Did you get any sleep at all, Gina?"

"I think so. I must have."

Our eyes met, and suddenly we began to laugh. Maddy said what was on both our minds. "Can you *believe* this, honey? Can you believe we are actually *doing* this?"

I shook my head. "No," I said. "I can't believe it."

"And can you believe that—" She lowered her voice and put her mouth close to my ear. "That *jackass* Donnie tearing up the name and address of the hotel in Rome right in front of our eyes!"

I timed my answer like a pro. "Well, now," I said, "*that* I can believe!"

That sent us both into unexpected hysterics. We bent our heads and laughed and laughed until tears rolled from our eyes. We put our hands to our faces, and our shoulders shook. Maddy finally gained control of herself, but then she took one look at me and broke up all over again.

"I've got to go to the bathroom," Maddy said after a few long moments. She wiped her eyes with her sleeve and stood up. "Do you think I can get by?"

While Maddy was freshening up, I began to worry just a little about where we would stay once we got to Rome. She was right; that Donnie *was* a jackass. I had gone with her to her office to meet Mr. Leonard Tater and pick up our money for the trip (the amount of which Maddy later described as "pretty chintzy"), and afterward we stopped by Donnie's office. Maddy knew he had called about reservations at an inexpensive hotel in Rome (he was *that* confident P.J. would win!), and she wanted to get the address. She also had to pick up the all-important demo kit of yo-yos that we were going to take with us.

"Is this the kit?" she asked Donnie, picking up the only demo case in sight.

Donnie nodded and turned his back.

"Now may I have the address of that hotel in Rome, please?" Maddy asked as polite as could be.

Donnie whirled around and really glared at her. "What hotel in Rome?"

"Oh, cut it out, Donnie," she said. "You told me you had made reservations for you and P.J. at some inexpensive hotel in Rome. So where's it at?"

"Oh, *that* hotel," he said. He walked to his desk, looked through a small stack of papers, and finally pulled one out of the pile. "You must be referring to *this* hotel," he said. And he deliberately tore the paper to shreds.

"You know, I've been thinking," Maddy said as soon as she came back from the restroom and buckled her seat belt. "Maybe we should change our plans. Maybe we should catch a train for Rome as soon as we land in Zurich."

"But Maddy, we already have reservations at that hotel in Zurich," I reminded her, remembering how my mother had not only insisted on knowing where we would be our first night, but had also wanted me to call her as soon as I could to tell her we had arrived safely.

"Yes, I know we have a reservation, honey," Maddy said. "But I'm sure I can call them and explain the situation. The problem is that this is Tuesday already, and we have to be back here in Zurich the day before our return flight, which is next Wednesday. Well, wait a second." She paused. "Can that be right?" She started counting the days on her fingers. "Tuesday, Wednesday, Thursday . . . God, there goes our whole vacation! No." She shook her head. "We really shouldn't waste a whole day just to spend the night. So what do you think, Gina? We can always nap on the train, you know. Are you too tired to keep on going?"

"Who me?" I asked, feeling like I was about to drop dead in a faint and wondering what she had just said about our whole vacation being gone. "Too tired? Not me!"

"Good!" she said just as the announcement came over the loudspeaker to prepare for landing.

Maddy got us through the busy customs and passport inspection lines at the airport as easy as pie, and then she found the currency-exchange place, where we each cashed in a small traveler's check for Swiss francs. "My travel book says there's a train depot right here in the airport complex." She glanced around a moment and pointed to some signs above our heads. "That way," she said, pointing straight ahead. "Follow those signs to the escalators."

The line of people waiting at the train ticket window was about a hundred feet long, so we decided to go first to the self-service store we passed moments before and get something to eat on the train. "Everybody eats on trains in Europe," Maddy said. "At least that's what my book says."

I was beginning to feel shaky, and I was also starving. We were both wearing our day packs on our backs, with our large bags slung over one shoulder. My large bag was a nuisance and a half, the way it kept slipping off. It was even worse for Maddy, since she had to lug around that brown demo kit full of yo-yos besides.

We walked stiffly through the turnstile into the self-service grocery store. It was difficult to navigate the narrow aisles without knocking things over with our packs. Maddy stopped to look at the yogurt section, and I hovered near the salami display trying to convince myself that salami was not really a *meat*, strictly speaking, since it wasn't in any recognizable form—like a leg, or a rib, or a wing. My stomach was growling so loudly I was afraid everybody in the store could hear it. I quickly looked through the salami selection and picked the largest size—in case Maddy wanted some—and also a package of cheese and a box of crackers. Now for some dessert. Maddy was already in the checkout line, so I just grabbed a tin of cookies and hurried to the end of the line. I looked at the unfamiliar money in my hand. Well, I would just have to trust the clerk. When my turn came, the woman rang up my purchases and said something in a language I didn't understand. I just handed her all my money and said, "I'm sorry. I'm not familiar with your money."

She smiled at me and picked out a few bills. Then she gave me a couple of coins in change.

"Come on, Gina!" Maddy was calling. "Hurry up!" She was several yards ahead of me and had to turn her whole body toward me in order to speak to me, since she was so loaded down.

"Hey," I said, catching up to her, "you look like a giant tortoise carrying all that stuff."

"My shoulder's killing me," she said. "How about you?"

"Yeah. Mine is too."

The line at the train ticket counter was quite a bit shorter than before. "They probably all went and caught the last train to Rome," Maddy joked.

"Do you think the ticket sellers speak English?" I asked.

"It doesn't matter. I'll just say 'Rome.' They should understand that."

"What if they ask you what time we want to go?"

"You've got a point there. I don't know how to say 'the next train.' " She squirmed around, trying to reach into her backpack. "If I could just get my guidebook out of here, it has a little foreign-language dictionary section that might help—"

I felt a slight tug on my arm and turned around to see a tall woman in a blue and white striped dress standing behind me. She was holding a toddler by the hand. "Oh, excuse me," she said with just a slight accent. "Are you from the United States?"

"Yes!" we both exclaimed. Her voice speaking English sounded like heaven.

"I thought so," she said with a smile. Then she pointed to the ticket window. "Don't worry. They do speak English. You shouldn't have any trouble."

"Oh, thank you!" we said.

The woman was very nice and friendly. We spoke with her for a few minutes and told her how cute her kid was and stuff, and then it was our turn at the ticket window.

Maddy did the talking. "We'd like two one-way tickets on the next train to Rome, please," she said. Then she added, "Second class, please."

The clerk spoke a few words to her and then told her the price. Maddy turned to me quickly and said, "Give me your money!"

I hauled it all out and put it on the counter. She examined the few bills and pieces of change quickly, muttering numbers to herself. Then she held out her hand and wiggled her fingers, asking impatiently, "Where's the rest?"

"That's all I have," I answered, slightly panicked.

"Are you kidding? My God! They must have shortchanged you at the store! Check your pockets again! Are you sure this is all you have?"

My heart sank. "That's it," I said.

The tall woman behind me pursed her lips and looked down at the floor. The little kid stuck a couple of fingers in his mouth and stared at me with his huge round eyes.

Maddy and the ticket seller were talking quickly back and forth and counting and recounting the money. Finally Maddy said in a desperate tone of voice, "Well, make it two tickets to Milan, then. Do we have enough for that?"

Apparently we did, because the ticket seller punched some numbers into his computer, pulled out two tickets from a machine, and pushed them through the little hole in the glass. Then he tipped his head to one side and surveyed us in a tired, bored sort of way.

Maddy was really upset. "Come on," she said, looking at her watch. "The train leaves in seven minutes." She picked up her large shoulder bag and grabbed the demo case.

"Let me have a turn carrying that," I said, reaching for the demo kit.

She didn't argue and just let me take it. Then she looked at me a second, biting the inside of her lip and frowning. "We don't have time to try to get your money back," she said. "So let's just chalk this one up to experience."

I gave my shoulder a hitching kind of twist, trying to readjust my bag. "Okay," I said softly.

"But I'm going to see to it that you learn to recognize *Italian* money, that's for sure!"

"Hey, Maddy," I said testily. "It wasn't my fault, you know."

She didn't answer.

Without speaking further, Maddy followed the signs to the trains, and I followed Maddy. I felt like I hadn't been to bed in a week.

11

Our train was just like the trains you see in foreign movies—with compartments. We were lucky to get seats together. Most of the compartments were full, but when we noticed a woman with two children coming out of one we hurried over to it and quickly hoisted our bags up into the overhead rack. I flopped down by the window and Maddy sat beside me. Across from us were three people—opposite me by the window was a heavyset, unpleasant-looking older man wearing thick reading glasses and thumbing through a stack of pamphlets; next to him sat a young blond kid who looked to be about seventeen or eighteen years old, and on the end, near the door, was a nicely dressed woman reading an Italian fashion magazine. The woman got off at the next stop, and as soon as she left, the blond guy moved over and took her seat near the compartment door. Then after a second he stood up again and got his backpack from the overhead rack and plopped it down on the middle seat where he had just been sitting. At the same time I noticed him direct a disapproving look at the older man by the window.

I wondered what the older man had done to get that kind of reaction from the blond kid, but I had other things to think about. Maddy and I were getting ready to have our lunch—and although we didn't know it then—our first big argument. It was over money. Swiss money, to be exact. She was still fuming over my carelessness in getting shortchanged when I reached into my plastic sack and pulled out all the stuff I had bought—the salami, then the cheese, crackers, and tin of cookies.

She stopped picking at the foil lid on her large container of yogurt. "Ka-ripes!" she said, looking up at me. "What's all *that* stuff, anyway?"

"Huh? What stuff?"

She grabbed the tin of cookies and looked at the small white price label. "Ka-*ripes!*" she repeated with more emphasis this time. Then she took the package of salami from my hand and looked at the price tag on that. "You weren't shortchanged, you idiot!" she said. "You just spent too much money!"

"Hey! Don't call me an idiot, stupid!" I shot back. "I didn't say a word about being shortchanged! That was your brilliant idea, remember?"

Her face turned bright red.

"And besides," I added, "how was I to know how much I could spend? You just said to get something to eat, so that's what I did!"

"Well, you didn't have to buy the whole store, for God's sake!"

"The whole store? What are you talking about? You call this the whole store?"

That stopped her. She just looked at me but didn't answer. I sat back, satisfied that I had gotten in the last word. But after a while she tapped me on the arm. "Listen, Gina, we're going to have to make a budget for this trip, okay? We have to figure out how much we can spend each day on meals, lodging, transportation—all of that stuff. Because if we run out of money, we'll be in big trouble."

I shrugged and said, "Okay by me."

So that's what we did. After we got it pretty well figured

out, Maddy announced that she needed a cup of coffee, but it would be a good idea, she whispered quietly in my ear, if I stayed there and watched our stuff, since her travel book said you should never leave your belongings unattended on a train. "And then," she added, "when I get back, it'll be your turn to go. Okay?"

"Okay." I nodded. "But don't get lost."

She touched me on the shoulder and grinned down at me. "Don't worry. I won't."

I smiled back at her, happy that we were on good terms again.

After she left, I settled back in my seat and started looking out the window, but my eyes kept drifting over to the other two passengers in our compartment. The old guy was still thumbing through those pamphlets of his and looking even more out of sorts than before, and the kid had closed his eyes and stretched out his long legs on the vacant seat opposite him, crossing his feet at the ankles. His shoes were untied and kind of ragged, and he wasn't wearing socks. Once in a while he'd open his eyes, let out a small impatient sigh, and glance out the window.

I liked the way he looked, though. I found myself looking at him quite a lot when his eyes were closed. But then it was hard *not* to look at him. You have to look at something. He wasn't bad looking, but I wouldn't call him handsome, exactly. His light blue eyes were too close together and his jaw too angular. But I liked the way his Adam's apple stuck out. (I had never really thought about it before, but P.J.'s neck was smooth and flat, almost like a girl's.)

Once the kid suddenly opened his eyes and caught me staring at him. That's when he decided to give up trying to take a nap, I guess. He put his feet back on the floor and started to examine his fingernails, filing and picking at them with his thumbnail.

The German man—at least that's what I imagined he was—finally finished reading. He put the pamphlets together with a rubber band and wedged them up against the armrest of his seat. His eyes met mine for a split second, but he quickly turned away.

I just couldn't stand the silence anymore. I decided to start with the old guy. I cleared my throat. "Do you speak English, sir?" I asked him very politely, as if he were a new teacher of mine.

He hesitated a moment, then shook his head. He looked very sad—and quite unfriendly. "No," he said gruffly. "Not well."

The blond kid stirred uncomfortably. I looked at him and asked the same question, with a look and a gesture. He too shook his head. "No," he said simply. "No English." And he turned away.

The tin of cookies was beside me on Maddy's seat. I removed the lid and picked out a cookie. Both the German man and the blond kid glanced at me as I bit into it. The cookie was chocolate and crumbly. I suddenly felt very self-conscious. Holding the open tin out in front of me, I smiled at the man and said very slowly, "Would you like a cookie?"

What a strange reaction I got. It was almost like he was afraid to look at me. And then he just extended his lower lip and shook his head. He fidgeted uncomfortably in his seat and began to toy with his digital wristwatch, pushing the little buttons and making the alarm go on and off.

The blond guy turned his head toward the man and gave him another disapproving stare.

"How about you?" I asked the kid, holding out the box to him. But he too just shook his head and then closed his eyes.

The minutes dragged by. I looked out the window again. The scenery was spectacular. We were in the mountains, and at every wide, curving turn there was another gorgeous view spread out before us. I couldn't help it; I had to try just one more time to get a conversation going. "It's beautiful," I said to the German man, enunciating as carefully as I could. "It's really beautiful—the scenery." I pointed. "Out the window."

He sighed deeply, as if he had finally resigned himself to performing some sort of sorrowful chore. Then he looked at me for several seconds. His eyes scanned my clothes, my face, my hair. He gazed out the window for a long, long time. "Yes," he said finally in slow, perfect English, "it is very beautiful."

Obviously the man did speak English after all. I couldn't understand it, but suddenly I was at a complete loss for words. I had no idea what to talk about. We rode along in silence for several minutes. The man kept watching me. His eyes seemed to narrow. "You are from America?" he asked finally.

His pronunciation was extraordinarily good. I wondered why he had said no at first when I had asked him if he spoke English. I smiled my brightest smile. "Yes, I am!" I said. "I *am* American."

He only stared at me some more and nodded. "Yes," he murmured in a voice so low I could hardly hear him.

"And you?" I asked. "I'll bet you're German, right? Those little booklets you were reading, they looked like they were printed in German."

That really seemed to upset the blond kid. He said something under his breath, but I couldn't make out the meaning. Then he began moving back and forth in his seat. He planted his feet wide apart, leaned over with his elbows on his knees and clapped his hands over his ears as if to block out the sound of our voices.

"Yes," the man replied quietly. "I am German."

"On your way home?" I asked.

"No. I have just attended a meeting in Zurich. I am presently on my way to another meeting."

"What sort of meeting?" I asked. He looked like he might be a doctor. I followed up quickly, taking a guess. "Are you a doctor? The man sitting next to me on the airplane was a doctor—"

"Oh, no," he interrupted, almost brushing aside the question. "No. I am not a doctor."

I was about to ask, "Well, what, then?" when he said, "I represent my country in an organization which is dedicated to promoting global health and eliminating hunger."

I must have had a very blank look on my face, because he obviously felt he should elaborate for me. "Our work is so very important, you know. Hunger *can* be erased. The suffering of millions of children throughout the world *can* be alleviated."

I noticed the blond kid had stopped his slow rocking back and forth and removed his hands from his ears.

"Oh, yes!" I said, nodding vigorously. "I agree."

The German sat up a little straighter in his seat. "And we must always be vigilant. We must guard against prejudice and injustice in all areas." He reached for the pamphlets he had been reading earlier and shook them at me. "This sort of garbage which was just shoved into my hands this morning as I boarded the train—this hateful literature, we must fight it with every bit of strength we have!"

His eyes looked directly into mine then. It was like they had finally come alive. "Do you understand that? As a young American, so far removed—by distance and time—from the terrible events earlier in this century, do you understand the importance of what I am saying?"

"Oh, *sure*," I said. But all the while I was hoping he wasn't about to get into a long, boring discussion about "the terrible events earlier in this century" and all their effects and manifestations.

Thank goodness, he wasn't. He stood up, reached for his

briefcase on the overhead rack, removed a newspaper, and began to read a long article.

I decided I would ask him about his family as soon as he put the newspaper down again. At least that might get a longer conversation going. Then maybe I could tell him all about the yo-yo contest and everything. Finally he folded the paper and put it on the middle seat next to the blond kid's backpack.

"Do you have a family?" I asked, catching his eye again. "Any *kinder?*" I smiled, suddenly remembering a question about the German derivation of the word "kindergarten" that I had recently heard on *Jeopardy*.

At my question his face slowly took on an expression of sadness. "I have one daughter," he answered at last.

Well, I thought, judging by that reaction, she must mean trouble with a capital *T*. I decided to drop that subject but quick.

"She is very gravely ill."

I was startled by his barely audible words. "Oh, I'm sorry!" I said.

"She has a tumor," he said softly. One hand touched his temple. "A tumor. Here."

"Oh, God! That's terrible," I whispered. "I'm so sorry!"

"The doctors say it is malignant. They cannot operate." He paused. "They say—they say she will die."

He removed his glasses and wiped his eyes with a large white handkerchief.

The blond kid quietly stirred in his seat. He must be wondering what we're talking about, I thought, that could cause so much emotion in such an unpleasant-looking man.

"My wife," the German continued, "she wants me to quit my work. She says I must not travel so much when Helga is so sick. The treatments, the radiation—" His hands rose up in a hopeless gesture and then fell back to his lap.

I somehow had the feeling—no, it was more than just a feeling. I was *certain* that this man never talked to anyone about his daughter's illness. But I was a stranger on a train. He could open his heart to me.

"Yes," I answered, my eyes beginning to brim with tears. "That's understandable, about your wife—"

"Ah, but my little Helga! She insists that I continue my work! 'It's all right, *Vater*,' she says—" His mouth began to tremble with pride.

The blond kid suddenly stood up and with one swift motion slid open the compartment door and swung his body into the aisle. He reached an arm behind him to close the door without giving us a backward glance.

Seconds later Maddy appeared on the other side of the door. She gripped the handle with both hands and slid it open. "Hi again," she said to me, picking up the cookie tin and sitting down beside me. "Sorry I took so long."

The German man nodded to her curtly. Then his eyes quickly flickered a plea to me. I knew the talk about his daughter was finished.

I stood up to stretch. "Well, I guess I'll go get a Coke or something," I said, pretending everything was normal.

"The bar car is three cars ahead," Maddy told me, looking at me strangely.

Oh, please, I thought. Don't let her ask me if anything is wrong! Not now!

"They have Coke," she said. "But no ice."

"Okay." I slid open the door. "I'll be back."

I found the bar car and drank a can of Coke standing up. My thoughts were all with that poor man and his daughter.

After I finished my drink, I headed back to our compartment. The train seemed to be slowing down. We must be coming to a station, I thought, but it's too soon for Milan. Up and down the aisles of each car I walked through compartment doors were opening and people carrying their luggage were starting to line up at the exits.

When I finally arrived back at our compartment, I saw through the glass door that the German man was also preparing to leave. I decided to wait in the aisle. He put his newspaper and those pamphlets into his briefcase and then took down a small suitcase from the overhead rack.

The blond kid was back in his seat by then. The German nodded a barely perceptible good-bye to him and to Maddy. I was surprised to see the kid lean forward and slide the compartment door open for the German man, who silently acknowledged that little kindness with another nod. The blond kid looked up at the older man almost shyly and pulled in his long legs to let him get by.

Then the German man and I were standing face to face in the narrow aisle of the train. We looked into each other's eyes. Hesitantly he reached one hand to my head, as if to touch my hair. But he didn't. "I wanted to tell you before your friend returned that your hair—all curly and blond—is so much like . . . hers," he said almost in a whisper. "So much like hers used to be . . . before her treatments . . ."

Then he extended his hand. "May I shake your hand, young lady?" he asked, his voice deep and low.

"Oh, sure!" I took his hand, but we didn't really shake. We just stood there clasping hands.

"I want to say good-bye and good luck to you wherever you go," he said like a blessing.

I wanted to answer, to wish the same to him, but I couldn't. I gripped his arm, and he patted me gently on the back in such an understanding, fatherly gesture that the tears already in my eyes spilled over onto my cheeks. Seeing that, his own composure broke, and he took me in his arms and hugged me gently. In another second he was gone.

I had some difficulty opening the compartment door. After

I stepped in, the blond kid helped me slide it shut. I sat down in my seat, completely spent.

"Now what was all *that* about?" Maddy asked, her eyes wide with bewilderment.

"Well, it was about his daughter," I said simply. "It was just something about his daughter."

The blond kid looked at me for a second and then stared out the compartment door into the aisle of the train.

"His daughter?" Maddy asked. "What about her? And why was he hugging you, anyway?"

But for once in my life I didn't talk. The man's words were still echoing in my head: "*Your hair—all curly and blond—is so much like hers*"; and later, "*Good luck to you wherever you go . . .*" I decided to trade the attention I craved from Maddy for something else. I decided instead to honor an unspoken agreement of silence, a kind of secret bargain of the heart between me and that stranger I met on the train.

"Well," Maddy persisted, "what did he say?"

"Maddy," I answered softly, "I really can't talk about it. Okay?"

I know I took her by surprise. But she looked into my eyes and saw that I was sincere. She reached over—proudly, I think—and gave my arm a little squeeze.

After the German man left, the blond kid changed his seat again, this time settling in the place across from me next to the window. After gazing out for a while, he got a beat-up sweater out of his backpack to use as a pillow and promptly went to sleep.

It takes about four hours to get from Zurich, Switzerland, to Milan, Italy, on a train. I tried to take a nap, but I couldn't get comfortable on that hard seat; besides, I guess I was still too excited to sleep. I spent part of the time looking at Maddy's travel book, especially the large foldout map of Europe in the back. I was trying to locate Assisi. I found Rome and Florence okay, because the print was so large, but I just didn't have any luck with Assisi. Finally I gave up. "Hey, Maddy," I said. "Where's Assisi, anyway? My grandmother said it was near Florence, but I can't find it anywhere."

"Well, give me that a second," she said, taking the book from my lap. She checked the map for a few minutes, running her index finger around from city to city, murmuring to herself. Finally she tapped lightly on the map, saying, "Here it is. See? Right there."

She moved the map closer to me, and I bent my head and looked at the spot she indicated. "Oh, yeah. I see it now. Listen, Maddy, are you sure it won't be too much trouble—you know, what my grandmother wants me to do—going to Assisi and feeding her sunflower seeds to those birds, and all that?"

Maddy ran her fingers through her hair, then folded her arms. "Well, truthfully, I'm not all that thrilled about it. But heck, we can do it. I mean, you promised her, didn't you?"

"Yeah, I did, but—" I shrugged. "Anyway, did I tell you that for some reason she wants me to do it on a specific day—the fifth of July, to be exact?"

Maddy nodded. "Oh, yes. You did tell me that."

I felt around the back of my neck. Yes, my grandmother's ugly necklace was still there. Naturally I wore it under my clothes, but at least I was wearing it. I figured that if I packed it away somewhere it would probably get lost, so I just said what the heck and kept it on. I almost told Maddy that if my grandmother hadn't *insisted* that I bring my camera up that mountain and take actual photos of Saint Francis's birds pecking away at her sunflower seeds, I could easily just skip the whole thing. But I decided not to. Instead I asked her what kind of publicity for Tater Toys she'd *really* like to get while we were in Rome.

"Well, Leonard won't be geared up for the overseas market for at least eighteen months, but if we could at least break the ice a little, you know, get our feet wet?" She smiled. "For instance, a nice big photo of you and your Fly-by-Nite in one of the large-circulation Roman tabloids would be perfect. I've been trying to work out the details of how we can accomplish that, but so far I'm coming up blank."

We stopped talking for a while, and pretty soon Maddy took out her little notebook and started jotting things down, probably ideas she was having about how she could get that publicity. I began to think about her job and decided I wouldn't like to be in her shoes at all. Even though I do like to talk and everything, I still wouldn't like a job like hers, where it would be my responsibility to get people to put things in the paper or on television and stuff like that. But then it's always easy to think of jobs you wouldn't like.

I looked at my watch. It said five minutes past six. "Maddy," I said, "what time is it *really*?"

"Well, we're six hours ahead of New York," she answered, looking up from her notebook. "What time does your watch say?"

"Five minutes past six."

"So you tell me. What time is it really?" She smiled.

"I'm on *California* time, Maddy," I reminded her. "I don't *know* what time it is in New York."

She grinned at me and shrugged.

"Well, I'm too tired to figure it out now," I said. "And besides, I'm so confused I don't even know if it's five minutes past six in the *morning* or at *night* back in California."

"Yes," she agreed. "It *is* pretty confusing, isn't it?"

She was no help at all! I sat and pouted for a little while. What did I care what time it was, anyway? But hey, I *did* care. I wanted to know if I was supposed to be hungry for lunch or dinner or what. I wanted to know how many more hours until nighttime, and bed. Blessed *bed*! I suddenly wished that that kid who figured out how many calories there were in a Gargantuan was sitting beside me instead of uncooperative old Maddy!

So okay, I thought. I would give it a try. I wasn't *that* much of a dummy. We were six hours ahead of New York, she had said. But what time was it in New York? That's what I had to know, since my watch was still set at California time. I felt so lightheaded it was difficult to think, but I was determined to work it out. First of all, I knew there were four time zones in the continental United States, but I could never remember if New York was four hours earlier or later than California. However, I was certainly not going to ask Maddy! She'd go into one of those now famous "Oh, dear! Oh, dear!" routines for sure, right there on the train.

I shut my eyes and thought about the map of the United States and how it is divided into four vertical time zones. Since the sun comes up in the east and sets in the west, New York has morning before California. So let's say it was sunrise in New York—five A.M., for instance. Since the sun hasn't come up yet in the next zone, it must be four A.M. there. Three in the next and two in California. Five A.M. in New York and two A.M. in California. But wait a minute. There are *four* time zones, but it works out to a three-hour difference! Now *that's* the sort of thing I can never understand!

I looked at my watch again. It was now eight minutes past six. So if it was eight minutes past six in California, it was three hours *later* in New York. But if New York got sunrise before us, it was *earlier* there. Or was it? How could it be both *earlier* and *later* at the same time? Jeez! Now I was *really* confused.

Okay, I said to myself. Erase everything and start over. Forget *earlier* and *later*. Instead try *ahead of* and *behind*. New York is *ahead of* California. Italy is *ahead of* New York.

So eight minutes past six in California. Count *ahead* three hours. Seven, eight, nine. That means it's eight minutes past nine in New York. Now I was getting somewhere! In Italy, where we were, it was another six hours *ahead of* New York. I counted on my fingers—ten, eleven, twelve, one, two, three. That was it! *Eight minutes past three!*

"Maddy!" I said. "I've got it! It's eight minutes past three! Right now! Right here! Altogether, we're nine hours *ahead of* California!"

She had taken off her contacts a long time before, so she was wearing those dark-rimmed glasses of hers. When I said, "I've got it! It's eight minutes past three!" she lowered them down her nose and peered over the rims. "Middle of the night or afternoon?"

"Oh, cut it out!"

"Only joking, darlin'," she drawled. "But thanks for figuring it out. Now I can set my watch." And that's exactly what she did.

12

A few minutes before our train pulled in to the Milan station, the blond kid suddenly woke up (as if he had some kind of inner alarm clock), got his stuff together, glanced at me for a second or two, and then left our compartment. For a minute I thought he might try to speak to me—in whatever language it was he spoke—but he seemed hesitant about it, and finally he just opened the compartment door and disappeared.

After we had changed a whole bunch of our traveler's checks for Italian money, Maddy and I decided to take turns using the restroom in the Milan train station. I went first, and then I guarded the luggage while Maddy took her turn. These were my thoughts as I was waiting for her: How could it be that this truly gigantic and beautiful place with all of these hundreds of people—some rushing by, some strolling, others simply standing, talking in groups—how could it be that all of this has been going on all this time without my knowing the slightest thing about it? This place is *real*, I thought. While I was back home, climbing up on the Thing that hot afternoon with P.J., for instance, or fooling around at Waterworld with Tammy, people just like these were rushing to catch trains, or sitting in that smoky restaurant way down at the end of this side of the building, or going up and down that huge flight of stairs directly in front of me . . .

Suddenly I spotted a vaguely familiar figure climbing up

the stairs. It was the blond kid from the train! Even though we hadn't spoken, just riding together in that little compartment for four hours made him seem like a long-lost buddy to me. I kept watching him, and then suddenly, just as he reached the top of the stairs, he looked over and saw me! He hesitated a moment, and then (surprise!) he began to walk over to where I was standing. Is he really heading over here? I thought. What could he possibly want?

I liked the way he walked, though—so confident and self-assured—weaving his way through the throngs of people. He looked as loose and graceful as a gazelle loping through the forest. His backpack hung from his shoulders as if he had been born with it there.

He came right up to me and clasped his hands behind his back. "Excuse me," he said, looking down at me, for he was quite tall. "My name is Stefan. You are Gina, right?"

What *is* this? I thought. Here he was, speaking *English*—and very good English at that.

"Hey!" I said. "What's going on here, anyway? First nobody speaks English, and then everybody does!"

"Oh, yes," he said with a sheepish little smile. "I must apologize for that. You see, I misjudged you at first, when you asked me if I spoke your language. Will you forgive me?"

"Misjudged me? How do you mean?"

"I thought you were just another one of those—" He paused as if trying to come up with the perfect word. "Another one of those stupid, spoiled American girls." He ran the backs of his fingers forward along the curve of his neck, as if to say he'd had it up to here with those so-called stupid, spoiled American girls.

For some reason that really ticked me off. "Well," I said, "what makes you think I'm *not* one of those stupid, spoiled American girls?"

"The way you spoke to the German gentleman," he answered, intensely serious now.

That surprised me. "The German gentleman?"

Stefan gestured with open palms. "You were so very kind to him. Right from the start. So sympathetic and understanding."

"I was?"

"Oh, yes!" he said, nodding. "You see, Gina, before you started speaking with him, I really disliked that fellow. How would you say it in English? *He was not my cup of tea.*"

"Not your cup of tea?" I repeated, smiling. "Why? Why wasn't he your cup of tea?"

"The way he looked, his attitude, but mostly that garbage he was reading." Stefan paused and looked down at his feet. I think he was blushing. "You see, I do read German a bit, and those pamphlets—well, I thought he was a fascist."

"A fascist? Did you say a fascist?"

He raised his eyebrows in a funny way and nodded, smiling a closed-mouth self-deprecating little smile. "Well, it turned out he was just the reverse. I jump to conclusions, you see. It is my main downfall."

All the while he was speaking I was trying to figure out where he was from. Although his grammar was perfect, his accent was definitely foreign. But what I noticed most of all was his sincerity—he sounded like the kind of guy you could actually trust (if there really *was* such a creature).

"It was my plan to speak to you about this on the train," he went on, "after the man had gone. But your friend was always present, and I didn't want to talk about the German gentleman and his poor daughter in front of her—"

"Maddy," I interrupted. "Her name is Maddy."

"Yes. Well, Maddy was always there, and I didn't want to open up again the closed subject, you understand, so I—" He stopped abruptly in the middle of his sentence and suddenly whirled his head around to the left. "What the—" he started to say. And at that same moment I felt myself being roughly pushed aside while the demo kit I was holding was suddenly snatched right out of my hand before I knew what was happening.

I was hit so hard that I was knocked completely off balance and sent sprawling sideways onto Maddy's large canvas bag. The wind was almost knocked out of me, and as I lay there struggling to get my breath, I caught a quick glimpse of a short wiry man dressed in a dark T-shirt and jeans disappearing into the crowd with the demo case clutched tightly in his arms. I quickly looked around for Stefan, expecting that he would help me up. But instead, all I saw was his back as he rushed off in the opposite direction, first in quick, giant strides and then in a full-speed run. In a moment he too had disappeared into the crowd.

I wasn't badly hurt, but I was dazed by the suddenness of the attack. But more than that, I was angry. How could I have been so deceived? Obviously that was Stefan's game (if his name really *was* Stefan!): to distract me while his accomplice made off with the loot!

I didn't even try to stand up. I just stayed there half lying on Maddy's bag and started to cry. That's how she found me a few minutes later. She leaned down and put her face next to mine. "Gina, what happened? What's wrong? Can you stand up?"

As she helped me to my feet I gripped her arms and cried, "The demo case, Maddy! They stole the demo case! *Now* what are we going to do? How can we—"

"Wait!" she said suddenly. "Look!" She pointed. "Over there. Isn't that the guy who was in our compartment on the train?"

"Stefan!" I practically shouted. "It's Stefan!"

He was hurrying toward us with a big smile on his face and one fist raised, and in his other hand was the demo case! As he got closer I could see something else—a growing red welt on his cheek.

"That sneaky little thief!" he said, handing the case back to me and pausing a moment to catch his breath. "I knew he'd probably try to make it down to the Metro, so I went the other way and caught up with him just as he was about to go through the turnstile."

I brought my hand up to his face, where the red welt seemed to be blossoming larger and larger each second. "But Stefan! You're hurt!"

"I am?" He touched his face briefly and then examined his hand. "No blood. I'm not bleeding, am I?" He touched his face again and then showed us his hand. "See there? No blood."

Maddy took a step backward. "Wait here," she said. "I'll go get some wet towels."

"No, no," he protested. "No need for that."

But Maddy was already on her way back to the restroom.

"Why did that guy take the case, anyway?" I asked Stefan. "Look," I said, pointing to our luggage, "he could easily have taken *both* of our small packs."

"Probably because it was the one you were holding. He probably thought it contained your most valuable things."

"Ha!" I said. "He sure would have been surprised when he opened it, then. It's full of yo-yos!"

"Yo-yos?" Stefan repeated. He moved his hand in an up-and-down motion. "You mean the little toy?"

"Yes." I laughed. "The little toy." I took a deep breath and began to explain. "See, my friend Maddy works for a—"

Maddy reappeared just then with a handful of sloppy wet toilet paper. "No paper towels," she said, starting to reach up to Stefan's injury. "Just this."

"Here," he said quickly, grabbing her hand. "Let me do it."

"All right." Maddy plopped the wet paper into his palm.

While he was busy applying the compress, Maddy quickly pinched my arm and whispered into my ear, "Let's invite him out to eat. It's the least we can do."

"Okay," I agreed quickly.

Maddy did the asking, and Stefan accepted. We picked up all our stuff and took off along the busy street outside the station. Maddy immediately began to complain about how warm it was, even though it didn't seem that hot to me. "She's from San Francisco," I explained to Stefan, "where it's always nice and cool."

"Ah, San Francisco," he said, his eyes lighting up with recognition. He turned to Maddy. "So it is usually cool in San Francisco?"

"Oh, yes. The temperature there rarely goes above—" Maddy started to say.

"Tell him about that headline in the paper," I interrupted.

Maddy looked puzzled and a little annoyed. "What headline? What paper?"

"Don't you remember? That headline in the San Francisco paper." I stopped walking and wrote an imaginary headline in the air, announcing loudly, "Thermometer Hits Seventy-three Again; No Relief in Sight.'"

"Seventy-three," Stefan repeated thoughtfully. "Ah, I see! On the Fahrenheit scale that would be quite cool, would it not? No relief in sight." He nodded and smiled. "Ah! I see the joke."

He looked so cute when he said that. *Ah! I see the joke.*

We were about to cross the street and had just walked past a bus that was parked at the corner, loading passengers. Stefan suddenly stopped walking and stared at the backs of a man and woman who had just gotten on the bus. He lurched forward, trying to get a better look at them. He kept staring even after the door shut with a hiss of air and the bus began to pull away from the curb. As it passed directly in front of us, a guy with the reddest mop of hair I'd ever seen leaned way out of an opened window, at the same time calling in an urgent voice, "Stefan! Hey! *Stefan!*"

Stefan immediately spotted the face in the window and

quickly raised both arms and shouted back, "Bluey! *Bluey!*"

The bus had picked up speed by then, but Stefan took off after it, running in the street, trying to keep abreast of it but losing ground fast.

"It seems like that guy is always running off someplace," I deadpanned to Maddy.

We watched as Stefan chased the bus down the street until it was finally forced to stop in the middle of the block because of a sudden crush of traffic. After a few moments we saw the exit door open partway and the redheaded man try to squeeze his way out shoulder first. He had someone by the hand and was trying to pull her out of the bus, too. There was a lot of confusion then, with the door folding shut again and then opening once more with lots of hissing and flapping of hinges. The man and woman got out, and Stefan ran up to meet them.

The three of them came together with shouts of joy. They separated for a moment and came together again, foreheads touching, arms clasped around one another's necks as passersby on the sidewalk turned to watch with curious smiles. Then Stefan and the man hugged alone, arms pounding on each other's back, and they whirled around in a little dance of friendship while the woman stood by beaming. They finally separated, and Stefan and the woman faced each other slowly, joining hands. They straightened out their arms and leaned back, feasting their eyes on each other, finally ending up in a close embrace. I doubt that I will ever again witness a reunion of friends quite so beautiful and moving as that. Even now I can close my eyes and still see a slow-motion replay of that circling dance of friendship, and I can remember my exact thought at the time: *Oh, what I would give to be one of those three!*

Their names were Bluey and Barb, but Maddy and I just called them the Australians. They were a suntanned, outdoorsy couple from Australia that Stefan had met two years before in Paris while on his first trip on his own.

After we had all been introduced, Maddy and I told them the story about the near robbery in the train station and how Stefan had saved the day. "We were just about to take him to get something to eat," Maddy said. "Would you two like to come along?"

"Wonderful!" they said, and quickly suggested a nearby self-service cafeteria that they knew about.

"Now, for heaven's sake, don't go and load up," Maddy warned me in a whisper as we entered the restaurant. "Then maybe the others will take the hint. We can't afford to buy these people a banquet, you know."

Following Maddy's advice and remembering the unpleasant incident in Zurich, I selected only a simple lettuce salad and a plate of spaghetti with tomato sauce and Italian sausage. Maddy got a bowl of soup and a plain cheese sandwich.

The Australians, however, really splurged. Every time they slid another dish of food onto their trays, Maddy grimaced at me and gritted her teeth. They finally finished up with a carafe of red wine, some kind of pudding, and a bowl of fresh strawberries for each of them.

Stefan took only the special of the day—which was a giant plate of eggplant Parmesan—along with two thick slices of bread and a carton of milk. I heard him speak to the server behind the counter, a simple one-word sentence. "*Carne?*" he asked, pointing to his plate. The server shook her head. "*No,*" she said. "*No carne.*" I wondered what that was all about.

Maddy and I got to the cashier first, ahead of the others. "I'll pay for it all now," she said to me quietly, "and then you can pay me back your half later."

But before she could even get her money out, Bluey gently elbowed his way to the front of the line, right behind us. "*Per tutto,"* he said, reaching over Maddy's head and handing a bunch of Italian bills to the cashier.

After we were all sitting down, Maddy started fumbling with her money. "Let me pay you back," she said to him. "And we want to pay for Stefan's, too." But the Australians wouldn't hear of it. Maddy and I exchanged looks. We were both embarrassed, I think, for suspecting that they were somehow going to try to take advantage of us.

While we ate, Stefan and the Australians entertained Maddy and me with stories of the adventures they had had two years ago in Paris. "It's so *good* to see you both again," Stefan said finally. "But then we *knew* we'd meet again somewhere, someplace, didn't we?"

"Righto, mate!" Bluey said. "That we did! So where are you staying?"

"Here in *Milano*, you mean?" Stefan asked. "No place yet. I just got off the train. But I thought I'd try the hostel again— where I stayed last year." He looked at Maddy and me. "What about you two? Do you have reservations for tonight? Where are you staying?"

Maddy and I exchanged another quick glance. "We don't know yet," Maddy said. "We still have to find a place."

The Australians suddenly put their heads together. After a moment Bluey spoke up. "It's all settled, then," he said. "You'll come and kip with us tonight. We've got a huge room, and the landlord's a beaut. He'll probably let all three of you crash for just a few hundred extra *lire.*"

Maddy gave me a questioning look. "What do you think?" she asked quietly.

"Sounds great to me!"

But Maddy was still a little cautious. "Well, wait. Where is this room, anyway? Is it far from here? Is it in town, or what?"

"We're just a few blocks from the *duomo*," Barb said. "Just a short Metro ride from here." She looked us in the eye. First

Maddy and then me. "It's okay," she said soberly. "Come on. There's no problem. It's really okay."

Well, that convinced us, and Maddy and I started to gather our stuff together. As we did so, Bluey and Stefan looked at each other in an amused, resigned sort of way, and then the Australian took hold of Maddy's large pack and swung it up effortlessly over his shoulder while Stefan did the same with mine. "Gee, thanks, guys," Maddy said, and gave me a big wink. They just grunted in return, and Stefan staggered around in a silly kind of way, pretending the weight of my pack was too much for him.

The Metro stop was not far from the restaurant. When we got there, Bluey grabbed Stefan's arm. "It's the *Cairoli* stop," he said. "Look, Barb and I will watch out for Maddy. You get Gina over there. Remember, that's *Cairoli*. It's about six stops away, but you've got to change lines, so check the Metro map. Right?"

"Right," Stefan said. And then he looked down at me, quite shyly, I thought, with his clear blue eyes. "Okay, Gina? May I be your guide?"

"Well, are we separating, or what?" I hesitated, beginning to feel just a little out of my depth.

Maddy moved toward me like a mother hen. "We're staying together," she said firmly. "Don't worry about *that!*"

That's when Barb stepped in to explain. "It's the *Milano* Metro," she said. "Of course we'll all try to stay together, but sometimes it's just impossible, especially for five people. There are *mobs* down there! You'll see. Sometimes the door will just *close* on you without any warning before you have a chance to step into the car."

"Oh," Maddy said, nodding hesitantly. "Okay, then."

We didn't even have to buy the tickets. Barb just reached into a money belt she had under her T-shirt and pulled out a little book of them. She tore out five tickets and handed one to each of us.

"How much do we owe—" Maddy started to say, but Barb just held up her hand and shook her head. "Forget it. We're leaving *Milano* tomorrow. They would just go to waste."

Barb was right about the Metro being really crowded, but somehow we all managed to clamber aboard the same car. Stefan stayed right by me all the time, and after just a few stops he told me we had to get ready to get off and transfer to another line. That's when I lost sight of Maddy. I saw Bluey's red mop of hair, though, and I figured Maddy must be there, too—just too short for me to see.

I took a quick look around me at all the people. I couldn't believe I was in a foreign country. The people looked exactly like the people I saw every day at home. The Italian writing on the advertisements was strange, of course. I had fun trying to puzzle out what they said. The walls of the Metro stations were plastered with posters advertising American movies. I stooped down a little so I could see them through the window as we zoomed past. That gave me a funny feeling, seeing those posters. It was sort of like there was a little part of America there in the Metro stations of Milan. But it was still hard to believe I was so far from home.

We had inched our way close to the exit by then, and Stefan grabbed me by the hand and pulled me off as soon as the train jerked to a stop. "That way!" he said, pointing to an escalator with his free hand. "We go up that way."

We were practically pushed along by the rushing mob of people. Up the escalator, around a corner, through a swinging gate, down some stairs, and right onto another Metro car—as fast as that. Unlike the first car, this one was practically empty.

"Gosh, that was fun!" I puffed as I entwined my arm around a chrome pole and tossed back my hair. "But where's Maddy? Do you see her?"

Stefan bent his head down close to mine. "She's *gone!*" he whispered. "Your friend is gone, and now you are my prisoner!"

For one tenth of a second I think I believed him. That's what made it so funny, I guess.

The car lurched to a stop at the next station, and we were suddenly engulfed by a laughing, screaming stampede of about a dozen schoolboys dressed in purple and white jerseys. At the same time, at the other end of the car, another group of boys stumbled aboard, pushing and shoving one another like panicked passengers on a burning airplane. They were screeching and carrying on as loudly as the first group, but their jerseys were blue and gold. And then, like opposing armies, the purple-and-whites and the blue-and-golds suddenly began hurling little objects at each other. At first I didn't know what type of ammunition they were using, but I soon found out. It was *bubblegum*, and Stefan and I were caught right in the cross fire!

Balls of half-chewed gum went whizzing by like bullets. Since the sticky wads would only bounce off the boys' jerseys, *heads* were their chief targets. More ammunition was continually being manufactured in the flapping, shouting mouths of the kids, while the colorful paper wrappers dropped to the floor like empty cartridges.

I knew I was hit as soon as it happened. The first pink missile landed on the left side of my head below my ear. I reached up to touch it, and I knew I was in trouble. The more I tried to free it, the more it seemed to spread its sticky tentacles throughout the surrounding area of hair.

The second and third direct hits occurred almost simultaneously. "Oh, God," I heard Stefan say. "Don't touch it! Oh, God, what a mess!" And then a moment later he said, "Hey! *Cairoli*! This is our stop! Come on!"

He grabbed me by the hand and pulled me toward the exit. We were the last ones out, barely making it before the doors shut behind us with a forceful snap. Stefan's hand was still holding on to mine as we again charged up some stairs with the rest of the mob, traveled down narrow corridors, tripped over blankets spread with gaudy bracelets and watches for sale, rushed around corners, pushed open chrome gates, climbed more stairs, and finally landed out in the daylight on a busy street corner somewhere in the middle of *Milano*, Italy.

13

At first Maddy was elected to do the cutting. "Gee, I don't know—" she said, watching Stefan as he reluctantly removed his red Swiss Army knife from a belt loop of his baggy gray trousers and handed it to her. "I was never very good at this sort of thing."

The room we were in was old and huge. It contained one double bed and a small cot. There was a cracked mirror on the wall next to the door, and below it stood a small brown-stained sink. The paint was flaking from the ceiling in patches the size of cornflakes, and there were wide cracks like rivers in the faded wallpaper. I was sitting on the cot, and Maddy, Stefan, and Barb were hovering over me. Bluey was still downstairs settling up with the owner of the little cheap hotel, or *pensione*, as it was called in Italian.

Maddy kept peering down at the army knife in her hand, turning it over and experimentally picking at one of the blades.

"No, no," Stefan said, taking it back again. "This way." And he pulled open a tiny pair of scissors. "They're small," he said, "but very sharp."

"And they're all we've got," added Barb. She gingerly lifted a gum-matted lock of my hair. "It'll just have to get cut. There's no other way."

Poor Stefan. He was acting like it was all his fault. "What

about ice cubes?" he suggested. "My sister told me once that if you put ice cubes—"

"Yes, but not on *hair*, Stefan," Barb said. "On clothing, perhaps, but not on hair."

"We could try alcohol or some type of solvent, maybe," he suggested.

"Hey!" I said, finally getting into the act. "Listen, I don't care! Just cut it! I was about to get it cut anyway at home." P.J.'s joking comment, "Cut that hair and we're through," seemed a hundred years away and miles ago. (At least that's how my poor brain—absolutely dizzy now from lack of sleep— thought of it.)

The three of them had been slowly walking around the cot, surveying me from different angles. Stefan happened to be right in front of me when I said that. What a look of surprise there was on his face!

"You mean this is not the end of your life?" he asked. "Such beautiful hair, and this is not like being doomed to a slow and agonizing death?"

I laughed. "Of course not."

He brought one hand to his forehead and let himself fall back onto the double bed as if in a faint. "What a woman!" he breathed in a half-serious, half-joking way. "A one-of-a-kind woman, right here in our midst."

His words filled me with a little bubble of happiness. Being referred to as "one of a kind" was part of it, but being called a *woman* (and I was certain that was how Stefan really thought of me), well, being called a woman was even more of a thrill.

Maddy made the first cut—a tentative little tweak that re-moved about three strands of hair. "I don't think I can do this," she said, taking a step back. "Hair cutting is just not my bag."

"I'll do it," Stefan said, suddenly raising himself from the bed and taking the scissors from Maddy's hand. "I have two poodles at home. I cut their hair all the time."

Both Barb and Maddy laughed. I guess they thought he was joking. But somehow I knew he was simply stating a fact.

"How short would please you, madam?" he asked, smiling a toothy smile at me and waving the tiny scissors over his head like a hairdresser gone berserk.

Suddenly remembering a line I had recently heard on television, I quickly replied, "Well, to quote Marie Antoinette's last words, 'Not too much off the top, please.' "

I happened to glance up into the mirror over the sink a second after I said that, and I caught a glimpse of Stefan's face. A little secret smile was hovering around his mouth as if he had just discovered something wonderful and had not yet told anyone about it.

Maddy had gone down the hall to shower and change into her pajamas before my haircut was finished. In the meantime Bluey and the *pensione* manager had quickly set up two more rollaway cots in the room. Now Maddy was resting on one of them with her arms across her forehead, shielding her eyes against the last slanting rays of the sun coming in through the open window. The Australians were stretched out on their backs, too, on the double bed, talking quietly to each other.

Finally Stefan took a step back and surveyed his handiwork. "Finished!" he announced triumphantly. Then he blew on the little scissors and ceremoniously wiped them on his pants before snapping them shut and returning the knife to his belt loop.

Barb raised her head a little and looked at me. "Gina," she said quietly, "that looks lovely." She sat up further, propping herself up on her elbows. "It really does."

"Gosh, Stefan," I said, fluffing up the ends and turning my head a little while I looked into the mirror from another angle. "Thanks! Thanks a lot! You really did a great job, you know it? I hope your two poodles appreciate you."

Stefan rolled his eyes around and finally focused on me

with a funny, cross-eyed stare. "Woof-woof!" he barked, so realistically that we all had to laugh. "Now," he said, "how would you like to take a little walk with me? To the *piazza*, maybe, and see the sights of *Milano*?"

"Well . . ." I hesitated, looking at Maddy, but she was out like a light, sound asleep.

"Oh, but perhaps you are too tired," Stefan said. "I have forgotten about your long airplane journey. You haven't been to bed last night yet, and now it's almost tonight."

"How's that again?" I laughed, suddenly feeling fresh as a daisy. "Sure, I'd love to go for a walk." I started scooping up great wads of hair from the bedspread. "As soon as I clean up this mess."

"Let me help." Stefan brought the wastebasket from under the sink and held it while I stuffed the gum-matted hair into it.

"Wait," he said. "I have an idea." And with that, he removed the entire bedspread and walked over to the large window. He opened the shutters all the way, stepped out onto the little postage-stamp-size balcony, and snapped the bedspread a couple of times, the way you'd do with crumbs on a tablecloth.

While he was doing that I asked Barb how I could get to the bathroom.

"Down the hall, to your right," she said. "It says 'WC' on the door."

"Thanks."

I got back to our room just in time to catch Stefan in the act of plucking a lock of my hair out of the wastebasket and proceeding to wrap it up in his handkerchief! The embarrassing part was, I *had* to confront him about it, since what he had just done was so obvious to both of us. Instead of saying something out loud, I just gave him what I hoped was a humorously puzzled look.

"For the authorities!" he said quickly, using a funny, nervous, high-pitched tone. "Hair clippers must always present a specimen of their work to the Department of, uh—the Department of Fleece and Bristles." He meticulously finished wrapping his handkerchief into a neat square and put it into his pocket.

I just stared at him suspiciously.

He clicked his heels, hands down straight at his sides. "It is the *rule*," he said. "You understand, miss?"

I turned away, hiding my smile. "Is it time for that walk yet?" I asked. "And hey, what's a *piazza*, anyway?"

But he didn't hear me. He was standing over the sink splashing water on his face.

I went over to take a closer look at Maddy. "Stefan and I are going out for a while," I whispered, feeling I should at least make an effort to let her know. She opened one eye and limply fluttered her fingers in a weak good-bye.

Bluey stood up and fished out a couple of keys from his pocket. "Here, Gina," he said, tossing them to me. "They lock up here at midnight. One key opens the downstairs door, and the other—with the number on it—is for the room."

I shoved the keys in my pants pocket. "Okay. Thanks."

Barb looked up from the bed. "It's going to be a lovely evening," she said kind of wistfully. "You two enjoy yourselves, now."

In a minute Stefan had dried his face and run his fingers through his hair. "Let's go," he said, and we were on our way.

In no *way* was I prepared for what I was about to see that night.

Stefan and I took the stairs down to the street, since the funny rattling little cage of an elevator didn't look all that safe to me. The front door of our *pensione* opened onto a narrow, noisy street. There was a sidewalk, but it was only about a foot

138

wide, and when you met another pedestrian coming the other way, one of you had to step down into the street to let the other pass. And stepping into that street with all those cars and taxis whizzing by just inches away—horns blowing like mad—was the next-best thing to suicide.

At first Stefan tried to lead me by the hand, but that was impossible. "We must go single file," he said finally. "Do you want to follow?"

"Oh, definitely!" I said loudly. "Since I don't know where we're going!"

After a few blocks, our street opened out into a small square crowded with people who all seemed to be going in different directions. Stefan stopped a moment and looked around.

"Do you know where we are?" I asked.

"I think so. I think we're almost there." After a few seconds, he pointed to one of the streets that radiated off the square. "That is the one," he said. And he took hold of my hand again, as if it were the most natural thing in the world.

I don't remember ever feeling as wonderful and free as I did that evening, walking along that street in *Milano*, Italy, hand in hand with Stefan. Part of it, I think, was the feel of his hand, slightly rough, but strong and dry and cool. And there was something about the early evening July air—a kind of softness about it—that I can't begin to describe. The air was so mild you didn't even have to breathe; it just flowed in and out of your body like a sweet, warm liquid. We walked a few minutes longer without speaking, and I know that I'll remember those few minutes as long as I live.

We passed under an archway and suddenly found ourselves in a huge and utterly magnificent high-roofed shopping mall crowded with people.

"My God," I breathed. "Look at this place!"

The shops were lively and rich looking, and there were restaurants galore, most of which had open-air eating areas blocked off by rows of colorful flower boxes. Gorgeous potted plants and trees were everywhere.

We continued walking until we came to the crossroads of two great passageways. The floor was a beautiful mosaic of colored marble, and the ceiling, so high above, was a splendid dome of tinted glass. I stood there breathless.

"We find ourselves presently in the world-famous *Galleria Vittorio Emanuele II*, completed in the year 1867 and designed by Giuseppe Mengoni," Stefan announced like a tour guide as he extended his arms, arched his neck, and stared directly up into the dome. After a moment, he straightened his neck and smiled proudly down at me like a prize pupil who had just recited his piece with no mistakes at all.

I joined in the game at once. "The *what*?" I asked. "Completed *when*, and designed by *whom*? Please, would you repeat that for me?"

"Certainly!" He laughed. "Designed by Mengoni, completed in 1867, and commonly called the *Milano Galleria*. Surprised at my knowledge, are you? Well, don't be. I read about it on the reverse side of Barb's map back at the *pensione*. It's tourist site number four."

"Gosh," I said, "there's a galleria back home in Stockton—at least that's what they call it. But wow! It's nothing like this! I've *got* to bring Maddy here. Too bad she was sleeping. Maybe we can come by again in the morning. Do you think we could?"

"Has she prearranged for the special all-day tour, or—"

"Oh, Stefan, cut it out!" I laughed.

We continued walking, and in a few more minutes we emerged from another archway into the open air again—and suddenly there it stood! The most beautiful and elaborate cathedral I could ever have possibly imagined!

The sun was just setting, and the whole facade of the church seemed to be basking in a soft, hazy golden glow. The roof was adorned with a countless multitude of graceful spires and pinnacles, and hundreds of statues were looking down upon us. The whole square was filled with people milling about, but they seemed like tiny dolls alongside the immenseness of the cathedral.

"The *Piazza del Duomo!*" Stefan announced grandly, still playing the part of a tour guide but now with a little tremor in his voice. "Cathedral Square! And there in front of us stands the *duomo* itself, one of the world's largest and most magnificent churches—" Stefan suddenly quit talking like a guide. "Just *look* at that, will you?" he whispered. "I have never seen it at sunset before."

I finally found my voice. "Why hasn't anyone ever *told* me about this place?" I said. And I wasn't joking, either. How could it be that before that moment I didn't even know that such a place existed? I felt strangely cheated and angry, too. But I didn't know who to be angry with.

The funny thing is, Stefan actually thought I *was* joking! "Yes," he said, smiling. "And why hasn't anyone ever told you about the moon?"

I decided I'd fake it. "That's right!" I said indignantly. "Why haven't they? Such a big round thing as that!"

We spent the next hour completely circling the outside of the church and then going inside to see the interior. Stefan pointed out the gigantic pillars inside. "I think there are over fifty of them," he said. "And I remember reading that those stained-glass windows are the largest in the world." He paused. "It is an amazing sight, is it not?"

Outside the church good-humored crowds of people were still milling about in a holiday atmosphere. The several rows of steps leading up to the front of the church were dotted with people our age, in their teens and twenties. There were two or three small groups centered around guys strumming on guitars, and pairs of lovers were openly caressing each other.

Stefan and I found a small expanse of empty step directly in front of the magnificent bronze doors of the church, and we quietly sat down together. I was insane with weariness. I slowly stretched out my legs and crossed them at the ankles. Then, closing my eyes with a tired sigh, I leaned over and clung to Stefan's arm with both of mine. I put my head on his shoulder and let the rest of my body go completely limp alongside his.

"Well, well," he said softly. "It finally seems that Gina from America has reached the end of her day." Then he patted his thigh with his hand. "Here," he said. "Rest your head here on my leg."

I opened my eyes for a second and did as he suggested, as if in a trance. I pivoted my body and stretched out on my back lengthwise along the step, with my head now resting on Stefan's thigh. I seemed to be floating on air.

"So where are you from, Stefan?" I asked, my words wafting up to him as if I were speaking in a dream. "Your English is good, but you still have an accent."

"My home is in Amsterdam. And thank you for the compliment. My parents are Dutch, but my mother grew up in England. I learned the language from her, you see." He paused, then added slyly, "But in my heart I am Italian."

I opened my eyes and smiled at him, and he laughed a short delighted little laugh, as if that were the first time he had thought of himself in that way.

"So what's it like in Amsterdam, Stefan? What do you do? Do you go to school?"

I felt his hand brushing my hair back from my forehead. "Yes, I go to school. I play with my dogs. I work—"

"You work? Where do you work?"

"I work in a restaurant near my home. On weekends, sometimes in the evenings. I save up money to travel."

"What kind of restaurant is it?"

"It is a vegetarian restaurant. But not so severe as some. We do serve eggs and cheese."

I opened my eyes and moved my legs a bit. "Well, hey!" I said. "That's what I am! I'm a vegetarian!"

Stefan leaned back with his elbows resting on the step above us. "A vegetarian," he said with a gentle laugh, "who eats spaghetti with tomato sauce and Italian sausage?"

"How did you remember that?" I asked, turning my head a little. Then I shrugged and added, "Well, sometimes I may eat a *little* meat, but I'm still a vegetarian."

Stefan was silent a moment. And then he said, "Oh, I see. And you are also against the death penalty except on every other Thursday. It's okay to lower the blade or flip the switch if we do so just *once in a while*."

"Hey, Stefan," I said, raising my head from his thigh and then letting it fall back with as much force as I could muster, "do I detect a little sarcastic streak in you?"

"Who, *moi?*" He laughed.

"Well, I still think I'm a vegetarian at heart," I said. "I saw a movie in one of my classes at school, and I agreed with everything they said—"

"You have to choose, Gina," Stefan interrupted. "If you eat meat, you are not a vegetarian. Just calling yourself one does not make you one, you know," he added a bit impatiently.

I tried to concentrate as hard as I could on what he was saying, but my brain was swimming in confusion. All I could say was, "I don't know. I really don't know. I'm just too tired to think about it now."

He didn't persist, so we just let the subject die. I think I dozed off for just a moment, because the sounds of the square suddenly fell silent and then resumed a moment later.

"So do you have brothers and sisters?" I asked, forcing my eyes to open. "Back there in Amsterdam?"

"Only one sister," he said. "She is thirteen."

"Oh, yes. She told you about ice cubes and chewing gum."

"Yes. That's the one."

I moved my head around a bit. Stefan immediately bent down close to look at me. "Comfortable?" he asked. "Do you want to walk again?"

I didn't want to change a thing. "No," I said quickly. "I'm fine. Just really fine."

After a few minutes, Stefan started talking about his sister again. "I think she is having some problems right now," he said thoughtfully. "Problems with friends and things like that."

"Like what? What do you mean?"

"She is too self-centered, I think," he said, nodding, agreeing with himself. "And also insecure. I think I can see that her friends, they get tired of her. She talks too much, always about herself, and she can *never* keep a confidence."

"Oh?" I asked softly. "Really?"

He touched my arm. "In that way she is very different from you," he said.

"Different from *me*?" I asked. Was I dreaming, or what?

"Yes, different from you. For instance, the German on the train. You didn't rattle his secret out just to entertain your friend, as my sister would have done. That's what I mean." He sighed. "But she is young. She may learn. She may yet grow out of it—"

Those were the last words I heard. My eyelids dropped shut, and I slept there on the steps of the *Milano duomo* with my head on Stefan's thigh.

14

Stefan woke me with a kiss. Not a passionate, sexy kiss, just a tender touching of his lips to my forehead. "It's late," he whispered. "We should go."

I sat up slowly, wondering why every muscle in my body ached. "Ooh, ouch," I groaned. "God, I'm so stiff. What time is it, anyway?" I raised my arms to the sky in a slow stretch.

"It's after eleven. You're shivering. Are you cold?"

"No, I don't think so. Not really." I paused and looked around—at the almost-deserted square, the cathedral, at the sky and the stars. "Oh, it's such a great night, isn't it, Stefan?"

He stood up first and helped me to my feet. I was standing on the step above him, so we were almost the same height then.

"It's a *wonderful* night," he whispered. And somehow our arms slowly encircled each other, and we stood together for a long moment, swaying gently from side to side.

We separated finally, and I moved my arm until I could see the hands of my watch in the glow of the dim light of the piazza. "It's twenty-five after two," I said. "California time." I was puzzled. "But is it day or night over there?"

And then I suddenly remembered something that I was supposed to have done but didn't—which was to call my mother as soon as we got settled and let her know that we were okay.

"Oh, *no!*" I said in a loud, agitated voice. "I forgot to call my mother!"

The distressed and anxious tone of my voice apparently attracted the attention of a middle-aged couple who were passing nearby, because they looked over at us and really glared at Stefan.

"They think I'm about to attack you," Stefan whispered in my ear. And then he grinned. "Not such a bad idea, no?" His grin turned into an evil smirk, and he muttered between his teeth, "I'll just wait until they disappear around that corner, and—"

"Oh, Stefan—"

"Shh!" He held up one hand, waiting, keeping his eye on the couple. "There they go! They are gone! Come here, my beautiful little American!" And he swept me into his arms exactly like Marcello Mastroianni did to his lover in an old Italian movie I saw once on the late show. The only difference was this kiss was real. God, was it real.

Neither one of us knew quite how to handle the situation—or what to do next. After that kiss, I mean. I know I was shaking, literally shaking, from my knees to my shoulders.

I think that scared Stefan, because he pulled away from me and looked at me with genuine concern. "Are you all right, Gina?" he asked. "You're trembling. Here, come on. Sit down again." He put his hands on my shoulders and gently started to push me back down on the steps.

"No, it's okay," I protested. "I'm okay, really. I'm just so *tired.* I've never *been* so tired!"

"Oh, yes. Of course," he said. "Well, come then. We must go back to the room."

"But I can't!" I wailed. "I have to find a phone! I was supposed to phone my parents hours ago! They'll kill me when I get home." I looked at my watch again. "It says two thirty now. Damn! Is it day or night in California? I figured that out once. Why can't I remember it now?"

"Because you are dead tired, that's why." Stefan spread his fingers and slowly placed both hands under my jaw, supporting my head and rubbing my neck with his thumbs. "We have a nine-hour difference, I believe. It is afternoon in California. But it is not so easy as that to place transatlantic calls from Italy, you know. We must find a telephone office. We will find someone to ask. Come, we will start walking back toward the *pensione* on the *Via Dante*. We can find a bar or fast food, and we will ask directions."

"Do you think so? Do you think we can?" I asked. God, I was so happy that he was going to try to help. And it turned out he was right. We only had to walk a few blocks before we came to a large fast-food restaurant. It was practically empty.

"Are you hungry?" Stefan asked, holding the door open for me.

"No, not hungry. I *am* thirsty, though. But can we ask about the telephone first? Maybe they close at midnight or something."

"Sure." Stefan went up to the counter and said something that sounded like "office of the telephones" in Italian. The girl started flirting with him right off the bat. She smiled and acted real cute, talking a mile a minute and pointing to her right. Stefan just kept nodding and saying, "*Sì, sì.*" Then he said, "*Grazie, signorina. Grazie.*"

She surprised me then by laughing and saying in slow, heavily accented English, "You are ver-y wel-come."

"We're lucky," Stefan told me. "The telephone office is just down the street. It's in the post office building, she says. And she says it should still be open."

It took us only a few minutes to get there. Following Stefan's directions, I went up to the desk and said to the woman, "Collect call to the United States, please." She nodded and gave me a piece of paper and a pencil and said, "Number." I wrote it down and gave it to her, and then she pointed to a booth and told me to go inside. I started walking toward it and Stefan followed me.

"You're supposed to wait, and she'll ring the phone when she has your call," he said.

I nodded. "Okay," I said. And then I went into the little booth and shut the door.

In a few seconds I was talking to my mother. She sounded like she was just around the corner.

"Hi, Mom!" I said, trying to sound bright and cheery instead of apologetic, hoping that might make her forget how late I was in calling. "We're doing fine, only we're not in Zurich like we planned. See, we had a little problem with—"

"Gina," my mother said before I could even finish my sentence. "Will you just listen a moment. I have some very, *very* bad news."

I knew immediately just by her tone of voice that someone had died. I felt a sudden burst of nausea rising up in my chest, and my arms turned cold and numb. Oh, no! Was it my father, Marie, one of my brothers . . .

"Your grandmother has passed away." The voice on the other end of the line began to fade, as if the phone were slipping away. "It happened yesterday afternoon. Marie was with her at the time, but your father and I—"

Only my grandmother! I thought as I felt the blood start to flow through my veins again. I took several deep breaths. Funny, but I hadn't even *thought* of her.

The line was suddenly quiet. Then, "Gina? Are you there? Gina?"

"Yes, I'm here," I answered. I didn't know what to say. Finally some words came. "She's dead? She's really *dead*? But she wasn't supposed to be that sick. Marie told me—"

"Well, I'm sorry," my mother said softly. "Marie was wrong. The funeral will be on Friday."

"Oh," I breathed, my heart sinking. That meant I would have to leave. I would have to fly back home immediately—

My mother's words interrupted my thoughts. "Your grandmother told Marie that you should *not* be called back home," she said. "She knew she was dying—" My mother's voice broke. "Just a minute, Gina," she said, and I could hear her blowing her nose. "Hello?" she said a moment later. "As I was saying, apparently she knew she was dying, and Marie told us that her last words were, 'Don't call Gina home. Gina must stay in Italy.' "

"Oh," I said softly, "it must be because of the seeds—"

"What seeds, Gina? What are you talking about?"

"Well, Grandma gave me some of those sunflower seeds, you know—her sunflower seeds? And she asked me to go feed the birds on that mountain in Assisi where Saint Francis used to go. I'm supposed to do it on Friday—on the fifth. She was very definite about that. My gosh, Friday. That's the day of the funeral, isn't it?" I paused, then added, "She didn't want me to talk about it. That's why I didn't tell you guys before."

"Oh, I see. Just a minute, Gina." I heard her put her hand over the phone. Then I heard muffled talking. The next thing she asked me was about the necklace. "By any chance do you know anything about her necklace? Marie thinks maybe you know something about it, because it seems to have disappeared."

"Well, I have it," I said, reaching up around my neck and feeling for the chain. "That's another thing she wanted me to do—to wear that necklace when I went up to the mountain. But you know, it's really a *locket*—"

"You were right," I heard her tell Marie. "Gina does have it." Then back to me again, "Well, I suppose she had her reasons, but I don't understand any of it."

"No. Me neither," I said.

"Well, all right, Gina," she said, changing the subject.

"Are you being careful over there? How's Maddy? Is she there with you now?"

I quickly glanced at Stefan, who was leaning against the wall, watching me. "Well, no. Not exactly." Then to avoid any more questions along that line, I asked about my father. "Is Dad okay? Tell him hello for me, okay?"

"Yes, I will," she said. "He's not here now. He's attending to some business at the funeral parlor."

"Oh." That's when the tears suddenly flooded my eyes. If anyone on this earth would really miss my grandmother, it would be my father.

"Well, you be careful over there now," she warned again. "Stay with Maddy, and don't talk to strangers."

"Yes. I will. Good-bye."

"Good-bye."

Stefan came right over as I left the booth. "My God, what's wrong?" he asked. "Bad news? Is it bad news?"

I was trying to find a tissue. I was pretty sure I had one in one of my pockets. I finally felt it squished way down in my back left one. I pulled it out, and all the Italian bills I got when Maddy and I changed money in the station fell to the floor. Stefan quickly stooped down and gathered them up.

I headed for the door, pushed it open, and went out to the street. Stefan was following close behind.

"My grandmother died," I said, blowing my nose. "She wasn't that sick, but she died."

I could tell Stefan didn't know what to do. "Here's your money," he said, pressing the bills into my hand. "These are large bills. There is quite a lot of money here."

"Thank you," I said, carelessly stuffing them all back into one of my pockets. If Stefan was alarmed at that, he didn't let on.

We started walking back to the fast-food place. I was still blowing my nose, holding my tissue with both hands, and

Stefan was kind of guiding me along by the elbow. "Did you say—" he started to ask, then hesitated and started again. "Did you say that your grandmother has died?"

"Yes," I answered. Even though I was still blowing my nose, I wasn't actually crying that hard. The whole scene was very weird.

In a few minutes we were back at the restaurant. "Do you still want that drink?" he asked gently. "Or do you want to go right back to the room?"

"No. I'm really thirsty. Let's get a drink."

"Okay."

It was easy to order. I just told the girl I wanted a cola, and she said in English, "Large or small?"

"Large, I guess," I answered. Then I started looking in my pockets for my money. I tried my left front one. My lipstick was in there, and some scraps of paper. Also the pull-tab from the Coke I got on the train. Then I tried my left rear one. I pulled out a comb, the keys that Bluey had given me, some paper clips, and a crumpled-up boarding pass from the airplane. I started piling everything on the counter. It was a good thing the restaurant wasn't busy, since I was taking so long. As it was, Stefan stood there beside me, fidgeting nervously as I went through my pockets one by one.

"Please let me pay," he said as I pulled out some American coins and a pencil stub.

"Oh, no, Stefan. I've got it right here." I emptied my last pocket—and there they were—all my Italian bills. "See? I have it right here."

I unfolded a couple of bills and showed them to the counter girl. She picked one out, held it up with her thumb and index finger for me to double-check (as if I could), said something in Italian, and gave me my change. I took my drink and walked to the nearest table and sat down. Stefan got his own drink and a large bag of french fries and joined me a moment later.

"It was my Grandma Gari," I said, swirling around the ice in my cup. "She's my father's mother." I took a sip. "*Was,* I mean. She was pretty old and had a bad heart."

Stefan nodded.

"It's terrible to say, but nobody liked her much," I said. "She had a habit of butting in to everybody's business, and she was always so disagreeable. She really had a very disagreeable personality." I sighed. "I know I sound terrible, but that's the way she was."

Stefan pushed the bag of fries over to my side of the table and shook some of them out. Then he sighed too, and said, "Well, that's too bad. Poor old lady."

I took a french fry, then closed my eyes. I was too tired even to chew it. I thought I was asleep for a minute, but then my head jerked up and I was awake again. "She gave me some sunflower seeds before I left." I reached for the chain around my neck and lifted the locket up over my T-shirt where he could see it. "And this, too. I'm supposed to go to Assisi and climb some mountain."

Stefan's voice came from far, far away. "Truly? For what reason?"

"I don't know, actually. Some kind of promise. A mysterious promise she made long ago, from two centuries ago, when she left to come to America. What do you think of that? Is that crazy, or what?"

There was no answer, and for one awful moment I thought maybe Stefan had gone off and left me there all alone. My eyes flew open, but naturally he was still there.

"What I think is that you must go to bed. Finish your drink, and let's go before I have to carry you back."

"What a wonderful idea!" I sang out, drunk with weariness, but Stefan only looked at me, shook his head, and smiled.

15

I didn't even get a chance to say good-bye to the Australians. By the time Maddy woke me up they were gone. But I knew that I would never forget them.

I had a horrible dream just before Maddy called me. I dreamed I was lying on the very top row of some bleachers watching a flock of frightened and hysterical white banty chickens being chased, decapitated, and thrown into a big stew pot by an old barrel-shaped woman all dressed in black. Suddenly the whole structure shook and collapsed, with me hanging on for dear life as it fell.

The first thing I saw was Maddy sitting on the edge of my cot looking down at me.

"Oh, Maddy," I said as soon as I realized where I was. "I had an awful dream. This old lady was killing chickens and throwing them into a pot one by one. The poor things—"

"We have to go," Maddy said softly. "They have to clean the room, and they're kicking us out. I let you sleep as long as I could, but we have to go. Come on." She pressed her hand on my shoulder and gave me a little massage with her palm. "If you can just pull on your jeans and blouse, we can stuff your pajamas into your backpack. I have your other junk all packed up."

I sat up and looked around the room. The beds were empty, with sheets and blankets half dragging on the floor.

My blue pack, all zippered up and bulging, was sitting next to Maddy's near the door.

"Where is everybody?" I asked.

"The Australians are gone. They wanted to catch an early train to Venice. They told me to tell you good-bye." Maddy smiled. "They said they knew they'd see you again—some other time, some other place." She paused and took my hand. "And Gina, I'm so sorry about your grandmother."

I closed my eyes for a second. "Yes. Well, it's all right." I hesitated. How do you tell someone that even though your grandmother just died, you're really not that sad about it? I was even starting to feel a little guilty, especially since I had been so devastated when my grandfather died.

"Stefan told me—about your phone call and everything—" Maddy was saying.

I felt a sudden rush of panic. "Where is he? Did Stefan leave, too?"

"Oh, no. He's downstairs getting our passports from the guy at the desk. Now will you please get up, Gina? Stefan will be back here any second."

I went to the sink and splashed my face with water.

"I already packed your toothbrush and stuff," Maddy said nervously. "If we're not out of here when Stefan comes back, they may charge us for another day."

"Do you think anyone is in the john?" I asked, grabbing my clothes off the chair.

"How should I know?"

I looked at her a second. She looked tired and a little frazzled. "Well, I'll be back in a minute. Don't go anywhere, okay?"

"I'll be here. Or at least I'll wait for you in the hallway right outside the door."

"And then are we heading straight for Rome, or what? Boy, Maddy, you should see that cathedral Stefan and I saw last night! It was so—"

"Damn it, Gina! Will you get going?"

"Okay, okay. You don't have to get so huffy about it. But listen—" And here I finally asked what was really on my mind. "Is Stefan coming with us—to Rome, I mean? If that's where we're going."

Maddy sighed and shook her head. "You take the cake," she said. "You really do. But to answer your question—yes and no. I think he'll at least take the same train we do, but I think he's headed for Florence." She paused. "I think he told me Florence."

"Oh." I was disappointed, but at the same time I was happy to hear that he would be with us for a little while longer, at least. "He's really *nice*, isn't he, Maddy?" I added just before she came at me with both fists swinging.

The bathroom was a mess. The shower didn't have a curtain around it, and there was water everywhere. The cracked toilet seat was wet, and even the few sheets of paper left on the toilet paper roll were damp. I couldn't find a dry place to put my pajamas after I took them off, so I tried to hold them with my chin while I put on my jeans.

Stefan and Maddy were sitting on the floor outside our room when I got back. They had their backpacks on and looked like they were all ready to go.

"G'morning, Gina," Stefan said, getting up first and then offering his hand to Maddy. She grabbed it and let him pull her to her feet.

"Good morning to you," I said.

Maddy just stood there brushing off the seat of her pants, watching as Stefan and I let our eyes linger on each other a moment. Something about him looked different, but I couldn't figure out what it was. I kept staring at him. He was wearing the same gray pants and T-shirt he had on the day before, so that wasn't it.

Maddy pointed to my backpack on the floor. "You want to put your pajamas away so we can get going?"

I unzipped the front pouch to see if I could make room for them in there, and my yellow yo-yo dropped out. I held it up for Stefan to see. "The reason we're here!" I said. "This is the cause of it all."

He smiled a puzzled smile. And then I saw what was different about him: it was his beard. Well, it wasn't really a beard. It was just that he hadn't shaved. There were tiny little silvery-blond bits of hair where yesterday there weren't any. "Hey, Stefan," I said, touching his face and recycling an old joke. "There's more of you!"

At first he didn't get it. "More of me?" he asked, slightly amused. "What do you mean?"

I didn't answer. I just raised my eyebrows and waited for him to catch on, which he did in about half a second.

"Oh, I see! More of me." He laughed, rubbing his jaw. "I see it now."

I shoved the yo-yo into one of my pants pockets and hurriedly decided there was no room for my pajamas in the front pouch of my pack, but when I tried to zip it shut, something got stuck in the zipper. Maddy was pacing down the hall by then, tapping her thigh with her hand in a little gesture of impatience.

"Just a second, Maddy," I called out. Then I examined the stuck zipper and discovered what the problem was. It was the little plastic baggie that contained my grandmother's sunflower seeds. I had to fool around with the zipper a moment before I got the baggie unstuck. Well, I don't need these anymore, I thought, and looked around to see if there was a trash container in the hallway somewhere. I didn't see one, so I just shoved the seeds back in and zipped up the pack again. Then I put my pajamas in another section of my backpack.

Stefan didn't offer to carry my big pack, but I think it crossed his mind. Maddy had a large pack too, and I guess he thought he would either have to carry both of them—which would be really difficult and awkward—or carry none. It was his idea to put the big bags on the elevator and send them down to the street floor, though. The three of us made a little game of racing down the steps to see if we could beat the elevator. It was fun, because the elevator was right in the center of the stairwell, and we could watch it as it rattled on down.

Maddy and I dragged our bags out of the elevator and banged and bumped our way out of the small front door of the *pensione*. Then the three of us stood near the doorway on the narrow sidewalk and looked up and down the street, noisy with traffic.

"What now?" I shouted.

"Back to the station, I guess," Maddy said loudly.

"But we can't!" I exclaimed. "Not yet! You've got to go see that cathedral, Maddy. It's—"

"I already saw it," she said. "While you were asleep. Stefan and I walked over there."

"Really? Well, what did you think of it? Wasn't it so *neat*?"

"To the station, then?" Stefan interrupted. "On the Metro?"

Maddy and I looked at each other and nodded.

This time on the Metro I felt like a veteran. I tried to look nonchalant and bored like everyone else. When we got to the *Stazione Centrale* Metro stop, Stefan led the way upstairs to the trains. He stopped in front of a glassed-in bulletin board. "All the departing trains are listed here," he explained. "See, it tells you what time they leave and what time and where they arrive."

All three of us looked at our watches. "It's about eleven twenty," Stefan said.

My watch said twenty-three minutes past two. "Twenty-three minutes after two A.M. in California," I said to no one in particular.

Maddy was running her finger along the glass. "Here's Rome," she said. "Let's see. The next train to Rome leaves at eleven forty. Can we make that one?"

"That's a TEE," Stefan remarked.

"What's that mean?" I asked.

"Trans-European Express. All first class, and very expensive."

"Well, scratch that one," Maddy said.

"When's the next one?" I asked.

"Twelve forty-five. It arrives in Rome at, uh—let's see—uh, eighteen forty."

"*Eighteen* forty?" I said. "What time is that, anyway?"

Stefan looked at me sharply, as if he didn't believe the question. "That's six forty," he said. "You know, twenty minutes to seven."

"Well," Maddy said, "shall we take that one?"

"It arrives pretty late to go hunting for a room," Stefan answered. "Unless you have reservations someplace."

"No," she said. "No reservations."

The strap on my large pack was starting to cut into my shoulder. I dipped toward the floor and slipped it off with a huge sigh of relief.

"That's a good idea," Maddy said, and did the same.

"So what shall we do?" I asked.

A man in a business suit who was standing behind me started to push against me. "*Scusi,*" he said, giving me a gentle nudge, inching himself closer to the posted train schedule.

"Oops, sorry," I said, dragging my pack and backing away. Maddy and Stefan backed up also.

"*Scusi,*" I repeated. "*Scusi.* That's cute. I just love the Italian language."

"So what shall we do?" Maddy said, echoing my question. "We've got to get to Rome." She looked at Stefan. "Do you really think it would be that difficult finding a room?"

He nodded. "So late, I think so. The inexpensive rooms go first."

I sat down on my large pack and decided to let them figure it out. I really didn't care what we did. Except eat, that is. I suddenly realized I was starving.

"Hey! When do we eat?" I asked. "I'm starving."

"Hold it, will you, honey?" Maddy said. "We've got to make some plans here."

"Well, what are our choices?" I asked. "If Stefan thinks it would be too late to get a room in Rome, we either have to stay here or go someplace else—"

"You know," Stefan suggested finally, "we *could* go to Pisa—"

Maddy looked up. "Pisa?"

"Hey, Pisa!" I said. "The Leaning Tower and all that!" Finally somebody was talking about something I knew! I looked at Maddy. "There's this pizza place at home—the Leaning Tower of Pizza. It's got a picture of the Leaning Tower on its sign, and on its take-home boxes and napkins and stuff. Let's go there, Maddy! It would be fun!"

Stefan fished out a little notebook from somewhere. He flipped some pages and nodded his head. "I could make a phone call. I stayed at a place last summer. It's cheap and a little out of the way. I could see if there's any room for to-night."

Maddy scratched her head. "You'd come with us?" she asked. "I mean, if you've already been there, you probably don't want to go again, do you?"

"Well, no. I mean, yes. What I mean is, I really wouldn't mind going there again," he finally ended up saying. "So? Shall I call?"

Maddy still looked a little doubtful.

"*Please*, Maddy!" I begged. "Let's do it!" All the while my heart was thumping. *Stefan is really going to be traveling with us! Stefan is going to Pisa with us!*

159

"Well, okay," she said. "But I didn't realize we'd waste half our trip just getting to Rome."

"Gee, Maddy," I said. "I don't think it's wasted. I mean, look at all the stuff we got to do so far! That train ride from Zurich, meeting those nice Australians, then the *Milano* Metro, staying in that *pensione,* and my God, that cathedral! The way I look at it, heck, this *is* our trip!"

Maddy kept looking at me very seriously after I said that. Then she nodded and said simply, "Yes, I think you're right. That's very wise of you. This *is* our trip."

As we were walking to the phone Stefan said the words I'd been dreading to hear. "After our night in Pisa," he said, "I think it is time I leave you and be on my way."

"How come?" I asked quickly. "I mean, where do you have to go?"

"It's not that I *have* to go anywhere," he said. "I have four weeks to travel this summer, but I shouldn't impose—"

"Heavens, you're not imposing, Stefan!" Maddy said. "I mean, you've helped us so much! You shouldn't feel that you're imposing at all."

Her reassurance seemed to please him, but all the same I began to worry that he really might decide to leave us after our night in Pisa, and my heart sank at the thought.

We arrived in Pisa at four forty-three P.M. In other words, sixteen forty-three. The reason I know that is because after we got settled on the train, I memorized train time—or military time, if you want to call it that. It was easy. Up until twelve noon, it's just the same as regular time. Then one P.M. is thirteen hundred, and you just go on from there all the way to twenty-three hundred, which is eleven P.M. The hardest ones for me to memorize were seventeen hundred and nineteen hundred (five P.M. and seven P.M.). So I just mumbled those over and over to myself until I got them.

Another thing I did on the train was to organize my pockets. I was so embarrassed at not finding my money for my drink the night before, and then when Stefan and I got back to the room, I had to repeat the same stupid performance all over again to find the keys. So I figured it all out on the train. I decided to keep my lipstick and any other miscellaneous stuff—like my yo-yo—in my right front pocket; loose change in my left front, my comb and tissues in my left back, and spare folding money, tickets, and any keys I might have in my right back. The way I figured it was that I didn't want anything valuable—like money or tickets or keys—in the same pocket as my tissues and comb, since I might lose stuff when I wanted to blow my nose or comb my hair. I was really proud of myself for finally doing something about being so disorganized that way.

And there was something else I was proud of, too. I finally decided to quit fooling around and really *be* a vegetarian. Stefan had something to do with it, but not that much, actually. He just made me realize—well, it happened when we went to the bar car in the train to get something to eat for lunch. It was set up like a small cafeteria. But the only choices were sandwiches. Maddy said to bring her back a ham and cheese sandwich, if possible, so I picked out one of those for her. Then Stefan picked out his, which was a cheese and tomato. Stefan saw me hesitating, and I know *he* knew what I was thinking.

Those blue eyes of his looked straight into mine. "You know all the arguments," he said. "So you are or you aren't. It's as simple as that."

I stood there looking at all the sandwiches lined up in rows, and suddenly everything became clear to me. I was only one little insignificant person in the world, but I had to make a choice. I couldn't decide for everyone else, but I could decide for me. I reached out for the cheese and tomato sandwich.

"I'm a vegetarian," I said to Stefan. "I'm not going to eat animals anymore."

When we got back to our compartment, I told Maddy. "I'm a vegetarian," I said. "I've quit eating meat."

"Really?" she said. "Since when?"

"Since now."

She shrugged. "Okay," she said.

After a few minutes, Stefan and I got to talking about it. "You know, Stefan," I said, "my not eating meat will probably not save even one animal's life. Directly, I mean. Realistically."

Stefan drummed his fingers along his upper lip and thought about that for a couple of minutes. I was beginning to think he wasn't going to answer. He settled way back in his seat, folded his hands over his lap, and began to snap his thumbnails together. "I had a philosophy class last year," he said. "We tried to come up with some definitions of a moral act."

Maddy crumpled up the stiff white paper from her sandwich and put it in the little garbage container next to the window. "Of a what?" she asked. "I didn't hear you."

"A moral act," he repeated. "We were discussing how to define a moral act, and the definition I liked best went something like this: A moral act is an act that if everyone did it, the world would be a better place in which to live. And conversely, an immoral act is an act that if everyone did it, the world would be a worse place in which to live."

None of us spoke for a moment, and then Maddy said, "Hey, I like that. That's good. Although I don't know if I would agree with the idea that if everyone quit eating meat, the world would be a better place."

For a second I thought Stefan might argue with her, but he didn't. Instead he just looked at me and said, "Well, your decision was probably a morally correct one *for you*, Gina. You can feel that somehow, can you not?"

"How do you mean?" I asked, even though I think I knew what he meant. I just liked to hear him talk.

He touched his breastbone. "Right here. You can feel it. There is a lightness here. The weight of your conscience is not sitting here on your chest. You understand me?"

I nodded. For a second I considered making a pun—saying something like, "That's *heavy*, man. Very *heavy*." But then I figured that would be pretty dumb, and besides, it wouldn't do justice to the serious point Stefan was trying to make. I didn't have to try to be funny all the time. So instead I said simply, "Yes, I do. I do see what you mean."

We had to change trains in Genoa—the birthplace of Christopher Columbus. What a strange feeling that gave me—the thought that hundreds of years ago Christopher Columbus might have been standing somewhere very near the spot I myself was standing on! Could that be the same shadowy, unreal man we recited poems about in the second grade? (*In fourteen hundred and ninety-two, Columbus sailed the ocean blue . . .*)

After we changed trains, Stefan, Maddy, and I had a compartment all to ourselves. We were able to adjust the seats and stretch out our legs across the aisle. Maddy and Stefan went right to sleep. I suddenly remembered my camera and thought it would be fun to snap their picture. I dug into my backpack and pulled it out. Those stupid seeds got stuck in the zipper again, so this time I yanked the little baggie out and quickly stuffed it down into the already overflowing garbage container next to the window. Then I snapped a picture of Stefan and Maddy, who were sprawled out on the seats like tired dancers.

After a while I tried to sleep too, but for some reason I just couldn't get comfortable. I wondered if I was catching something, because there seemed to be a slight obstruction in my chest and an unexplained heaviness somewhere around the edges of my heart.

16

Less than ten minutes after our train pulled in at Pisa, I discovered something deplorable and rotten about myself, and in probably one of the fastest turnabouts in recorded history, I attempted to make amends.

It began as soon as we stepped off the train. I followed Stefan and Maddy out of the depot, and the three of us stopped and formed a loose circle in a shady spot overlooking a small *piazza* filled with buses and taxis. It was not yet five o'clock on a beautiful, wonderful, gorgeous blue-sky afternoon in Italy.

"Well, where is it?" I asked, referring, of course, to the famous Leaning Tower.

Stefan laughed and slid his backpack off with a graceful dip of his shoulders. Then he got down on one knee and extracted a small packet of maps bound together with a rubber band. He pulled one map out and stood up again, straddling his open pack with those long legs of his. God, I thought, his shoes are so ragged and cute.

"Look here," he said, opening the map.

There was a slight breeze, so Maddy and I each grabbed a corner to keep it from blowing away.

"This is where we are now," Stefan explained, pointing to a spot on the map. A sudden gust of wind came up, almost snapping the map from our hands. Stefan made a grab for it, and our fingers touched for a second. His eyes met mine, and his mouth moved slightly. "Anyway, here's the tower," he said, tapping the map, "and around over here is the *albergo* where we'll be staying."

"What's an *albergo*?" Maddy asked.

"I think I know," I said. "It's like a *pensione*, isn't it, Stefan? Because I noticed signs along the street in *Milano*— and some said *pensione*, and some said *albergo*. And I noticed some that said *locanda*, too. So they're all types of hotels, aren't they?"

Maddy looked up at me quickly. "Hey, I like your pronunciation, kiddo! You sound like a real Italian! *Milano*, even! Ka-*ripes!*" And she playfully punched my shoulder with her open palm.

Stefan gave me a sweet smile. "You seem to have a natural—oh, how would you call it in English?—a flair, yes. You seem to have a natural flair for language, Gina."

I looked at him closely. There wasn't even a hint of hidden sarcasm in his expression. He actually meant it! I was complimented—for *talking!* As Maddy would have said, ka-*ripes!*

"So shall we walk to the *albergo* first?" Stefan asked. "You saw on the map it's not very far from here. We can drop off our things and then go to visit the tower."

"Great!" Maddy and I said, and off we went. We left the little *piazza* by the depot, and in a few minutes we came to another. "This is the *Piazza Vittorio Emanuele II*," Stefan said.

"Hey, the same name as the galleria in *Milano*," I remarked as we stopped to look around. "That Vittorio Emanuele character must have been pretty important," I added. "I wish I knew something about Italian history."

Maddy groaned and set down the demo case and examined her hand, slowly flexing her fingers. "Numb," she said simply. "My fingers are just numb."

"Let me carry that," Stefan suggested. "I'm sorry, I should have—"

"No, you shouldn't," I interrupted. "It's really my turn. Remember, Maddy? I *promised* I'd lug it to our room this time. So give it here."

And that's when it happened—one of those weird chance encounters that seem to set up a whole chain reaction of events. But the timing of this one was so delicate and so precise it still sends a chill through my body whenever I think about it. "*Scusi, scusi,*" a feminine voice said, and I felt a hand touch my arm. The woman was pushing a wheelchair, and as I stepped back to get out of her way I stumbled on one of its large chrome wheels.

Stefan quickly reached out a hand to steady me. "And you always keep your promises, right?" he said lightly at the exact same moment that I looked down at the person sitting in the wheelchair. She was an old woman all dressed in black. Our eyes seemed to lock, and her long squinty stare gave me the chills. It was as if my grandmother were speaking to me from beyond the dead.

And that's when it hit me. "*And you always keep your promises,*" Stefan had just remarked—simply stating a fact, he thought. But was that true? Did I always keep my promises? Of course I didn't. A sudden question flashed through my mind: *If everyone didn't keep their promises, would the world be better or worse?* I knew at once what I had to do.

I set my large pack down near a flower bed in the *piazza* and said to Maddy and Stefan, "Listen, you guys, I have to go back to the train. I'll be back in a minute. Stay right here, okay?" And then I took off running.

"Gina!" Maddy yelled. "What's wrong? Where are you going?"

I stopped for a second. "Wait for me right there!" I shouted back to her. "I forgot my grandmother's sunflower seeds on the train! Remember, I told you about them and the promise I made to her? I have to go back and get them!"

But what if the train is not there? I thought. What if it has already gone?

I ran mostly in the street, since the sidewalk was too narrow and crowded. I dodged the speeding motor scooters that seemed to come from nowhere and twisted my way through crowds of strolling tourists led by guides wearing funny hats. Old people turned to watch me with disapproving scowls, and young Italian males called out and whistled as I ran past. I realized I should have taken off my backpack, too, but it wasn't that heavy, and in a few minutes I was back at the train station.

I rushed through the door and headed to *binario* number three—the track our train had come in on. Thank God the train was still there! Two men in overalls were checking the underside of the engine, and one of them turned to stare at me as I ran past. I climbed up the steep step of the first car and yanked on the door handle. "Oh, no!" I breathed. "It's locked!"

Two nuns were saying good-bye to each other on the platform by the door of the next car. I jumped down and ran over to where they were standing. "*Scusi! Scusi!*" I said, beginning to panic. "I have to get back on that train! I forgot something! *Scusi!*"

The nuns stopped talking and looked at me. "You'd better hurry," the younger one said in a distinct Irish brogue. She checked her wristwatch. "The train's about to leave."

Just then one of the men in overalls shouted something in Italian to another guy way down at the other end of the train, and the other guy waved and shouted something back. A uniformed man holding a small red flag walked up and signaled impatiently for us to get on board.

"Oh, God!" I said. "Now what?" But I really had no choice.

I followed the older nun aboard, my mind racing like mad, wondering what I was going to do about Maddy and Stefan waiting for me in the *piazza*. Also, I was thinking that Stefan and I didn't even get to say good-bye. It was all I could do just to keep myself from jumping right off the train again. But I didn't. The trainman slammed the car door shut practically in my face.

I leaned out the window and waved my arms to attract the attention of the nun left behind. She was still standing on the platform below, blowing her nose. "Oh, uh—miss—I mean madam—uh, *Sister!*" I said frantically. "Could you do me a big, big favor, *please*? See, I have to find something on this train—" All of a sudden the train jerked and started to move!

"The *Piazza Vittorio Emanuele II*," I shouted hysterically out the window. "Would you go there and tell my friend I got stuck on this train and to meet me—" I quickly turned to the older nun, who was standing at my side. "Where is this train going?"

"*Rome!*" she said excitedly, no doubt sensing my urgency. "It's going to Rome!"

"Tell her to meet me in Rome!" I turned to the nun at my side again, foolishly grabbing at her shoulders. "But *where* in Rome?" I asked loudly. "Where shall I tell her to meet me?"

"The Trevi Fountain!" she answered quickly. "Everyone meets at the Trevi Fountain!"

"Yeah!" I screamed as the train began to roll slowly in fits and starts. "The Trevi Fountain! Tomorrow! In Rome! I'll wait there for her! I'll wait all day! Her name is Maddy!" I shouted. "*Please* do it, okay?"

The nun on the platform looked bewildered, but I knew she understood me. She cupped her hands around her mouth and shouted, "What does she look like?" I was momentarily amazed. I had never heard a nun shout like that before.

"She's short with reddish-brown hair. *Piazza Vittorio*

Emanuele II! She's with a boy! He's tall and blond!" I was screaming then as the train started to pick up speed. *"He's Dutch! And thank you, Sister! Thank you!"*

I was out of breath and my heart was pounding. Finally the platform was no longer in sight.

The nun started to walk on ahead, and she held the little swinging door that led into the narrow corridor of the train car open for me.

"Thanks," I breathed, wiping the sweat off my forehead.

She kept walking until she passed an empty compartment. Then she turned into it and stood aside, obviously making room for me.

"Oh, no!" I said. "I can't sit down. Not yet. I have to find some sunflower seeds that I left on the train a little while ago. It's really important. I'm not exactly sure what car I left them in, but I think it was quite a bit farther back."

"Maybe I can help?" she suggested.

But I was just anxious to get going. I was sure I'd be able to spot the seeds if I just got into the right compartment, and that's what I told her.

I walked through car after car, stopping at the door of every compartment and staring at the trash container. The train was fairly crowded, and I was sure that the other passengers thought I was nuts, but I didn't care.

I made my way through the entire length of the train, but I didn't find the seeds. I knew the little trash containers hadn't been cleaned out, because some of them were almost overflowing.

I decided I was going to have to actually poke around in every container. The seeds *had* to be there somewhere. After I had done that in three or four cars, I was stopped by the conductor, who blocked my way with a raised hand and a stern look. *"Biglietto?"* he said.

At first I thought he was asking me what I was looking for.

So I said, "Seeds. I'm looking for a little plastic baggie of sunflower seeds—"

He held up one hand, frowned, and shook his head. "*Biglietto!*" he said again a bit more firmly.

"What?" I asked, looking around for help. "I don't speak Italian."

The people in the adjoining compartment all began to stare at me. Finally one of them leaned forward and said, "He's asking for your ticket."

"Oh!" I exclaimed, turning to the conductor. "I don't have a ticket."

The conductor looked extremely out of sorts. He started rattling off in Italian and opened what looked like some kind of receipt book. Then he said "*Roma*" and murmured something else I didn't understand.

"I'm sorry," I began, very flustered. "I don't understand—"

The man who translated a moment before tried to help again. "He says you have to *buy* a ticket."

"Oh! Well, just a minute." I took off my backpack and got some Italian money out of my right back pocket. The conductor took a whole wad of it and gave me back a little stub. Then he sighed a big tired sigh and stepped into the compartment.

I poked my head in after him and thanked the guy who translated for me. He just nodded and shrugged, but I was glad I thanked him anyway.

Then I continued my search. I just swallowed my pride and went through that routine in compartment after compartment. It was *really* embarrassing the way the people just stared at me like I had a screw loose. Trying to explain what I was doing only seemed to make it worse.

Finally I came to a compartment with just a woman and a little boy. The kid was about six, I guess, and he was sitting cross-legged by the window. I couldn't believe what I saw.

The plastic baggie was in his lap, and below him on the floor was a scattering of sunflower seed shells. That kid was eating my grandmother's seeds! The woman, probably his mother, was in the seat beside him. There was a magazine spread across her lap, but her head was falling forward and her eyes were closed.

Quick as a flash I stepped into the compartment and snatched the baggie right out of the little boy's lap. He stiffened suddenly and pressed his body against the back of his seat like a frightened kitten. His eyes opened wide and he made a squeaky little cry of surprise.

I didn't hang around to explain. I just held that little baggie tight in my hand and hurried through the train until I got back to the compartment with the waiting nun. "I got them!" I said breathlessly. "Sister! I got them back!"

She seemed very happy for me but a little confused. She touched the baggie gently, turning it over and examining it from the other side. "But they are just seeds," she said. "Why are they so important to you?"

"Well." I hesitated. "It's a *long* story, and I've been known to—well, I have this habit I'm trying to break. I just go on and on sometimes," I admitted, "and never know *when* to stop."

"It's a long way to Rome, my dear," the nun answered with a smile, "and I am ready to listen."

I smiled too and settled back in my seat. "Well, in that case, it all started with a promise I made to my grandmother back in the United States. Actually she's dead now. She died—well, I guess it was two days ago, now."

The nun's eyes widened. "Oh, bless her soul!" she said, reaching for my hand. "What is your name, my dear? I am Sister Mary Louise."

"Gina. Gina Gari."

"I'm so sorry, Gina, to hear this about your grandmother." Suddenly and unexpectedly the tears welled up in my eyes.

I got out a tissue and blew my nose while Sister Mary Louise very calmly folded her hands and patiently gazed out the train window. I think the real reason I started crying then was mostly because Sister Mary Louise was so *nice*, and not because of my grandmother. And then I felt guilty about *that*, so I cried even more.

After a few minutes I settled down, though, and I put the tissue back and said, "I'm sorry. I'm okay now. Really."

Sister Mary Louise smiled gently. "That's good. But maybe it is too upsetting for you to talk about this—"

"Oh, no. It's all right. See, my grandmother was Catholic. So I think she would *want* me to tell you about it. She was born right here in Italy—in Assisi, actually—and these sunflower seeds are descended from some that she brought to America when she came over on the boat. She used to go and feed the birds up in the hills there, where Saint Francis used to go, and she made me promise that I would go feed them, too." I lifted the locket from under my blouse. "This is a locket my grandfather gave to her. She wanted me to wear it while I fed the birds. And oh, yes. She said I had to do all this on the fifth of July. But she didn't say why the date was important."

"That is indeed an interesting story. One cannot help but wonder about the reason for such a sentimental journey."

"Yes, I know. But anyway, after I found out that she died— see, I telephoned my mother just to tell her I was okay, and that's when I found out that my grandmother had passed away." I cleared my throat. "The next part is sort of embarrassing."

Sister Mary Louise looked at me as if I had already been forgiven. "You don't have to tell me if—"

"No, no, it's okay," I said. "It's just that after she died, I mistakenly thought I was no longer bound to—you know, like I didn't have to *keep* my promise because, after all, she was dead now, and it wouldn't make any difference to her."

"And what changed your mind about that? Because obviously you are here—"

"Well, that was very strange how it happened. This friend of mine—he's a new friend, actually. I'll tell you all about him later, maybe. Anyway, he was just complimenting me on how I always keep my promises at the very same moment that I saw an old lady in a wheelchair that reminded me a *lot* of my grandmother. And then it hit me! Just because somebody dies, that shouldn't cancel out any promises you made to them."

Sister Mary Louise nodded slowly. "Yes, that is very true. But the seeds. What about the seeds?"

"Well, that's just it. See, I threw them out on the train ride to Pisa. I put them in the little trash container in our compartment. So I had to come back. And Maddy and Stefan— they're my friends—they're waiting for me back in the *piazza*. Oh, I hope your friend can find them and give them my message!"

"I'm sure she can, my dear. Sister Agnes is *most* dependable. I'm sure you will meet your friends tomorrow at the Trevi Fountain."

"Friend, *singular*, I'm afraid," I said. "The boy, Stefan, is going on to Florence. So it will just be me and Maddy again for the rest of the trip."

Sister Mary Louise and I talked for a long time after that. She was really nice. She told me she was on an assignment in Rome, working at a hostel for foreign Catholic young women. Then she suddenly reached over and put her warm, soft hand on mine. "You must stay with us tonight in Rome," she said.

"My gosh! That's right!" I said. "I didn't even *think* about that! What a dummy! I didn't even think about where I would stay tonight. But hey," I added, "I *can't* stay with you. I'm not even a Catholic. My grandmother was a really good one, like I told you, but, see, I'm not, and—"

"Shhh!" she whispered, smiling and putting a finger to her lips. "That is all right. You will be our welcomed guest."

"Wow. This must be my lucky day, for sure. Thank you. Thank you *very* much!"

She nodded and brought out her little black prayer book, which she started to read, and I kind of dozed off until we arrived in Rome.

As we were walking along the platform leading into the station I saw the woman and the little boy who had been eating my grandmother's seeds. When the kid saw me, he clutched the woman's arm and tried to hide behind her skirt. I had to smile to myself, wondering what the poor little guy must have thought of this crazy teenage girl suddenly pouncing on him and snatching his trash-can snack right off his lap.

Once we were inside the station Sister Mary Louise had to call the hostel for a ride, and while she was making the call, the woman and the little boy passed right by the phone booth. Suddenly, on the spur of the moment, I got an idea. I took the yellow yo-yo out of my pocket and stepped up to them as the boy ducked behind her skirt again with a little scream.

Now, how do I say "gift"? I thought desperately. And then I remembered one of the posters in the *Milano* Metro, which showed a man presenting a woman with a bottle of perfume. I remembered the words *profumo* and *regalo*. If *profumo* meant perfume, perhaps *regalo* meant gift. I decided to take a chance. I tapped the woman on the shoulder and showed her the yo-yo in my hand. Then I did a quick walk the dog along the floor. I removed the string from my finger and handed her the yo-yo. I pointed to the little boy, who was peeking out from around her back by then, and said, "*Regalo! Regalo* from America!" She understood me immediately, because she took the yo-yo from me with a big smile and gave it to him. "*Grazie!*" she said. "*Molto grazie!*" As they disappeared into the crowd the little boy turned to give me one last look. I smiled and waved, and he responded with a shy, self-conscious smile of his own. I felt a lot better after that.

Pretty soon Sister Mary Louise and I were picked up in a car and driven to the hostel. My room was small and spare. The only decoration was a large crucifix hanging above my bed.

Sister Mary Louise knocked lightly on my door a few minutes after I got settled in. "Will you be all right, my dear?" she asked. "Do you have everything you need?"

"Oh, yes. And thank you *very* much. You saved my life. I really don't know what I would have done here on my own—alone here in Rome."

"You are welcome, I'm sure. But this is good-bye for me. I must leave again early in the morning. I trust you will meet your friend tomorrow at the Trevi Fountain. You can easily walk there from here. Sister Florence at the desk will show you a map of the city."

"Thank you, Sister," I said again. "Thank you very much."

My bed was hard, and the muslin pillowcase was rough and coarse. I am alone in Rome, I thought, and so far from home. And I will never see Stefan again.

17

I was awakened by the odor of coffee and the sounds of the city below. I opened my eyes and gripped the sheets, staring at the gray ceiling as the room spun around and around. At first I thought I was back home in my own bed, but the room was too small and the window and door were in the wrong places. After a few moments, when the room stopped spinning, I started to remember bits and pieces of my adventures during the past several days. I tried to sort it all out in my mind: We left San Francisco on Monday, arrived in Zurich on Tuesday, spent Tuesday night in *Milano*, and traveled to Pisa on Wednesday. So now it was Thursday morning. And I was all alone in Rome.

I got out of bed and stared at my reflection in the small mirror over the sink. I looked much older somehow, and at first I thought it was because of my haircut. But no, it was more than that. My face seemed thinner and my eyes more deeply set. Whatever it was, I liked what I saw.

I splashed my face with water and dried it with the skimpy towel I found folded neatly on the rack. Then I sat back down on the bed and wondered why I'd never seen a sink in a bedroom at home in America.

I slipped on my jeans and went down the hall to the bathroom in my bare feet. I tried the door, but it was locked. A girl's voice called out, "Just a second, all right?"

"You speak English!" I called back. "You sound American! Are you American?"

I heard the toilet flush and then the door opened. There stood a slight dark-haired girl about my age, dressed in a denim skirt and a red and white Stanford University T-shirt. She was grinning at me.

"Hi!" I said. "You're from California!"

She tipped her head sideways and gave me a puzzled look. "No. You're only about a thousand miles off, though. I'm from Denver."

That was a bit intimidating, her saying in such a confident tone that I was "a thousand miles off." I mean, I hadn't the foggiest notion of how far Denver was from California. But I just motioned to her T-shirt and said, "Well, your T-shirt—"

"Oh!" She laughed, pulling on the shirt with a little pinch and letting it go again. "I see what you mean. But no, one of the girls staying here gave me this a couple of days ago. *She* was from California, but she went back home yesterday."

"Oh, well, that explains it."

"Actually, everybody went back home yesterday."

"Really?"

"Yes. See, it was a kind of a study-group thing. We were all here on a six-week art-appreciation program, but there was a mix-up with my charter. It's too boring to go into, but anyway, now my flight home isn't until next week." She paused. "But what are you doing here? The next group isn't supposed to arrive until tomorrow."

"Well, I—" I started to say, but then she lowered her head and looked up at me from under her thick black brows.

"Hey, listen to *me*!" she said sheepishly. She imitated her own voice. "*What are you doing here?*" It was really funny the way she did that. Then she added, "You'd think I owned the place! Sorry, just don't mind me."

"Oh, no," I said. "That's okay." I clasped my hands behind

my back, sort of like Stefan did with me that first day. "My name's Gina," I said. "And I *am* from California."

"Cecilia." She smiled and extended her hand. "But everybody calls me Ceci. It's very nice to meet you."

We shook hands a little self-consciously and then just stood there a moment, neither one of us speaking.

"Well," I said finally, glancing at the bathroom door, "I guess I'd better get going." I didn't mean to make a joke of it. It just came out that way.

"Hey, yeah!" She laughed. "But listen, my room's that way." She pointed. "Around the corner, number 412. Come by and see me after you get dressed and stuff, okay? We can go down to breakfast together. Do you know anyone here? Are you alone?"

"I'm supposed to meet my friend later, over at the Trevi Fountain—wherever that is. But sure, I'll come by in a minute. And boy," I added before closing the door, "it sure is nice to see someone from home!"

After I got back to my room and before I put on my shoes, I made a little note on my hand with my pen, just for fun, to help me remember. DEN TO CA, I wrote. 1,000 MI.

Later, downstairs in the dining room, over a breakfast of just orange juice, bread, jelly, and a mixture of strong coffee and milk, Ceci offered to take me to the Trevi Fountain, which she said was only a short walk away. We figured we should be there by noon, since it would take Maddy at least that long to get there if she left Pisa that morning—that is, if everything went right, and if she got the message from the nun.

"I can't believe this is happening," I said. "It's all so weird. I mean, sending a nun to give Maddy a message like that and everything. The one thing we didn't *want* to do on this trip was get separated, and now that's just what happened. Whew! I sure hope she got my message!"

"Oh, I'm sure she did. It's too bad you didn't know the name of that *albergo* in Pisa, though, because you could have called her there. But you told that other nun where Maddy was and what she looked like and stuff. Nuns are very resourceful. I'm sure she found her okay." Ceci spread more jelly on her bread and took a bite. "How long will you be in Rome?" she asked. "You and your friend, I mean."

"Well, we have to catch our plane back home early Wednesday morning in Zurich. We already have reservations at a hotel there for Tuesday night—the same place we were going to stay at the first night we arrived, before Maddy changed her mind and wanted to get on a train instead . . ." Oh no, I thought suddenly, maybe I'm talking too much. "Anyway," I finished, "to answer your question, we have to leave here Tuesday morning, I guess."

Ceci nodded. "Yes. Rome to Zurich. That's quite a long ride. I have to leave Rome on Tuesday, too. But my flight is from *Fiumicino*. You know, where the airport is," she added when I looked at her quizzically. She passed the bread basket to me. "More bread?"

I took another slice. "Thanks." I spread some jelly on it and took a bite. "I'm kind of surprised they don't have a better breakfast here, though," I said softly. "I mean, I really *shouldn't* complain since they were nice enough to let me stay, but—"

"Oh, listen," Ceci said, putting her elbows on the table and leaning toward me. "Nobody eats breakfast in Italy. I mean, American-type breakfasts—eggs and all that junk. Just bread, like this, or a little pastry—and coffee, of course—that's all they usually eat. It's funny, though. You get used to it. Now just the thought of a big breakfast—yuk!" She bugged her eyes out and puffed up her cheeks.

I laughed. Ceci was cute and funny.

"So, what-all do you plan to see while you're here?" she

asked. "Are you into art, or music, or literature, or architecture, or what?" Then she added, "I'm into art myself. Early Italian religious art in particular. I don't know why, but it just fascinates me."

I had never before met a person my age (or any age, actually) who said they were interested in early Italian religious art! I immediately decided to level with her. "To tell you the truth," I confessed, "I don't know what I plan to see. I don't know beans about Rome."

She seemed surprised to hear that, but then she shrugged and said, "Well, there's something here for everybody, that's for sure. But you really don't have a lot of time, you know. So you'll probably just want to hit the usual tourist spots."

"Probably." I cleared my throat. "Like what, for instance?"

She wiped her hands on her napkin and kind of waggled her finger at me. "Maybe you want to come up and see some of my guidebooks. You could get a lot of ideas from them."

"That's a great idea," I said. "But you know, I would really like to get over to that fountain as soon as possible. I want to *be sure* I'm there first. Before Maddy, I mean. I don't want *her* to have to wait for *me*, since it was my fault that we were separated in the first place. Can we bring your books along with us? Then I could look at them while we're waiting."

"Super!" she said.

I read about the *Fontana di Trevi* in bits and pieces as we strolled along toward that famous site. "Hey," I said, looking up from the book, "it says here it's called the Trevi because of the three streets that come together right there at the fountain. *Tre vie* means 'three streets.' This is really interesting."

"That's right," she said. "Do you know any Italian?"

"No." Then I laughed and corrected myself. "Wait a minute. That's not quite true. I know *scusi*. And I know a bunch of words that sort of mean 'hotel.' And I know *regalo*."

"Oh, yes." She nodded. "Gift. How do you happen to know that?"

"Hey, Ceci," I said, touching her arm. "That's a *long* story."

"So tell me!"

Well, I filled her in as best I could without dragging it on and on, and I guess I did a pretty good job, since her eyes never got that glazed-over look I'd grown so used to seeing in others.

Just as I finished we turned a corner, and suddenly I heard the splashing of water and felt the spray on my face, and in another second, the beautiful *Fontana di Trevi* was laid out before us in all its splendor. For several minutes I was so overwhelmed I couldn't even speak. I felt like a little mouse who had been plucked from the dry fields of California and set down right in the center of the world.

"That's Neptune," I said finally, "god of the sea. And those other guys are called the Tritons." I smiled at Ceci. "According to your guidebook, that is."

Ceci smiled back at me. "It's great, isn't it? I just love it here, with that large, gorgeous fountain and all the tourists and everything."

And that's when it hit me—like a ton of bricks, actually. *The large fountain. The god of the sea.* I took another look at the large male figure at the center of the fountain. His right arm was extended slightly, and his hand was positioned in exactly the right way. "Oh! Oh!" I breathed, bringing my hands to my head in disbelief. "That's it! That's the fountain my grandfather dreamed about! Oh, Ceci! This is so great! This is so—" I collapsed on the steps, just a bundle of pure joy.

After a moment Ceci sat down beside me, grinning. "Uh, Gina," she said, tapping me on the arm. "If it's not too much trouble, will you *please* tell me what this little fit of ecstasy is all about?"

"Oh, it's so *neat*," I said finally. "It's about my grandfather. About my grandfather's last dream just before he died. See, he told me that he dreamed he was a boy again. A boy again, here in Rome. And he was running past *the large fountain—*

181

that's what he called it. He didn't mention it by name. But he said in his dream he heard a familiar sound—a sound he knew. And what it was—well, see, first you have to know that my grandfather was crazy about yo-yos." I paused a moment to make sure she had understood me.

She was nodding. "Yes," she said. "Yo-yos. Go on."

"Well, that was it," I said. "The familiar sound he heard in his dream was old Neptune there, playing with a yo-yo." I had to wipe a tear from my eye before I added, "He said that the sea god was very, very good."

I looked at the beautiful central figure in the fountain again, at the look of concentration in his face, and I could almost see the yo-yo in his hand. "I just can't believe I'm at the very same spot where my grandfather played as a boy," I said. "I just can't believe I'm at the very same fountain he dreamed about."

Ceci looked at me for one long moment and clasped both of my hands in hers, and now there were tears in her eyes, too.

"Oh, Ceci," I said, "don't cry." And I had to laugh, because now we were both crying, but gently, and half-laughing, too.

Finally we dried our eyes and settled down to watch the spectacle around us. I quickly scanned the faces in the crowd, but Maddy was nowhere in sight. It was still early, though, so I didn't worry about it.

Ceci was busy looking at something else. She leaned over and cupped one hand over my ear. "Look down there," she said gaily. "By that bottom step."

I looked where she pointed, at a young couple sitting near the water, directly in front of that huge, fabulous statue of Neptune. The girl had her hands on the boy's face, both thumbs pressed against his skin.

"Ka-ripes," I said, using Maddy's favorite expression. "It looks like she's squeezing his blackheads!"

Ceci covered her face with her hands and giggled like a little kid. "Isn't that *bizarre*! Squeezing blackheads at a place like this! I love it!"

"And look over there!" I said, pointing to the other side of the fountain, where a middle-aged woman in a red skirt was sitting with her shoes off applying a Band-Aid to the back of her ankle.

"She's putting on a Band-Aid!" Ceci sputtered, burying her head on my shoulder. "Can you believe it? The most glorious fountain in Rome—maybe even in the world—and people are squeezing blackheads and sticking Band-Aids on their feet! Darn! I wish I had my camera! I love to take photographs like that. You know, with that kind of weird contrast."

"Yes," I said, nodding enthusiastically. "I know what you mean. For an album of inappropriate behavior. That would be perfect. It would be a great photo. Squeezing blackheads and putting on Band-Aids, with the Trevi Fountain in the background."

"So what does this Maddy look like?" Ceci asked after a while. "I'll help you look for her."

"Oh, she's short, in her late twenties, with reddish-brown hair. She's got a nice figure. She's really cute."

Ceci nodded. "Well, I don't see anyone fitting that description yet."

Time passed, and I grew more and more nervous. I kept looking at my watch and figuring the hour. Maddy surely should have arrived by now, I thought, and I began to truly worry. What if she hadn't received my message? That *was* possible. The nun could have missed them. Maybe Maddy and Stefan left the *piazza* before the nun got there. Maybe they tried to follow me back to the station. Anything could have happened.

Ceci was being really nice, trying to keep me distracted but still sympathizing with my plight. "Down there," she said, pointing. "Look. Someone's going to get a ducking."

She was right. Several people—and they weren't kids, either—were frolicking in the water of the fountain. One man was holding a laughing woman in his arms and was threatening to drop her in. He didn't, though. He was just fooling around. I was so involved in watching what was going on down there, I didn't see Stefan until he tapped me on the shoulder. I turned around and there he was.

"Stefan!" I said, jumping up. He grabbed me in a tight hug and kissed me on the cheek. He still hadn't shaved, and the roughness of his face against mine was a thrilling new feeling for me. (P.J.'s face was smooth as a baby's.)

When we finally separated, I looked around for Maddy.

"Maddy is not feeling well," Stefan said before I could even ask about her.

"Oh, *no!*" I started to say, but he gently put his hand over my mouth. "Don't worry," he said, touching his stomach with his other hand. "It's just a little upset. Here, in her stomach. We were lucky to find two small adjoining rooms near the station. She's waiting for us there."

"But what are *you* doing here, Stefan?" I asked. "I thought—I mean, we thought you were going on to Florence."

"Maddy became sick late last night. I think part of it was worrying about you," he said with just a slightly accusing tone, "but I couldn't leave her. She—" he made an awkward motion. I think he was trying to say she was throwing up.

"Yawning in Technicolor?" I suggested. "Decorating her shoes?"

Stefan stared at me, his head tipped sideways, his face a blank. And then he caught on. "Oh, God!" he said, laughing and turning away. "American comedy! I can never get used to it!" He turned to me again. "But did you find those seeds on the train?" he asked. "I remembered about them, and about your grandmother's wish—"

"Yes!" I said. "I did find them! It was kind of funny, too, where they were. But I'll wait until we're together with Maddy to tell you about it, okay?"

I introduced Ceci and Stefan then, and the three of us took off, heading for the place Stefan and Maddy had found not far from the train station. It was quite a long walk, but we were in the mood for walking.

"We checked the big bags and the yo-yo case at the depot," Stefan said. "We can pick them up now, on our way, if you like."

"Sure. Let's do that."

"Now let me tell you something about her, your friend Maddy, I mean," he continued. "Even though she felt so sick, when we happened to walk past a large toy store, she marched right in and arranged for a yo-yo demonstration for Monday. She didn't even have the sample case with her, since we had checked it at the station, but she talked the manager into it anyway."

"How could she do that?" I asked. "She doesn't know any Italian."

"I helped a little, in my meager way," Stefan said modestly. "And the store manager, he spoke a bit of English." He smiled and shook his head. "Maddy was very persuasive. I was so impressed."

"Well, that's my Maddy, all right," I said proudly. "But I sure hope she's all better by Monday. My god," I added, "that will be our last day in Rome! We have to catch a train back to Zurich on Tuesday morning."

Stefan, who was holding my hand (did I mention that?), gave it a squeeze, and we hung on to each other just a little bit tighter after that.

18

Stefan kept calling it our Assignment in Assisi until Ceci made him stop, saying that made it sound like a spy story when it wasn't that at all. The tarnished silver locket was still hanging like an albatross around my neck, and the packet of sunflower seeds was safely tucked away in my backpack. And it was Friday, the fifth of July.

I felt terrible about leaving Maddy alone in Rome, and I know she felt terrible about seeing me go without her.

"Now *be sure* you all stick together," she said weakly, staring up at Stefan, Ceci, and me with her eyes sunken away somewhere in the depths of two dark, shadowy caverns. It was very early in the morning in Ceci's room at the "nunnery" (as we had started to refer to it) and Maddy was trying to tell us good-bye. Stefan, Maddy, and I had spent the night before in the little hotel by the station, and we had just splurged on a taxi to transport Maddy to Ceci's room, where she would spend the day eating only rice and white bread in sparse amounts, avoiding all fruit juices, and visiting the john at regular ten-minute intervals. (Sister Florence had promised to check in on her from time to time, and should she make a miraculous recovery, any one of the off-duty nuns would be more than happy to show her around the city.)

"Now, are you sure you know where to go once you arrive in Assisi?" Maddy asked, at the same time frowning and massaging her temples with her fingertips.

"Please, Maddy," I begged, "stop asking the same questions over and over, okay? We're going to be fine. Really."

"Gina's right, Maddy," Stefan said, "there's no cause for worry."

"And you'll be back here in Rome *tonight*? Is that right?" Maddy interrupted, squinting at poor, sweet Stefan, who had somehow metamorphosed from a nice Dutch boy to a suspected terrorist-rapist-maniac. "You'll all three go directly back to those two rooms we rented last night by the station— the two girls in the double room, Stefan, and you in the single?"

"That's right, *Mom*," I said pointedly, finally bringing a faint smile to her lips.

On the bus to Assisi we discovered that Stefan played the harmonica. I was the one who noticed something in his shirt pocket, and I reached in and grabbed the instrument during an unguarded moment and waggled it in his face. Then the three of us huddled together in the rear of the bus, arms and legs entangled, and sang away the miles. Sometimes the other passengers would hum and clap along.

When we got off the bus in Assisi, we followed the crowds up the hill to the great basilica. "What lovely old cobblestone streets!" Ceci exclaimed. Stefan tapped my arm and wordlessly pointed up a side street where jumpsuited men were busy with cement mixers and trowels putting in brand-new "old" cobblestones. "Much too touristy for me," he whispered, and I agreed immediately.

The narrow streets were lined with souvenir shops, and the others waited while I stopped to buy a guidebook of the town, complete with color photographs and a map. Arm in arm, pairs of young monks dressed in brown robes walked serenely to and fro in perfect swaying rhythm. Oh, how I wished then that I had asked my grandmother more about the city of her birth! I wished that I knew the name of her old street; then maybe I could find her old neighborhood, and perhaps even her old rooms there on the cobblestone streets of Assisi.

The basilica was magnificent. It was crowded with tourists, mostly in groups accompanied by guides. We soon found ourselves tagging along behind a British group, and we eavesdropped on their guide. Pretty soon we came to the small chapel that contained certain relics of the saint, including his poor, ragged gown. It was then that I remembered my grandmother's anger, and for the first time I think I really understood it.

After the tour was over, we sat down to rest outside on the steps to the upper church.

"Did you guys *see* those old paintings by Giotto?" Ceci asked, since she had wandered off by herself several times during the tour. "Did you see the crib-scene one? Did you know that Saint Francis *originated* the custom of the manger scene? I never knew that before!"

I flipped open the pages of my new guidebook. "It tells all about that in here," I said. "Look, with pictures, even."

Ceci was fascinated. "Oh! May I see that a minute?" She flipped the pages, stopping here and there for a longer look. "Look at this one! It's Saint Francis and the birds!" She began to read the words of Saint Francis. " 'My little brothers, you should greatly praise the Lord. He has covered you with feathers and has given you wings for flying.' That's very pretty, isn't it?"

"Yes, it is," I agreed, "but you know, I think we'd better find out how to get up to that hermitage. We don't want to be stuck up there after dark. Maddy would flip out for sure."

Stefan pointed to the guidebook, which was still in Ceci's hand. "May I take a look at that, Ceci? It has the map."

She held up one hand. "Okay, but just a sec, Stefan. Look at this mosaic. It's of Saint Francis and his friends before his conversion . . ."

That's when I decided I would go back to the tourist shop and buy another book as a gift for Ceci. I was almost out of money myself, but thanks to Maddy's careful budgeting, we were going to make it okay.

"Be back in a minute," I said as they continued to turn the pages of the guidebook. "I'm going back to the souvenir shop."

It was crowded with tourists now. I was fascinated by the variety of souvenirs I saw. There were key chains, pens, bracelets, ashtrays, night-lights, necklaces, pillboxes, pencils, letter openers, thermometers, bud vases, and even shoehorns—all imprinted with the familiar figure of the saint. Finally I paid for another guidebook and went outside again to study the map. The hermitage itself was off the map, but an arrow and notation pointed to a road on the eastern edge of town, stating that it was four kilometers away from the eastern gate. The basilica, where we were, was on the western edge of town.

"Well," I said, walking up to Ceci and Stefan, "it looks like we have to go clear across the town. And after we get to the town gate on the other side, we will still have another four kilometers to go." I hesitated, then looked at Stefan. "I guess I should know this, but how far is a kilometer, anyway?"

"A little over half a mile," he answered. "So that's over two miles, all uphill, and steep. It could take us quite a while."

"Okay, get up, you guys!" I said. "Let's go!" But to myself I was repeating over and over, determined to remember it: *A kilometer is a little over half a mile.*

As we started walking, Ceci thumbed through the guidebook in her hand for an extra few seconds and then reluctantly started to hand it back to me.

"Keep it!" I said. "It's yours. A *regalo*," I added with a smile.

She immediately noticed the other book in my hand. "Oh, Gina," she said, holding the book against her chest, "thanks!

Thank you so much! I *love* this book, but, well, I'm almost out of money, and—"

"Just something to remember me by," I said. "You know, when you're back home in Denver."

She bit her lip and gave me a little hug. "Well, it was very thoughtful of you, and of course I'll remember you. And I hope you'll remember me, too."

I had the idea of buying some food to take up to the mountain with us so we wouldn't have to go to a restaurant. We stopped at a tiny store on our way through the town and picked out some bread and cheese, pears, some kind of funny apricot pies, a couple bottles of orange soda, and water. All three of us dug into our pockets for *lire*, but when Stefan and I saw Ceci's little pile of coins, we made her put them back into her pocket.

We had a great time walking through the town and hiking up the wooded mountainside. We kicked loose rocks and stopped often to admire the view below. We locked arms and walked three abreast on the empty road, doing a silly walking dance step Ceci had learned at camp when she was nine years old (*step, step, step—heel, step, heel, step—dip, pause, dip, pause*). Groves of olive trees flanked the curving road, and an occasional breeze lifted their leaves and exposed their silvery undersides in rolling, wavelike sweeps.

Up ahead we saw a picnic table off the road at the point of a hairpin curve. Stefan staggered over to it, clutching his throat as if he were seeing a mirage in the desert. "Water!" he croaked. "Orange soda! Funny little apricot pies!" He used the bottle opener on his Swiss Army knife to open the soda, and afterward he touched my hair and smiled.

After lunch we didn't have much farther to go, and for some reason we grew less talkative the closer we got to our destination. I stopped once along the way and took the baggie of seeds from my backpack. "You know," I said quietly, "my sister and brothers and I have been making fun of these seeds all my life."

I was interrupted by the sharp *toot-toot!* of a taxi filled with tourists, who stared at us with their tired faces pressed up close against the windows. We had to make room for the taxi by quickly moving to the edge of the road. We walked the few remaining yards in complete silence.

Before we could get to the actual spot where Saint Francis fed the birds, we first had to wait in line with eight or ten others for several minutes. When our turn came, we had to pass single file through a cramped ancient cavelike structure that contained a large flat stone with a small sign identifying it as the bed of Saint Francis. Back outside again we followed the shady, winding trail that led to a small table made of stone, the actual spot ("according to tradition," as a bearded monk explained) where Saint Francis asked the birds to "greatly praise the Lord."

Nearby, a boy dressed in a flowing brown robe tied with a piece of rope was softly strumming on a guitar. Two smiling old nuns were tossing birdseed on the ground to half a dozen doves, and an assortment of tourists was milling about, taking deep breaths of the mountain air and lazily looking first up at the sky and then down into the valley below. I thought that the two nuns feeding the birds would make a nice photograph, and that's when I suddenly remembered that I had forgotten to bring my camera. I was devastated at first, until I realized I no longer needed proof that I had been there. Stefan and Ceci were standing nearby, waiting, I think, for me to do my thing.

"Well, this is it," I said to myself.

I carefully adjusted the tarnished old silver locket, making sure the side with the etching of Saint Francis was facing out, and opened the little baggie of sunflower seeds. The moment had come at last, I thought. A tame white dove landed at my feet and looked up expectantly. Could that bird be an actual descendant of one of the birds my grandmother fed so long ago? I wondered. I bent down to let him eat from my hand.

Somewhat self-consciously I looked up to see if the others were watching me, and that's when I first saw the old man. He was staring at me so intently it made me blush. He had been sitting on a blue folding chair just a few feet away from me in a little protected nook near the side of the mountain, but as soon as our eyes met he rose from the chair and slowly started walking over to me as if in a trance. Ceci noticed him too, because she quickly stooped down beside me and whispered anxiously in my ear, *"Who's that?* He looks like he *knows* you!"

What I noticed first about him were his eyes, which were so dark they were almost black, and as he got closer I could see they were bathed in that same cloudy, mucuslike film that I remember seeing in my grandfather's eyes. His cap, too, with its badly frayed visor and worn leather band, reminded me of the one my grandfather used to wear on occasions too formal for Yo-Yo Man. In spite of the heat the old man was wearing a loose-knit dark green cardigan sweater with several buttons missing. His beard was mostly gray, and the expression on his face was a strange mixture of sadness and surprise. He had a cane in his left hand, which he seemed to use more for balance than support.

I instinctively rose as he approached with little shuffling steps, and the closer he got, the more emotional he seemed to become. His deeply lined face was actually quivering as he took the final step that brought him directly in front of me. But now his eyes had left mine, and he lowered his gaze, peering intently at my chest. His cane fell to the ground, and he reached out to touch me with his two trembling hands. This was such a surprise and shock to me, I automatically took a step back, at the same time protectively crossing my arms over my chest.

Ceci became immediately alarmed at this. "Stefan!" she shouted in a loud, agitated voice. "Come here, quick!"

She must have startled the old man, because suddenly his legs seemed to give way, and he started to fall. But both Ceci and I saw what was happening, and we were able to grab him before he hit the ground.

Stefan hurried over to us then. "Here, let me take him," he said as he put one arm around the old man's waist and held on to his elbow with the other.

"His chair is over there," I said, pointing to the folding chair where he had been sitting before.

Ceci immediately fetched the chair while I got a bottle of water out of my backpack.

Apparently it was just a dizzy spell, because after sitting down and having a few sips of water, the old man seemed as good as new. In fact, he kept trying to stand up again, saying something in Italian that even Stefan couldn't understand at first. Finally Stefan caught on. "His pocket," Stefan said. "He wants to get something out of his pocket."

We helped him to his feet again and held on to him while he pulled out a key ring chock-full of keys. One by one he examined them, until at last he held the correct one between his shaking fingers. It was a tiny, tiny key of tarnished silver. His eyes fell on my chest again, but this time I knew what he was looking at. My heart was pounding so hard it felt like it was going to explode. I bent my head and slipped the necklace from my neck.

"Sì! sì!" The old man nodded, his eyes absolutely glowing. His hands were shaking too much for him to fit the tiny key into the keyhole, so Stefan did it for him. The locket fell open and Stefan gently placed it in the old man's hands. The tears ran out of his eyes even as he closed them. He kissed the locket and cupped it in his hands and repeated the same Italian phrase again and again: *"Finalmente, finalmente. . . ."*

"He's saying, 'At last! At last!' " Stefan said quietly, looking at us all with obvious amazement. "And now he's asking, 'Where is she? Where is she?' What shall I say to him, Gina?" Stefan looked at me helplessly.

"You have to tell him she's dead," I whispered, my throat swollen and dry. "You have to."

So then Stefan told him what I think the old man already feared—that my grandmother was dead. He was surprisingly serene. He closed his eyes and bowed his head in prayer. After a long while, he opened his eyes again and tapped me on the hand. Then he showed me the tiny pictures inside the locket. Now it was my turn to be amazed, because one of the photographs was of me.

Of course, it really wasn't me. It was a photograph of my grandmother, before her heart was broken. And opposite her, imprisoned in the locket for sixty years, was the ever-young likeness of the handsome boy she had to leave behind forever.

We tried our best to talk with the old man, but he only knew a few words of English, so it was difficult and very frustrating. Without Stefan it would have been impossible. Finally Ceci and I just stood by and let the two of them work it out.

"It is true," Stefan told us after a particularly long session of words and gestures. "He has been coming here on this fifth day in July for sixty years. *Sixty years!* Can you *imagine* that? It was an agreement they had made on the day they had to part. Nevertheless, he knows that once she was married, she could never—" Stefan broke off in midsentence and asked the old man another question in his halting Italian. After the old man answered, Stefan told us his reply. "He says that he himself has never married."

Stefan asked yet another question, and the old man nodded, a faint hint of a smile crossing his lips.

"He says he had *many* chances but passed them all by," Stefan translated as the old man almost smiled again while he eagerly watched our reactions.

The worst of his grief seemed to be over by then. It was replaced by a kind of wonder—a feeling of wonder that we all shared. We sat for several minutes in silence, and then the man crossed himself and smiled at us, a slow, disbelieving smile, and shook his head and wiped his eyes again.

"What's his name, Stefan?" I said. "Ask him his name."

But the old man understood that question. "Salvatore," he answered, and added in slow and heavily accented English, "My name is Salvatore Vittore."

His answer took my breath away. "Salvatore! That's my father's name," I said softly. "Stefan, tell him that she, my grandmother, named her only son after him."

How happy he was to hear that! How happy and yet how sad.

But the shadows were starting to fall, and the time had come for us to leave the mountain. I was worried about Salvatore, though, and how an old man like him would be able to get home without some help.

"Ask him how he will get home," I whispered to Stefan. "He can't walk down that mountain alone, and I'm sure he doesn't drive."

"I have already asked him that," Stefan answered. "He said his nephew will come for him. His nephew has been coming for him for many years, ever since he has been unable to walk down the mountain road."

I could hardly bear to tell Salvatore good-bye, and I knew he felt the same about me. I insisted on leaving the locket with him, of course. I was sure my grandmother would have wanted it that way. And together, before we left, Salvatore and I scattered the last of the sunflower seeds to the cooing doves under the trees.

*   *   *
195

My head was so full of questions as we made our way back down the hill! And my heart was overflowing with all sorts of mixed-up emotions. I had been so concerned about Salvatore and my grandmother up on the mountain that I hadn't even thought about my grandfather. Then all at once it hit me. Poor Grandpa! I thought. Did he know about Salvatore? Did he know he had a rival all those years? Probably not, I concluded. He probably never knew. Oh, how could she do that to him?

We walked along for several minutes before I could even speak. Finally I said, "And all this time I thought my grandfather had given her that locket. How could she keep a secret like that for all those years?"

"Do you think *anyone* knew?" Ceci asked. "Maybe she told—"

"Someone *did* know!" I said suddenly. "Father Rossi knew! He was her priest. I remember now. At my grandfather's funeral he took me aside and said something about how she had had a heavy cross to bear for many years. He said it was heavier than I would ever know. So he *must* have known. I'm sure she would tell him everything."

"But do you think your grandfather knew?" Ceci asked quietly. "Do you think he was married to her for all those years and didn't know that she—well, that she had left someone behind like that. God, it's so *sad*, isn't it? Why do you think she married him, anyway?"

"Well, actually, now that you mention it, I think she sort of had to," I said. "I remember when I found her old wedding picture on the day she moved, she told me the marriage was more or less arranged. She said my grandfather *wanted* to marry *her*, but that she was only seventeen and just did what her family told her to." Oh, I suddenly found myself thinking. Poor Grandma! She had to get married, even though she knew Salvatore was waiting for her all the time. How could she stand it! What must it have been like for her every fifth of July, knowing that he was up there on that mountain waiting?

"How awful!" Ceci said, mirroring my feelings. "Can you imagine what her life was like?"

Stefan tightened his grip on my hand. "Maybe that explains a little bit the reason for your grandmother's unpleasantness," he suggested. "I remember you told me no one liked her very much—"

"Well, someone certainly liked her!" Ceci broke in. "Someone liked her well enough to wait for her sixty years!"

I couldn't help but wonder if maybe my grandfather had been waiting, too—waiting and hoping for all those years that he might someday find a way to break through that thin hard shell around her heart.

19

Back at the nunnery the next morning we found Maddy had greatly improved. After we told her all about the strange and heartbreaking meeting with Salvatore and reliving those moments all over again, the four of us sat in Ceci's room and talked about what to do next. After what we had been through, we all agreed we wanted to spend the rest of our time in Rome together.

"Well, do you have to stay here, Ceci?" I asked. "Here at the nunnery? Like, I mean, is your rent all paid up or anything?"

"Oh, no," Ceci said. "I just pay by the day." She opened a drawer and pulled out an envelope. "My rent money is here, enough until Tuesday. That's when I fly back home."

"And you and Maddy take the train back to Zurich also on Tuesday, isn't that right, Gina?" Stefan asked.

I nodded but didn't answer. I couldn't. Maddy did, though. She said, "So that means if we want to stay together, we need a place for tonight and Sunday and Monday. Three nights."

Stefan stood up and shook the kinks out of his legs. "Okay. I'll see what I can do."

Maddy turned her head and looked at him. "I do feel a lot better, but I'd prefer not to have to walk *too* far. And don't forget, Gina and I are on a budget, too, okay? No Hiltons or Hyatts."

Stefan took off then, and Ceci and I went to the little grocery store around the corner and got some bread, cheese, yogurt, grapes, and pears. We were surprised to see Stefan return in less than an hour. Somehow he had managed to locate a *pensione* with a very inexpensive four-bunk dormitory room in a section of Rome called *Trastevere*. "They said on the phone they'd hold it," Stefan said, "but we should get out there as soon as we can. We can take the Metro, Maddy," he added. "It is not far to walk."

Our room was large but stifling hot, and the bunks were hard and small. They weren't made up, but there was a pile of worn blankets and torn sheets haphazardly piled on a chair. We had our very own bathroom, though, right off our room, and a balcony overlooking a small *piazza* crowded with children at play.

We spread out the food we had bought and began to make our plans. Because she knew the city better than any of us, Ceci became our leader. This was her list of "must-sees": the Colosseum, of course; the Pantheon; the Spanish Steps (whatever *they* are, I thought); and St. Peter's Cathedral, the largest Christian church in the world. It was late on Saturday afternoon, and we had Sunday and Monday, two days left—two whole days in which to tour the city of Rome, try to get some free publicity for a yo-yo that glows in the dark, and make memories we would never forget.

We started our tour with the Spanish Steps. Ceci led us up around the back way so we could see them from the top down. Oh, what a magnificent sea of gracefully curving steps and ramps, crowded with people and flowers—an area as large as a football field, it seemed—all spread out below us!

"But why do they call them the *Spanish* Steps, Ceci?" I asked after I had caught my breath.

"Well, the Spanish Embassy is around here someplace.

That's where the Spanish ambassador has lived for a couple of centuries."

"He must be a *very* old man by now," I remarked while the others all groaned.

"Hey, look! There's a McDonald's!" Maddy said as we were walking along the wide street in front of the steps. So we went in and had fries and drinks, and afterward we walked on over to a huge square called the *Piazza del Popolo*, where something very funny and wonderful happened. It was late afternoon by then, the time the Italians call the *passeggiata*, which is like their "strolling hour." It's really great; whole families just go strolling around eating *gelati*, the old people talking to their friends and the young ones flirting. Ceci and Maddy and I were having fun checking out the latest fashions; Stefan was kind of leading the way, walking a little ahead of us. Directly in front of him a heavyset, middle-aged Italian woman with a bouffant hairdo was walking her little dog—a kind of cute, stuck-up little dog that would be a real pain in the neck if he were a person.

That's when the fun began. Stefan started it by trying to tease the lady's little mutt. He put his hand over his mouth and barked "Yip, yip, yip!" in a very realistic, high-pitched, strident tone. The little doggie immediately snapped his head back and answered with a frenzied "Yip, yip, yip!" of his own.

Then Stefan, flush with success, grinned and put both hands over his mouth. Out came a deep, guttural "Woof! Woof! Woof!" that sounded exactly like Slugger, my next-door neighbor's big German shepherd back home. A handsome young Italian guy on a bicycle smiled and waved at Stefan, and as he rode past he gave *his* imitation of what sounded like a hound dog in heat.

Immediately from somewhere way in the square came the mournful howl of a mangy stray. And then, like magic, the whole *piazza* seemed to be filled with dogs of all sizes and temperaments—whining, squealing, roaring, and yapping. I had no idea so many people could imitate dogs so well. God, if I ever felt that people are basically funny and congenial and wonderful, it was that evening in the *Piazza del Popolo.*

Later Ceci led us to the Roman Colosseum, because she said the best way to see it for the first time was in the moonlight. And she was right. I never thought that just looking at a huge old monument like that could make me feel like I was somehow enlarged and expanded—like there was a big rubber balloon in my chest and someone had blown it up as large as a house. Standing there on the ground looking up at those massive stones and jagged ruins, I could almost hear the ancient, faraway sound of the voices of my Italian ancestors, screaming and yelling and calling out to their friends in those bygone days. Pretty soon we found a place to sit where we had a good view, and the four of us stayed there a long time just talking quietly about a lot of different things. Once, after several minutes of silence, I laughingly told them about the Thing back home (deleting completely the part about P.J.) and how neat I had thought it was at the time. "San Joaquin County's answer to the Colosseum," I said. "But definitely less crowded during the tourist season."

On Sunday morning the first thing on our list was a visit to the Pantheon. I will be honest and admit that I was expecting something completely different. That's because I had the Pantheon confused with the Parthenon, which is in Greece. In fact, I didn't even know we were *there* until we were practically inside this wonderfully symmetrical high-domed building, lit only by an opening at the very center of the dome.

Ceci started to read out of her guidebook in a soft but distinct voice as the rest of us stood around gaping like all the other tourists there. "The magnificent dome of the Pantheon," she read, "ranks as the supreme achievement of Roman interior architecture."

I was utterly overwhelmed by the entire experience. How could I have known, just a month before, slumped in my chair in Mr. Costello's room at old San Joaquin High, that such things really existed in countries I only knew about from misplaced and forgotten outline maps?

After our visit to the Pantheon, Maddy suggested that we find the office of a newspaper called *La Bandiera*. She said that the manager of the toy store where I was supposed to give my demonstration the next day told her it was the kind of tabloid-type newspaper that might be a good prospect for some free publicity.

"*La Bandiera?*" Ceci said. "Hey, I've seen that place! It's not far from the Forum. Come on, let's go!"

The person who greeted us was a chic young woman photographer named Sofia, and Stefan immediately made a hit with her. Maddy and Ceci and I tried to do our part by admiring her photos, which were haphazardly pinned up all over the walls. Well, once Sofia understood about the yo-yo demonstration I was going to do at the toy store, she picked up a clipboard and went over and spoke a few words to a man who was smoking a cigar and talking on the phone the whole time we were there. He scowled and looked at us over his reading glasses and then held the phone with his thick neck and shoulder while he gestured all over the place with both hands.

"God, he'll never let her do it," Maddy whispered, putting her hands in her pockets and looking at the floor. "How can a yo-yo compete with half-clothed Italian starlets?" she asked, glancing at the stack of papers on the counter.

But Maddy was wrong. Sofia came walking back to us, scribbling something on the clipboard. "It is all settled," she said in English. "This is eleven o'clock tomorrow, then, at the toy store. I will be there."

And then she smiled at Stefan and said something in Italian. It took him a minute to catch on, probably because she spoke so fast, but finally he understood, because he laughed and blushed and said, *"Gràzie, signorina."* And then (I couldn't believe it!) she kissed him, the Italian way, on both cheeks.

"Jeez," I said after we were back on the street. *"Friendly,* wasn't she? What did she say to you, anyway?"

God, he was so cute. He rubbed the back of his neck and looked at the ground and said, "She told me she liked my shoes."

We were up by eight on Monday morning. Maddy and I put on our Tater Toys outfits—white pants, Tater Toys T-shirts and caps—and then Maddy grabbed the demo case and the four of us hopped on the Metro. We still had lots of time when we arrived at the toy store, so we got pastries and coffee from the sidewalk café next door and sat down together at a table in the shade.

Sofia came riding up on a red moped at ten minutes to eleven. She locked it to one of our table legs, kissed Stefan, and sat down with us and had a beer.

I was getting pretty nervous by that time. There had been no prepublicity, of course, but the store was on such a busy street, I knew we could gather up quite a large crowd. The manager, a dapper, fussy little man with a mustache, came out of a back room to greet us, and then he clapped his hands and gave some orders in Italian. Two or three employees in green and red smocks came running up, and after a lot of words and gesturing, they went into some sort of storeroom and came out with a kind of heavy crate box that was meant for me to stand on. Maddy was trying to explain to him that I needed six or seven feet between me and the audience, but I don't think he was catching on. We all went out to the sidewalk, and Maddy snapped open the demo case.

"*Oh, my God!*" she said, and I knew it was something really serious.

I looked at the contents inside the open case, and my heart sank. It was chock-full of Sailing Circles, from the little baby four-inchers to the regular-size ones, but not a yo-yo in the lot.

Neither one of us could speak. Maddy turned absolutely white, and I thought I was going to faint.

"This is the case Donnie pointed to, isn't it?" she asked me. "It was the only one I saw. This was the one, wasn't it?"

"I—I guess so!" I sputtered. "It was the only one I saw, too."

"That snake! That *slime!* I don't believe this! Ka-*ripes! Ka-ripes!*" She suddenly grabbed me by the shoulders. "Gina! Your yellow yo-yo! Where is it?"

For a second I felt a surge of relief. *Of course! I could use my*—and then I remembered. *Oh, no! The little boy on the train!*

"I don't have it!" I said, practically crying. "Oh, Maddy! I don't have it anymore! I gave it away to a little kid on the train!"

In another five minutes the store manager was back in the store, shaking his head and rolling his eyes in disbelief at those crazy Americans, and Sofia, camera case still strapped on her back, had sped off on her red *moto* with an unconcerned wave and a cheerful "*Ciao!*" Stefan and Ceci were extremely sympathetic, but other than saying they were sorry, what could they do?

Ceci suggested that if we wanted to, it would be a good time to visit Saint Peter's Cathedral. We all agreed, and on the way over I put my arm around Maddy's shoulder and gave her a little hug. She reached up and touched my hand. "It's okay," she said, biting her lip. "I'll live." Then she stuck out her jaw and gritted her teeth. "But just *wait* until I get a hold of that Donnie! I'm going to wring his *neck!*"

When we arrived at Saint Peter's, Ceci asked if we wanted her to read to us from the guidebook. "Oh, if you *must*," we said, teasing her, and she began: "On either side of the most imposing church in Christendom are semicircular colonnades, formed by two hundred eighty-four columns and eighty-eight pillars. Above are one hundred forty colossal statues of saints . . ."

I tapped Stefan's arm. "Look!" I pointed. "The way some of those saints are holding their arms, with their middle fingers extended like that! They look like they're playing with invisible yo-yos!"

Stefan laughed and nodded, but Maddy turned away and quickly swiped at the corner of her eye with her finger, and then I was sorry I said it.

Before we left the square, Stefan looked up at the statues of the saints again and shook his head in amusement. "Playing with yo-yos," he repeated. "Where do you get such ideas?"

I looked up at the statues again. Maddy was a short distance away, talking with Ceci. "From my grandfather, I guess," I answered quietly. "He dreamed once that Neptune—at the Trevi—was yoing. And he said Neptune was very, very good," I added.

Stefan cocked his head and put his forefinger to his temple. "Ah, yes!" Then he struck a pose, imitating the posture of the Trevi Neptune. He extended his right arm and stiffened his fingers just like the statue. "Like this!" he said, and I could almost visualize the yo-yo in his hand.

We toured the Vatican museums next, ending with the famous Sistine Chapel. It was beautiful, but I could tell that Maddy's heart still wasn't in it, so that sort of spoiled it for me, too.

When we finally got back to our room in *Trastevere* late

that afternoon, everyone was so tired we just didn't feel like doing much of anything.

"What are we going to do with these?" I asked Maddy, opening up the case full of Sailing Circles and playfully tossing a couple of them over to Stefan and Ceci.

Maddy didn't even answer. She just shook her head helplessly and shrugged.

"Maybe we could make big yo-yos out of them," Stefan said, holding two of the same size up to each other. "All we need is a shank of some sort . . ." He studied the two large disks in his hands and suddenly got up and headed for the bathroom. I could hear him rummaging around in the little wastebasket in there, and in a few seconds he returned with a couple of cardboard toilet paper rolls. "If we could cut and glue this between—" he started to say, and then he jumped up again and left the room.

"What does he want to do?" Ceci asked sleepily. "Cut and glue what?"

"I think he wants to turn these Sailing Circles into big yo-yos," I said. "Don't ask me why."

Stefan returned in a few minutes with a little plastic bottle of glue and a ball of heavy twine. He got out his Swiss Army knife, and after some cutting and glueing, he came up with a couple of "yo-yos," one five inches in diameter and another one even larger.

"We can try them off the balcony!" he said, pulling me up by the hand. "Come on, I want to see if they will spin."

Ceci and Maddy didn't seem too excited by his handiwork, but I got up and followed him over to our small balcony. The two of us spent about half an hour trying to make those big yo-yos behave. By the time we went back into our room Maddy and Ceci were fast asleep.

"Come on," Stefan whispered, "let's leave these two tired persons to rest here, and you and I can take a walk."

We went up to the ridge of the *Gianicolo* hill, which overlooks *Trastevere*. Right away I noticed that the name of the street we were on was *Via Garibaldi*.

"Hey!" I said. "That's *my* name! My real name, I mean. Garibaldi!"

"You should be proud. He was a genuine Italian hero."

Soon we came upon a splendid equestrian statue of Giuseppe Garibaldi himself, and I remembered Mr. Costello's words—*a very noble name*. That's when I decided that when I got back home, I was going to see how complicated it would be to change my name back to Garibaldi, in honor of my grandfather. I also resolved to read up on old Giuseppe and see what he did to make himself such a hero.

When we got down from the hill, we picked up the others at the *pensione* and went to a little outdoor café there in *Trastevere* for our last evening together in Rome.

It grew later and later, but no one wanted to leave. It was Ceci who suggested we all exchange addresses so we could keep in touch. "Can I borrow your little notebook, Maddy?" she asked eagerly.

"That's a good idea," Maddy said, taking her red notebook out of her shirt pocket.

"Here," Ceci said, beginning to write. "I think all of our addresses will fit on one piece of paper. So we can just write our names and addresses four times on four different sheets, and then we can pass the little papers around and everyone can keep one."

Stefan quietly got up from the table, walked over to the tree next to the curb, and gazed up at the stars.

"Hey, Stefan!" Ceci called. "Come and sign!"

He looked over at her and just shook his head.

"What's wrong? Come on!"

I caught a glimpse of his face then, in the dim light of the street lamp. His expression was so sad and forlorn that it actually hurt me to look at him.

"Ste-fan!" Ceci insisted. "Come *on*—"

"Shh," I said to her. "I'll go see what's wrong with him."

But he wouldn't let me come near him. Each time I took a step closer, he would take a few steps back, until I'd followed him clear around the corner. As soon as we were out of sight of the others he took me gently into his arms and kissed my hair and then my lips. "I think it would spoil everything," he whispered softly. "It would spoil everything to exchange addresses now."

"But why?" I asked, trying to hold back my tears. "Why would it spoil everything? Stefan, I—well, I've really come to like you very much, and—"

"And I like you, too, Gina. That's why I think it would be better to just say good-bye—until we meet again, someday, someplace—"

"Oh, Stefan! That would never happen just by chance!"

"But we could always hope it would, don't you see? We could always hope that somewhere, like maybe in a little train station somewhere, or on a busy street—"

I remembered the Australians and began to understand.

"Besides, you know what would happen, don't you, Gina," he asked, "if we did exchange our addresses?"

I sniffed a couple of times and answered with a quiet, "No. What?"

"I think you would write to me from the airplane. And then when you got home, a time or two again. But soon you would run out of things to say. And surely you would avoid to tell me many things, your dates, your—"

I started to say something, to interrupt, but he gently put his hand over my mouth. "You must know what I am speaking is true. Oh, I could receive a card at Christmastime. And maybe next year also. But then you would forget me. You would go away to college and misplace my address in your papers. I would become a blurred memory, and finally I would be forgotten." He touched my hair, brushing it back from my face the way he did on the steps of the cathedral in *Milano*. "I don't want you to forget me, ever. I am selfish that way."

"Oh, Stefan," I said, my voice breaking.

He put his arm around my waist, and we started walking slowly down the quiet, almost deserted street. My heart was racing. I was starting to have crazy thoughts. I could move to Amsterdam. I could get a job. I could . . . No. No, I couldn't. Of course I couldn't.

Pretty soon we stopped walking and held each other close. Then he tipped my head and tried to smile at me, and I could see his eyes were glistening with tears. "You will forever be my beautiful, intelligent, unspoiled American girl. Every July—especially on the fifth of July—I will remember you and look for you."

We got up on Tuesday morning before the sun came up. No one spoke as we quietly took turns in the bathroom and packed up our things. Ceci had to be at the train station at six thirty to catch the bus to the Rome airport, and Maddy and I had tickets for the seven ten train to Zurich.

"Now remember," Ceci said, hugging me for the tenth time and patting my back with both hands. "*Write to me!* I'll be watching for the mail every day."

We were standing on the southwest side of the huge *Stazione Termini*, and Ceci was about to board the bus to the airport. Stefan had seen that her bags were stowed in the baggage compartment in the side of the bus, and we were standing close to her, taking turns hugging her and snapping pictures in the early morning light.

We watched her as she climbed aboard and sat down at a window seat opposite from where the three of us were standing. She tried to open the window, but either it didn't open or it was stuck. She smiled at us and shrugged helplessly. The driver started up the engine, and as we backed away from the curb she suddenly tapped on the window and waved at us frantically. "Gina! Gina!" she called out, cupping her hands around her mouth. "Thanks again for the book! Thank you!" The driver shifted gears and in a few seconds she was gone.

"Oh, God, I hate good-byes," I said, wiping my eyes with my sleeve and grabbing on to Stefan's hand. "And I really dread the next one," I whispered, looking up at his face.

"Yes," he said, releasing his hand from mine and throwing his arm across my shoulder. He bent down and lightly kissed me on the temple. "Yes. I know."

Maddy looked at both of us and started to cry.

Our train was waiting on the track, and the seats were filling up fast. Stefan helped us get our stuff on board and into our compartment, and then he hugged me very tightly and said hoarsely, "This is it for now, Gina. But we will meet again. I'm sure of it."

"But *when*, Stefan?" I whispered. "When and where?"

He looked deep into my eyes for a long, long moment. "We will know!" he said. "If it is right, we will know!" And then he quickly turned and left the train.

Maddy lowered the window of our compartment and leaned out, looking up and down the platform. "He's coming over here, Gina," she said, pulling me over to the window. "See? Here he comes."

Stefan and I stood staring into each other's eyes—he on the outside of the train and me on the inside—the tears running down like a river. As the train started to move he quickly stepped forward and grabbed my extended hands with his. We must have held on for three or four seconds before we had to let go. The train lurched forward for maybe a hundred yards or more and then inexplicably slowed to a stop. I could still see Stefan standing on the platform.

"Your camera!" Maddy said. "Here's your camera! Take his picture! Quick!"

I grabbed my camera from her hand and raised it to my eyes. "Oh, no! I'm out of film!" I said quickly. "Get my other roll out of my backpack, will you?" I asked, quickly removing the used roll and setting it on the window sill. "It's in the little pouch there. Hurry! The train's going to start again!"

A guy in the next compartment was waving to someone on the platform with his handkerchief. I guess that gave Stefan the idea, because just as the train jerked forward I saw him pull his own handkerchief out of his pocket and wave it in the air. And then, even from where I was, I could see the look of utter dismay on his face as strands of my hair were freed and blew away like petals in the wind. I didn't notice until seconds later, as the train began to pick up speed, that my only exposed roll of film had fallen onto the roadbed below.

20

"Now this is a *nice* airplane," I said as I followed Maddy down the aisle to our assigned seats. "A wide-bodied Boeing 747, I believe," I added with exaggerated nonchalance.

Maddy turned her head and gave me a sweet, knowing little smile. We stuffed our backpacks under the seats in front of us, and Maddy sat down while I reached up to put our large packs and the empty demo case in the overhead rack. We had left the Sailing Circles (now all turned into yo-yos) in Rome for Stefan to give to the kids in the *piazza*.

"You know something, Maddy," I said as we were sitting there waiting to take off. "I'm going to learn five languages and then get a job in the travel industry—after I get out of college, that is."

She smiled at me, raising her eyebrows in surprise. "Really? I think that sounds wonderful!"

"I love traveling," I said. "I just love everything about it."

"Even bathrooms down the hall with no shower curtains?" She laughed.

"*Especially* bathrooms down the hall with no shower curtains!" I paused then, remembering Bluey and Barb and our room that first night in *Milano*. "Weren't the Australians just so great?" I asked her. "I mean, weren't they the *greatest*?"

Maddy smiled at me again. "Yes, they were," she said. "They were very, very nice." She kept looking at me, waiting for me to say more.

I swallowed and blinked several times. "And Stefan, too. Wasn't he—" I faltered.

She put her hand over mine. "Stefan was very, very nice, too, honey."

Just then a flight attendant came by with an armful of newspapers. "Papers?" she asked. "Would you ladies care for a newspaper?"

"Hmm. What do you have?" Maddy asked, stretching her neck to see.

"Well, there's *The International Herald Tribune*, in English, and this other one—but it's in Italian."

As Maddy reached out for the *Herald*, I noticed the name of the Italian paper; it was *La Bandiera*. "May I have that one, please?" I asked, pointing to it.

"Oh, that one's in Italian."

"I know. May I have one anyway?"

"Well, certainly," she said, handing it to me.

I showed the cover to Maddy and smiled. It was a full-page photo of a very chubby Elizabeth Taylor, all dressed in pink and popping out of her bodice. The large headline slashed across the page said: LIZ—ANCORA GRASSA.

The pilot suddenly revved up the engines.

"Here we go!" Maddy said, and we held on tight as our plane soared out of the mist and into the cloudless blue sky high above Zurich.

"You know, Maddy," I said after the roar of the engines had subsided and the FASTEN YOUR SEAT BELT sign was turned off, "I've been thinking. Isn't it strange how *different* people are?"

"Different from what, honey?"

"Oh, you know. Different from each other. Like, take that old man at Assisi—well, you didn't meet him, of course—but even as old as he was, I could tell how different he was from my grandfather. My grandfather was always joking around, a real playful sort of a guy, you know? But Salvatore—that was

213

his name, did I tell you about that, how my grandmother named my father after him? Isn't that just so *sad*?"

"Yes." Maddy nodded. "You did tell me that."

"Well, anyway, Salvatore just seemed to be a different type of person altogether. I could *never* picture him playing around with a yo-yo, for example. And he's religious, too, like my grandmother. Like my grandmother was."

Maddy snapped off her reading light and rested her head against the back of her seat. "I wonder how often your grandmother thought about Salvatore during all those years she was married to your grandfather—comparing them, you know?"

"Yes. I wonder about that, too. But the really sad part is that she couldn't *help* it. I mean, she couldn't *help* getting married in the first place, and then she couldn't help how she felt about both of them."

"That's right," Maddy agreed. "But then it's the same with the rest of us, isn't it? When you come right down to it, when can *anyone* help how they feel about other people?"

"Sure, that's what I think, too. It's mostly all luck, isn't it? I mean, if people happen to like each other and get along, it's just the way things are. And if they don't, well, it's the same thing. It's nobody's fault, really. You can't order love like a pizza, huh? Either it's there or it isn't."

We didn't say anything for a while, and I started to think about home and my mother, and it suddenly occurred to me that she, too, like everyone else, couldn't really help how she felt about people—how she felt about me. "You've been nothing but a royal pain in the ass since the day you were born," she had said in a moment of frustration. What really made her say that? I wondered. Was there a "Salvatore" in her past that I knew nothing about? Oh, I don't mean a real person waiting on a hilltop for her. I mean, what combination of events and circumstances in her life made her how she is today? I had always resented her for being so careful with money, but maybe she *had* to be—like Maddy and me this past week. Plus, she *had* to watch her budget—with seven kids! Why hadn't I realized that before? I pictured my mother in her garden, quietly pruning her roses or tending to her violets, and I had to admit that I had never once shown an interest in the one thing that interested her most—her garden. Maybe I could ask her something about her plants—the name of a rose, or something. Of course, I would have to start slow. I wouldn't want to shock her or anything. I smiled to myself, picturing her expression of surprise. *The name of that rose? Well, yes, that is a pretty one, isn't it?*

I leaned over in my seat until my forehead rested against the cool glass of the window. The steady hypnotic hum of the engines seemed to fill me with a wonderful sense of calmness and well-being. I don't know how to explain it—except that I felt forgiving, mostly—and free, too. I felt free and light, like a kite at the end of a broken string, sailing off into the blue.

Soon an attendant came around with our breakfast trays. As we were comparing our omelets, Maddy happened to glance at me. "Hey," she asked, "what's with you? You're positively glowing."

"Really? I guess I've just been thinking about stuff. Listen, Maddy," I said. "How long is our stopover in New York?"

"About three hours, I think. I'd have to check the tickets. Why?"

"Well, I was just thinking, if there was time, maybe I could call Tammy while we're there. I could ask her how she was doing and if she was getting along okay with her father's new wife and stuff. She was pretty worried about that."

Maddy nodded. "I'm sure there would be time."

After the attendant came by and picked up our breakfast trays, Maddy said she was going to take a little walk around the cabin. I picked up the copy of *La Bandiera* and started looking at it. That cover photo was really eye-catching. I idly turned the page and suddenly got the shock of my life. Staring me in the face was another full-page color photograph, but this one was of the *Fontana di Trevi*—and there, dangling from the right hand of Neptune, the god of the sea, was a yellow yo-yo in perfect proportion, just like in my grandfather's dream! In the bottom right corner of the picture were two lines of credits.

FOTO: *Sofia*
YO-YO: *Fly-by-Nite, Tater Toys, U.S.A.*

Of course it had to be Stefan's doing! I could just see him scampering around on that fountain with his homemade yo-yo and then talking Sofia into taking the photograph.

Maddy returned a moment later, and I waited until she was sitting down and had buckled her seat belt before I sprang it on her.

"Close your eyes!" I said. Then, "Okay, open!"

I think they heard her shriek of delight all the way back to Rome.

"You know something, Maddy?" I said. "I'll bet you anything that Stefan sends a copy of this to your office in San Francisco. He knew how much you wanted that publicity."

She grabbed me by the hand. "I'm sure you're right! It's just too wonderful, isn't it?"

Later, after Maddy had settled down for a nap, I took out my copy of *La Bandiera* and turned again to that wonderful photograph on page three. But wait! Whose back was that in the somewhat blurred foreground? I raised the paper closer to my eyes and scanned the photograph like a detective. Yes! It was him! It had to be! I would know the back of his head anywhere. And suddenly, as clear as the sun and sky overhead, his voice came back to me. *"Every July—especially on the fifth of July—I will remember you and look for you."* And later, *"We will know!"*

And so I did. I knew that Stefan was the most romantic guy I could ever hope to meet, and that we had a date in the years ahead as surely as summer follows spring. Some fifth of July in the future, at the *Fontana di Trevi* in Rome, Stefan and I will meet again and twirl around and around in a wonderful dance of friendship—maybe, even, of love.

Hours later, as our plane circled low in its final approach over San Francisco Bay, my thoughts returned once again to the old swing in the shady corner of the porch, and I could almost see my grandfather cupping his hands around his mouth and calling out to me in one of those yoing metaphors he loved so well, "Your string's finally untangled now, Papushka, and you're ready to shoot for the moon."